"You can sit," Ivy said. "I promise I don't bite."

Austin settled himself next to her. He immediately wished he hadn't because there was way less space between them now.

"Every time I've been someplace where I can see the night sky like this, I'm always in awe," Ivy said.

"Yeah. I admit I don't take advantage of this view enough."

"I'd tell you not to work so much that life passes you by, but I'd be saying that from a place of privilege. I know you work as much as you do out of necessity. But hopefully you won't forget to do this from time to time."

He looked over at Ivy, and his heart thumped a bit harder when he saw her smiling at him.

"You seem to be deep in thought," she said.

He averted his gaze, staring up at the sky. "Just trying to remember when I sat out beneath the stars with anyone."

Dear Reader,

Welcome back to the picturesque small town of Jade Valley, Wyoming, where you'll find gorgeous mountain views, delicious pies at Trudy's Café and opportunities to find happily-ever-after.

I've always loved stories of starting anew, both as a reader and a writer. I also enjoy thrift shopping (it's like a treasure hunt!) and seeing old buildings renovated and given new life. So the fact that all of those things play a part in Ivy Lake's life makes her a character near and dear to my heart.

It also takes a special person to make you believe in love again when your heart has been broken. For Ivy, that person is Austin Hathaway. And as fate would have it, Ivy is that person for him as well.

I hope you enjoy Ivy and Austin's journey to happily-ever-after.

Trish Milburn

HEARTWARMING

The Heart of a Rancher

—

Trish Milburn

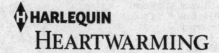

HARLEQUIN
HEARTWARMING

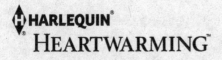

HARLEQUIN®
HEARTWARMING™

ISBN-13: 978-1-335-47583-1

The Heart of a Rancher

Copyright © 2024 by Trish Milburn

Harlequin Enterprises ULC
22 Adelaide St. West, 41st Floor
Toronto, Ontario M5H 4E3, Canada
www.Harlequin.com

Printed in U.S.A.

Trish Milburn is the author of more than fifty romance novels and novellas, set everywhere from quaint small towns in the American West to the bustling city of Seoul, South Korea. When she's not writing or brainstorming new stories, she enjoys reading, listening to K-pop music, watching Korean dramas and chatting about all these things on Twitter. Hop on over to trishmilburn.com to learn more about her books, find links to her various social media and sign up for her author newsletter.

Books by Trish Milburn

Harlequin Heartwarming

Jade Valley, Wyoming

His Wyoming Redemption
Reclaiming the Rancher's Son
The Rancher's Unexpected Twins

Harlequin Western Romance

Blue Falls, Texas

Her Perfect Cowboy
Having the Cowboy's Baby
Marrying the Cowboy
The Doctor's Cowboy
Her Cowboy Groom
The Heart of a Cowboy
Home on the Ranch
A Rancher to Love
The Cowboy Takes a Wife
In the Rancher's Arms

Visit the Author Profile page
at Harlequin.com for more titles.

CHAPTER ONE

Ivy Lake entered the small ballroom and immediately spotted James on the other side talking to their boss and his wife. Ivy took a moment to appreciate the scene. Friends, family and colleagues were gathered at one of the company's hotels to celebrate her engagement to James. Since the hotel had an art deco design, they'd decided to have fun with their party and go with a 1920s theme. Black and gold Gatsby-esque decorations covered the white tablecloths, and lively jazz music filled the air. She was even wearing a flapper dress, a crystal-covered headband and Mary Jane pumps.

James looked dapper in his suit, and it hit her anew just how lucky she was to have a successful career, good friends and a handsome fiancé.

With a smile for the people she passed, she headed straight for him.

"Don't you look beautiful," Mrs. Sterling said as Ivy approached.

"Indeed she does." Mr. Sterling, who had built

up an impressive collection of themed boutique hotels beginning here in Louisville and expanding to several other cities, gave James a friendly pat on the arm. "You're a lucky man."

"I am indeed."

"Is that right?"

They all turned to see a woman Ivy didn't recognize. In fact, there were two unidentified women, and neither of them looked happy. Ivy started to ask if there was a problem, if perhaps they were disgruntled hotel customers, but she stopped when she saw the look on James's face. It had drained of anything remotely resembling color, and shock wasn't too strong a word to describe his expression.

"James? What's wrong?"

"I'll tell you what's wrong," the second woman said with a smirk. "We just ruined his plans."

Ivy shifted her gaze to the woman. "I don't understand."

"Of course you don't," she said. "He's pretty good at hiding all his girlfriends from each other."

"But not good enough," the other woman said.

Ivy wanted to push the two women out of the ballroom, to clear up whatever lies they were telling, away from the eyes and ears of Mr. and Mrs. Sterling and all the other guests, but that would likely draw even more attention.

"What's going on, James?" Ivy asked instead.

"I can explain."

Those three words sent a chill through her body. It was such a cliché coming from a man caught cheating that Ivy almost laughed.

No, this couldn't be happening. She refused to believe it.

"Why are you doing this?" she asked the women. The sympathetic looks on their faces were almost worse than if they were hostile toward her, as if she was the one stealing their man. Instead, they pitied her. The woman who had spoken first, a cute blonde, extended her phone. On it was a photo of her and James at the Kentucky Derby, which had taken place only two weeks ago. She could tell it was recent because third-place finisher Sunrise on Sunday was clearly visible in the background.

Then the other woman, who was more voluptuous and had long, black hair, presented her Instagram feed filled with photos of her in a skimpy bikini and James in swim trunks. It was obvious they were vacationing in some tropical locale.

One photo stood out, and Ivy grabbed the phone to enlarge it. Sure enough, it was taken on Valentine's Day.

She slowly looked at James and pointed at the photo.

"You said you went to visit your mother that

weekend because she'd fallen. This does not look like your mother or Wisconsin."

"I can explain," he said again, as if he had no other words.

White-hot shame washed over Ivy as she handed back the phone.

"Somehow, I don't think you can."

Feeling as if she might actually pass out or die of embarrassment, Ivy turned her back on James and headed toward the exit. Air, she needed air. The ballroom felt smaller with each step she took, as if the walls and ceiling were closing in around her. The murmur of voices was like the buzzing of bees in her head.

Suddenly, her sisters, Lily and Holly, were next to her.

"Ivy, what's wrong? You're as white as that tablecloth," Holly said, pointing at one of the tables set with beautiful china and crystal goblets.

"The engagement is off." Ivy could barely get the words out.

"Off? Why?"

"He cheated on me. With two different people." If not more. That idea horrified her, but if there were two, logically it could be more than that. She suddenly wondered how he had the time. And why he'd bother getting engaged and eventually married. It wasn't as if he was marrying into a fabulously wealthy family.

Without any further questions, her sisters ushered her out of the ballroom and then out of the hotel.

Right out of her engagement.

IVY SHOVED ANOTHER spoonful of chocolate ice cream into her mouth, not caring that she'd probably gained five pounds over the past couple of days. Why did it matter? She no longer had to fit into her wedding dress.

If there was one thing to be thankful for, it was that she'd accumulated a lot of days off and had decided to take them all at once. Maybe by the time she'd exhausted them she'd have enough courage to face her coworkers again.

But right now, the thought of having to see James made her physically ill. He hadn't called, hadn't even tried to keep her from leaving the hotel after the truth bomb had landed. Either he didn't care about her enough or he knew there was no way to talk himself out of the Grand Canyon–sized hole he'd dug for himself. The fact that it was likely both had led to her losing count of how many pints of ice cream she'd eaten.

A mirthless laugh escaped her. Not only had James's response been a cliché, but now she was living one. How many movies had she seen where the heartbroken woman drowned her sorrows in ice cream?

That thought propelled her to the kitchen, where she tossed what little was left of the ice cream in the sink and washed it down. Even when it was gone, she stared at the stream of water coming out of the faucet until she heard her mother's voice in her head telling her to stop wasting it. She shut off the tap and returned to the couch. Her apartment seemed quieter than ever now that she'd convinced her sisters and mom that she was fine and they should return home to Lexington. They'd tried arguing that they didn't want to leave her by herself, that she should come with them, but she'd declined.

In all honesty, she'd sent them on their way because she'd been on the verge of cracking. She'd needed to be alone to cry her heart out, to punch things, to send all the pictures of James through her paper shredder. She hadn't wanted an audience for any of that.

But with all those things done, now what? How in the world was she going to go to work every day and see the man who'd cheated on her and with everyone knowing it? She felt like the biggest of fools. If there was a major award for being an idiot, she'd have it on lock.

When nothing on TV caught her attention, she resorted to scrolling through social media. She'd already removed James and hidden his family members. It wasn't their fault he'd done what he had, but she also didn't want to see their posts. She'd probably end up removing them as well, but it felt wrong to do so now, as if she would be punishing them by association.

She watched kitty videos, read random posts about household cleaning hacks and urban gardening, got sucked into watching tours of tiny houses, colored a few pictures in her coloring app that appeared under the label "Zen." Unfortunately, she still didn't feel very Zen after she finished.

As she scrolled away from a video about a woman who lived in a converted grain silo, something caught her eye.

Click here for a chance to win a historic building in beautiful Wyoming.

With nothing better to do, she clicked.

The more she read, the more excited she got. The building was so cool. And the little town it was in looked charming. Her mind started racing with possibilities until it stopped on the perfect one. She could already imagine the building filled with handmade quilts, beautiful fabrics, endless baskets of yarn and sewing supplies. The dream her grandma Cecile had long had about opening her own quilt and fabric store settled in Ivy's brain as if it had been hers all along. Grandma Cecile had never realized her dream, but Ivy could do it for her.

Before she could talk herself out of it, she wrote the required paragraph about why she wanted to win and paid the fifty dollars to enter the contest. Maybe she was being a fool again, but she was pretty sure she'd already eaten that amount in ice cream and chips. At least if she was making another mistake, no one was around to witness it. But a chance at a fresh start far away from her cheating ex sounded way better for her peace of mind—and her waistline—than continuing to eat boatloads of self-pity food. If nothing else, it would be fun to daydream of the possible rather than remember what she'd lost.

IVY WOKE WITH a painful crick in her neck. She guessed that's what she got for falling asleep on the couch watching TV instead of actually dragging herself to bed. She rolled onto her back and grabbed her phone to check the time. A little number one next to her email icon drew her attention. She considered ignoring it, but what else did she have to do?

Congratulations! You have been chosen as the winner of the Stinson Historic Building Giveaway.

Ivy sat up so fast her head swam. She really should eat something remotely healthy. Protein would be good.

She scrolled through the message, then read

it a second time. Alarm bells threatened to ring. Despite the research she'd done the night before, was this really just a scam? How had they chosen a winner so quickly? Was there something obvious she'd overlooked and, because of that, she was the only entrant? But the law firm handling the giveaway and transfer of the property was a real one in Casper. Jade Valley was a real town, and she'd found an article about the Stinson Building's past as the town's first grocery store. She'd tried finding a street view, but Jade Valley was one of those small towns that evidently hadn't received such a drive-through yet. Nothing in town had a street view online.

Still, she called the number in the email and paced as she talked to a woman at the law firm who told her that the owner had been reading the entries as they came in so that it didn't take long to pick a winner.

"He connected with your desire to start over, because that's what he's doing," the woman said.

Just to be sure, Ivy contacted the county government and found out that if she accepted the property, it would be hers free and clear of any debt or liens.

She stood in the middle of her living room, stunned at the turn of events. She'd seen that contest notice literally an hour before the deadline. And she'd encountered it right when the idea of a fresh start somewhere else seemed like the perfect solution to her current situation.

She squealed and did a little excited dance.

Her friends and family might think she'd lost it, but she was moving to Wyoming!

AS SOON AS Austin Hathaway walked in the front door of his house, he heard his mother sneeze. He followed the sound to the kitchen and found her pulling a bowl of soup out of the microwave sitting on the rolling cart so she could reach it from her wheelchair.

"Are you sick?" he asked. "Do you need to go to the doctor?"

Sure, they had a stack of doctor bills that rivaled the tallest peaks in the Rockies, but he wasn't about to let his mother fall ill and not give her proper care either.

She shook her head as he took the bowl and placed it on the table for her.

"I'm fine. Just a bit of the cold since it's been damp."

Damp was an understatement. They'd had an abnormal amount of rain for May, more than twice the typical average. His muddy boots sitting on the front porch were proof of that. But ranch work didn't wait until it was sunny and dry. And there was always work.

"Are you sure? Because—"

"I said I'm fine." She sounded a mixture of tired and irritated.

It was strange how the irritation was actually a good sign. He knew his mother was depressed a lot, even if she did her best to hide it from him and his younger sister, Daisy. While it was understandable why she felt that way, he nevertheless felt helpless in the face of it. How did you help someone get over losing both her second husband and the use of her legs at the same time? It didn't matter that the loss of both had happened more than a year ago. They were still gone and always would be.

Deciding not to push her anymore, he didn't ask anything else.

"I'm going to take a shower." Between cleaning out a barn stall, replacing a couple of rotting fence posts and cutting up a tree that had fallen over the driveway when it uprooted from the wet soil, he'd gotten quite sweaty and dirty.

He was halfway down the hallway when he'd swear he heard his mother murmur that she was sorry. It wasn't the first time he'd heard those words, but he always hated them. His mother used to be so active, first helping out on this ranch when she was married to his dad and later working with her second husband, Sam, in running his river rafting business. It didn't take a high IQ to figure out that she now felt like a burden, both physically and financially. And though the financial burden weighed him down like a stack of anvils on his shoulders, he would not let her or Daisy see that. They'd been through too much already. All he wanted to do was make their lives easier.

But that was difficult on what money ranching brought in, especially when it felt as if things kept breaking around the place. Fence posts, a tractor tire, the starter on his truck. Then there was the unexpected jump in the property taxes. That was why he took every extra job he could while still being able to keep the ranch afloat. He would keep this home for his family if it was the last thing he did.

He stayed in the shower longer than he should, but the hot water felt good and he was honestly too tired to move. But he finally did because he still had to go pick up Daisy from school. Her geography club, all three members, were meeting with their sponsor, Sunny Wheeler, to plan some projects for the summer and the next school year. Sunny had traveled the world with the job she had before moving back to Jade Valley, and Daisy loved hearing about all the places she'd been.

Daisy was typically a shy, quiet girl, but her eyes lit up and she talked more when she learned about a new place or bit of culture that she wanted to share. Even as a toddler, she was entranced any time there was a travel, history or nature documentary on TV. He knew she wanted to travel, and he hoped that whatever path she chose in life would allow her to do so. Yet something else he couldn't provide for her.

When he pulled up outside the school thirty minutes later, Daisy was waiting for him.

"Did you have a good meeting?" he asked.

"Yeah. We're going to focus on Antarctica over the summer and then cover various parts of Asia next year."

"Sounds interesting." Those places seemed like they existed in another universe to him. The farthest away he'd been was Seattle once to go to a baseball game with a group of friends. None of them had much money, so they'd pooled their resources and six of them had shared one hotel room. But it was still one of the most fun times he'd ever had.

"I also won the end-of-year prize for doing the most projects." She held up a certificate and an envelope. She tapped the latter. "I got fifty dollars. Can we stop at Trudy's?"

"Sure."

If she wanted a piece of pie or a milkshake to celebrate her hard work, she deserved it. But when they stepped up to Trudy's front counter, Daisy ordered not only one but two full meals then looked at him.

"Order whatever you want."

"I'm okay." She didn't need to be spending her money on him. It was supposed to work the other way around. She wasn't his child, but he was still in charge of keeping her safe, fed and clothed until she reached adulthood in four years.

"Please."

The tone of that plea, however, had him ordering a pork chop with sides. Daisy might be on the shy side, but she possessed that same stubborn determination to not be a burden that their mother did. He wished he could make them understand that he didn't see either of them as a burden. They were the only family he had, and he'd almost lost his mother.

"You're kidding." He glanced over and saw Jonathon Breckinridge, Sunny Wheeler's dad, chatting with a couple of his buddies. "I'm surprised anybody took that bait."

Trudy stepped up to the counter in front of Austin with the bag containing the desserts and bread that went with Daisy's order. She nodded toward the older men.

"You heard about what has everyone talking?"

"No. My cows aren't big on gossip."

Trudy chuckled. "They're probably smarter than

we are. But this is actually interesting. There's a new owner of the Stinson Building."

"Really? Someone finally bought it?" John Young had been trying to unload that building for probably ten years.

"Not exactly. Seems John ran a contest online where people could enter for a chance to win it for fifty dollars."

Okay, so the building needed a lot of work, but a fifty-dollar price tag seemed like a steal. Whoever bought it could get enough salvage out of it to make that back and more. Or maybe they could afford to fix it up and flip it, sell it to someone with money to burn.

"Evidently there are a lot of people out there who want an old building," Trudy said, "because John made out like a bandit and is moving to one of those fancy retirement communities in Arizona."

"Maybe I should raffle off my barn," Austin said. "Then I could afford to build a new one."

Not to mention pay off all the debt, reminders of which arrived in his mailbox almost daily.

"You know," Trudy said, leaning in closer so others couldn't hear. "If whoever won that building wants to try fixing it up, they're going to need help. I can give them your name and number."

His heart skipped a beat at the idea of how much work that would be, how much income it might bring if the person didn't just hire a contractor to handle it.

"I would really appreciate that. You're the best."

Trudy waved away the compliment. "I'd be doing whoever the new owner is a favor. You're a good worker. I think I could tap dance on the new steps you built at the house and they wouldn't budge."

"You should have replaced those shaky steps ages ago."

"I know, I know. Just always too busy to think about stuff like that."

"You have to take care of yourself." He saw in her eyes that she knew he was thinking of his mom, so he decided to lighten the mood. "You don't want to give Alma an opportunity to snatch all your business."

The two older women, who had competing cafés directly across from each other on Main Street, had some sort of long-standing feud. The cause was a mystery that kept everyone in the county guessing. But neither Trudy nor Alma ever spilled the truth.

Trudy huffed. "Not darn likely."

Even Daisy laughed a little at that response.

Once he and Daisy were back in the truck that was now filled with the delicious smells of Trudy's cooking, he glanced over at his sister, who was sneaking a french fry.

"Go ahead and eat them while they're hot."

"I'll wait."

"I wish you had saved that money for something you wanted."

"This is what I wanted."

Just as he hadn't pressed his mother earlier, he let the topic go with Daisy. She had a few years before she was an adult, but she wasn't a little kid anymore either. And she was more mature than a lot of fourteen-year-olds, but then tragedy tended to make you grow up quick. He knew that from experience, having gone through losing his father as well.

He forced his thoughts away from the sadness of the past. It did no good to dwell. Instead, he allowed a little hope to flicker to life. If he could get a long-term renovation job and no more unexpected expenses popped up, he could start to chip away more significant chunks of debt. While Daisy dreamed of traveling the world, he had simpler dreams.

He wanted to make sure his mom and sister were always safe, had a roof over their heads and never had to go without necessities. He wanted to find a way to make them happy.

And he wanted to breathe that first breath of debt-free air so much he could taste it.

CHAPTER TWO

WHEN IVY SAW the sign for Jade Valley, she half expected it to be a figment of her imagination. That would be on par with how her cross-country trip had gone so far. First had been a flat tire halfway across Missouri. Then her car overheated in the middle of nowhere Kansas. It had been so windy there, however, that if she'd had a sail to attach to the car she could have coasted into Colorado on wind power alone, if only it had been blowing the right direction. While she'd waited for a tow, she'd tried counting how many times the blades of one of the nearby windmills went around. After losing count, she looked up how long those huge blades were. Half the length of a football field!

It took two days to have her car fixed in a little town where the repair shop was one of exactly three businesses—the other two being a convenience store with a single gas pump and a dingy little motel with half a dozen rooms that had made her seriously consider sleeping outside on

the grass instead. When she'd finally gotten back
on the road, she'd given considerable thought to
retracing her route right back to Louisville.

But no. She'd come too far, sold off too many
of her belongings and made too many life-
altering decisions to back out now. So she forged
ahead, and when she'd made it through Colorado
without incident, she'd very nearly stopped to
kiss the Welcome to Wyoming sign. After one
last on-the-road night in Laramie, she'd driven
the final three hundred or so miles to this, her
new home.

Jade Valley was definitely a small town, but
compared to where she'd stayed in Kansas it was a
booming metropolis. Like so many Western towns,
it was laid out on a simple grid. As she drove down
Main Street, she glanced at the various businesses.
She spotted the two restaurants—Trudy's Café
and Alma's Diner—she'd seen advertised on her
approach to Jade Valley and her empty stomach
grumbled.

First things first, however. She made a right
turn off Main onto Yarrow Street and drove another block.

And there it was on the corner, the building she
had won. The historic building she now owned.
Where she would live and hopefully be able to
make a new start and an actual living.

But as she pulled over on the side of the street

and stared at the building, panic threatened. The exterior looked more worn and abandoned than it had in the photos she'd seen. Even the windows appeared as if they hadn't been washed in several seasons, if not years. One had plywood covering what she assumed was a broken pane. How old had those photos with the contest listing been?

What had she done?

All the worried questions lobbed at her by her friends and family came rushing back in a jumble, but she shoved them away. Thinking positively was the key to her new future. Whatever it took, she would make a happy life for herself.

Surely the inside was better maintained. The outside was simply exposed to the elements and only needed some sprucing up. At least she hoped that was all.

Ivy took a slow, deep breath before getting out of her car. Then she stretched to rid herself of the kinks in her back and shoulders. One huge positive was that she was finally done with her days-long drive. She was well and truly tired of the driver's seat and staring at endless interstates. There sure weren't any interstates in or anywhere near Jade Valley.

She took a few moments to look at her surroundings. The street seemed to have a few other small businesses before it gave way to homes.

She'd gradually get to know her neighbors, but first things first.

When a quick look in both directions revealed not a moving car in sight—that would take some getting used to—she crossed the street and retrieved the key to the front door from beneath a brick set next to the foundation on the side of the building. She'd thought it had been a joke when she'd been told that she wouldn't be picking up the key from the lawyer's office or even a realty company. This was the commercial equivalent of hiding a key in the flowerpot on the front porch of a house. She was genuinely surprised the key was actually there.

She wiped the dirt off the key and returned to the front, climbed the two stone stairs to the door. As she slid the key into the lock, she spotted the engraved stone square set into the exterior of the building.

Stinson Building, Built by E. M. Stinson, 1902.

The number of people who had walked through this historic structure lit a flame under Ivy's excitement again. She looked forward to learning more about the building's history. Maybe she'd even create an exhibit inside to appeal to history buffs. She'd spent some of those long hours driving from Kentucky brainstorming ways to get people through the front door with their wallets.

With renewed determination, she unlocked

the door and tried not to wince at the resulting screech as she opened it. She stepped across the threshold and was greeted by the smell of dust and disuse. Her heart sank as she saw how much dust coated the floor, some old store furnishings and several boxes that looked like they were on the verge of actually collapsing and becoming dust. The floor below the broken window appeared to have suffered some water damage.

"No going back," she said, then put one foot in front of the other, advancing slowly to make sure the floor was sound.

When it felt spongey in spots, she couldn't help some worry about the structural soundness of the building. Had she given up everything for a money pit, even if it had only cost fifty dollars to acquire?

Don't borrow trouble.

She heard those words in Grandma Cecile's voice and took them to heart. Things didn't look awesome, but it was to be expected for a building this old to need some repairs and upgrades.

She felt as if her thoughts were attached to a yo-yo. One moment she told herself that whatever needed tackling, she'd tackle it. But then she discovered a disturbing stain on the wall and thought she heard a decidedly rodent-like scratching. A chill raced down her spine. She hated mice, and the idea that it might be a rat truly freaked her out.

Trying to keep calm, Ivy crossed to the stairs at the back of the main level and tested the first one by pressing on it with the toe of her sneaker. It felt mostly solid, so she eased her full weight onto it. When it didn't collapse, she continued upward in the same manner. Her surroundings didn't get any less dusty. If anything, it worsened as she climbed. Plus she had to dodge thick cobwebs. The last thing she wanted was to run into one of those, causing the spitting, "I have ancient cobweb on my face" dance that might send her tumbling back down the stairs.

She reached the top of the stairs and emerged into a large, open room that mirrored the one below. Only this one was stuffed with the detritus of decades. The dim light filtering through the dirty windows allowed her to see a mishmash of furniture, more boxes, what seemed to be leftover construction supplies, a rack of flowerpots of all shapes and sizes, and—strangest of all—a random toilet.

This…this was supposed to be where she would live. It was a long way from livable. Where did she even start to make it so?

Again, careful in case the floor might send her falling through to the first level, she walked toward a small room in the corner that was obviously added later on. When she opened the door, it fell off the hinges and she had to jump out of the way to avoid getting hit. Dust erupted in a big whoosh when the door smacked the floor. Ivy coughed as she eyed the interior of the small room and saw where the toilet was supposed to have been installed.

The sudden urge to cry came over her, but she shoved it away. Crying wouldn't solve anything. What she needed was an action plan.

Her stomach growled so loudly she'd swear it echoed off the brick walls. Evidently, her first order of business should be getting some lunch. Maybe everything would look better once she wasn't hungry anymore. The growling happened again, as if her stomach was agreeing with her assessment of things.

She sneezed three times before she made it outside, and even though she hadn't been inside that long, she felt as if she needed a shower.

With a shake of her head, she began walking the block toward Main Street. She had to adjust her thinking. Her old apartment in Kentucky with an updated bathroom, her comfortable advertising job, easy access to anything she could possibly want—all those things were gone. They were the old Ivy. Today she was the new Ivy, and new Ivy could accomplish anything she set her mind to.

What she couldn't do was make money appear

from thin air. She had some savings and earned a bit by selling off everything she couldn't fit in her car. Her reasoning had been that it would be easier to replace furnishings once she arrived and assessed the space rather than try to maneuver a moving truck across six states. But considering how much work her new home needed, her furnishings might be an inflatable mattress for the foreseeable future.

Since Trudy's Café was on the side of the street Ivy was already on, she headed there. The sooner she got food, the better. Because if her stomach kept growling as it had been the last few minutes, her new neighbors were going to think a bear had wandered into town. She wondered if that ever actually happened.

Trudy's was exactly how she'd imagined—quaint with a mixture of wildlife, scenery and local faces in frames on the walls. It was also busy, and many of the patrons looked up with curiosity at the unfamiliar person who'd just entered their familiar space. Ivy smiled then slid onto a chair at a two-seater table next to the wall.

A waitress arrived with a glass of water and a menu, then pulled out a pad and pen from her apron and stood waiting. Okay, not the friendliest person ever. Maybe…Katelyn, according to her crooked name tag, was having a bad day.

Service work also came with verbal abuse that wasn't deserved from customers.

Ivy smiled and said, "Can I have a couple of minutes to look over the menu?"

Katelyn didn't eye roll, but she might as well have before she shoved the pad and pen back in her apron pocket and retraced her steps to the area behind the counter and then through the swinging door to the kitchen.

"It's not you," a middle-aged woman at the next table said. "Katie's just got a bad attitude. Chip on her shoulder."

Ivy didn't know quite how to respond to this unsolicited information, so she simply nodded and gave a quick smile before turning her attention to the laminated menu. Carbs, carbs, so many carbs. But then healthy offerings with low carbohydrates and fat content would have been more surprising than food meant to keep people fueled for ranch and other outdoor work.

Well, apparently she was going to be doing a lot of physical labor as well, so she could indulge without worrying too much.

She looked up to see an older woman approaching from the direction of the kitchen.

"Hello," the woman said as she reached the table. "You must be our new neighbor."

Surprise must have shown on Ivy's face because the other woman chuckled.

"I'm guessing you're not from a small town. You'll get used to everyone knowing everything soon enough. I'm Trudy, by the way."

Ivy glanced toward the front window where Trudy's name was painted.

"Yeah, that's me, the one and only Trudy in the whole county."

"It's nice to meet you. I'm Ivy Lake." Ivy extended her hand for a shake.

"Well, that's a pretty name if I've ever heard one."

"Thank you."

Trudy gestured toward the kitchen. "Sorry about Katelyn. Her parents made her get this job, and she's hated it from day one. Today's her last day, thank goodness. So I'm in need of a good waitress if you hear of anyone looking for a job."

"Well, considering I don't know anyone here, I'm afraid I can't help much."

Unless…

She hadn't waitressed since college, and she didn't yet know what kind of price tag she was looking at regarding getting her new building repaired, renovated and ready for business. Her head was suddenly filled with huge floating dollar signs. She knew from being in the hotel business that repairs and renovations always ended up costing more than anticipated. Always. She didn't know how much she was going to have to spend, but her gut told her it was more than she had in her savings.

"I'm interested." Sure, she'd been in town less than an hour, didn't have a place to sleep or shower and didn't know anyone, but she could be friendlier than Katelyn. "I have experience."

The surprise on Trudy's face almost made Ivy laugh.

"Let's just say the building I now own needs a bit more work than I was led to believe."

"Don't tell me John lied about it just so he could finally off-load it?"

"Was that the previous owner's name?"

Trudy parked herself in the chair across from Ivy.

"Yes. John Young has been trying to sell the building for close to a decade with no takers."

Ivy couldn't help the sinking feeling that she'd made another colossal mistake, that once again she was proving herself a fool. She sighed and ran a hand over her face. Trudy patted Ivy's other hand where it lay on the table.

"One thing at a time," Trudy said, sounding so much like Grandma Cecile that Ivy felt an immediate fondness for her. "I'm happy to give you the position, but maybe you want to get things assessed first, make a plan?"

"Trust me. Whatever my plan ends up entailing is going to cost me more than I have saved. Right now, I'm feeling quite the idiot."

"Still, take a day or two to get settled then get back with me."

Ivy's stomach grumbled audibly.

"I have faith you'll figure it all out," Trudy said. "For now, let's start with satisfying your hunger. Do you know what you want yet?"

Forget calories and carbs, Ivy needed some comfort food. Some "I can't do this" food.

"I'll take fried chicken with mashed potatoes. And a salad so I feel remotely healthy."

Trudy chuckled as she patted Ivy's hand again. "Coming right up. And when you've eaten your fill, I've got a suggestion for a person to call about the building repairs."

As Trudy headed toward her kitchen, Ivy saw the woman at the next table smiling.

"You're going to be okay," the woman said. "Trudy has adopted you. That's like the Jade Valley official seal of approval."

Chalk one up in the "win" column for the day.

AUSTIN PARKED HIS truck on the side of the street behind a small, cranberry-colored crossover SUV with a blue-and-white Kentucky license plate. Judging by how much stuff was packed into the car, there was no mistaking who it belonged to. The new owner of the Stinson Building sure had traveled a long way. He wondered why someone would do that, pick up and move across the country to a place where they knew no one.

But her story didn't really matter to him beyond how it impacted what she wanted done to the building and whether she was willing to pay to have it done. He hoped that her not knowing anyone local would lead to her trusting Trudy's recommendation of him for the job.

He got out of the truck and waved to Gavin Olsen as he drove by. Gavin was going to hand over the title of newest transplant to Jade Valley, if Ivy Lake decided to stay in town.

Ivy Lake. Sounded more like a vacation spot than a person's name.

But her name also didn't matter. He knew how long the Stinson Building had sat empty and therefore how much work likely needed to be done to make it habitable. What he could earn from a job like this would take care of a lot of bill payments, and was why he'd hopped in his truck and practically sped to town after Trudy called to tell him the new owner had arrived.

"She's a sweet little thing," Trudy had said. "But she's going to need a lot of help based on what she found inside. John ought to be ashamed of himself."

"Well, she got it for only fifty bucks, so hopefully she can afford to fix what he neglected," he'd responded.

He hurried to the front door and knocked. He tried to see inside, but the windows were too grimy. However, he did think he heard the thud of footsteps on the wood floor.

"Oh, hey."

It took Austin a moment to realize the voice was coming from above him. When he looked up, a woman was roughly a third of the way out of the window. He shaded his eyes against the sun and could see that she was fairly young, maybe early thirties like him.

"Are you Austin Hathaway?"

"Yes, ma'am."

"Come on in. The door's unlocked. I'll be right down."

Her Southern accent wasn't something he heard often. Though it wasn't as pronounced as that of characters in movies set in the Deep South, she would definitely stand out in Jade Valley sounding like that.

The work that would need to be done struck him the moment he opened the door with a creak worthy of a haunted house. It became more evident as he stepped inside and his nostrils were assaulted by the stale, musty air—the odors of neglect and abandonment. As he scanned the interior, he noticed the lack of color. Everything was coated in a thick layer of dust, making the palette of the entire space range from shades of gray to a vague brown. As he walked to the middle of the room, he started estimating what would need to be done and how much it would cost.

He hoped Ivy Lake had a comfortable bank balance or credit card limit.

He supposed he'd soon find out as the woman in question appeared at the bottom of the stairs at the back of the room.

"You got here quick," she said as she approached and finally stepped into the light filtering in through the dirty windows.

Ivy Lake might be dressed in a T-shirt that said Thunder Over Louisville and loose workout pants with her reddish brown hair pulled back in a knot held by what looked like chopsticks, but there was no mistaking that she was pretty. He predicted it wouldn't be long before any eligible men within driving distance would be coming to make her acquaintance.

He might be one of those single men, but he wouldn't be in that line. The last thing he had any interest in or time for was dating.

"Trudy called me at the right time." The right time being any time he might pick up a well-paying job.

"Great."

"What exactly are you looking to do?"

She laughed a little and gestured at their surroundings. "Make this habitable for humans instead of spiders, mice and ghosts."

"You'll want to address safety first—foundation, supports, roof, electricity."

"And plumbing. I'm in serious need of usable plumbing and bathroom facilities. I'd like the commode in the middle of the floor upstairs to be more functional than a weird conceptual art piece."

"Sounds reasonable."

"So, what's next? You look around, see what needs to be fixed, then tell me a total that I hope doesn't make me stroke out?" The little laugh she tacked on the end held a hint of hysteria, like she was second-guessing all her life choices.

He needed to give her a reasonable enough quote that she wouldn't bolt immediately, because at some point the scope of this renovation project was probably going to overwhelm her and she'd go back to where she came from. At least he could do enough work that it would be easier for her to sell it than it had been for John. Still, he was curious about her intentions as they existed now.

"What do you plan to do with the place? Knowing that will help me quote the job properly."

"I intend to turn this into a quilt and fabric shop."

Making something like that profitable in a town as small as Jade Valley seemed like a flight of fancy to him. But there were other businesses in town that surprised him by making it from year to year, combining sales to locals and tourists alike, so what did he know? His business acumen didn't extend much past ranching and physical labor.

"Is that what you did before?"

She shook her head. "No, I was the advertising director for a chain of boutique hotels."

Yeah, she wasn't going to last here. He'd be lucky if she stuck around long enough for him to totally repair and renovate the place to sell it rather than abandoning the project midway or before.

He nodded once but didn't voice his thoughts about how ill-equipped she likely was for this undertaking.

"Well, I'll get started inspecting everything." Best to begin before she had second thoughts and that needed income slipped through his fingers like water.

Austin began with an examination of the exterior of the building. Coming from somewhere inside he heard music, not the country he was used to hearing but rather pop music. He thought he recognized a song that he'd heard coming from his younger sister's room. It amazed him sometimes just how much of a difference the seventeen years between their ages made. Often, he felt more like Daisy's father than her brother, even more so since her father's death.

Despite their age difference, however, that was the thing that really bound them together—the fact that they'd both lost their fathers and had witnessed their mother's sorrow in the wake of those losses.

Austin shook off those thoughts and focused on a careful examination of the building and writing down everything that absolutely had to be done in one column and things that should be done in another. Maybe if he gave her options, she would be more likely to hire him. It became evident that if she did, this would be the biggest job he'd ever undertaken. He tried not to get too excited about the potential income so that he wouldn't be as disappointed if it didn't work out.

Hours passed as he checked stone and brick, wood and glass, plumbing and a cursory look at the electrical. He wasn't certified to do the type of electrical work Ivy would likely need, but he intended to suggest Rich Tucker for that part of the job.

At one point, while measuring the square footage of the first-level floor, he caught himself humming along to Ivy's music. He stopped and listened, realizing it was an old bluegrass song.

He supposed that made sense, considering where she had lived before. Her playlist seemed to be quite eclectic.

Once he'd examined everything on the lower level, he made his way up the stairs, announcing himself as he neared the top. What he saw when he stepped into the light of the upper floor, however, surprised him. Ivy had obviously swept and mopped the floor, and now was struggling to set up a tent.

"You do realize those are supposed to be used outside, right?" he asked.

She spun at the sound of his voice, making it obvious that she hadn't heard his approach despite him having called out as he climbed the stairs. Her sudden movement caused her to lose hold of the tent and the progress she'd made in setting it up. Her sigh of frustration made him feel bad.

"I've been battling with this thing for fifteen minutes, and so far it is winning." She glanced toward him, showing that she had several streaks of dirt on her face. "As for why I'm assembling a tent inside, as you can see I don't have a bed yet. Plus this will hopefully keep away any critters who have called this place home before today."

"You're staying here?" The idea would be comical if it wasn't ridiculous.

"Yes. It's my new home, after all."

Austin looked around. Though she'd made an attempt to clear away the worst of the dust and fresh air was flowing in the open windows, this still wasn't an ideal place to spend the night.

"There are some nice cabins outside of town a few miles, right on the river. Pretty place."

"I'm sure they have a nice rental rate too. As you have no doubt gathered, I need to save my money for other things."

Dread started to form in his stomach. No matter what he quoted her, was she not going to be able to pay? He'd have to require at least half the amount up front. He couldn't afford to devote the time to a job and then not get paid for the work.

Still, the idea of her sleeping in a tent in this old building didn't sit well with him.

"I'm not sure it's healthy to stay here yet."

"Don't worry. I plan to keep the windows open. It would be better if they had screens, but I'm willing to risk a bird flying inside if I can have fresh air. And I'll give you that, the air here is really fresh."

"You're going to get cold at night."

"I once walked three miles home in an ice storm when the roads weren't passable, so I think I'll be okay."

Some people had to learn the hard way.

CHAPTER THREE

AUSTIN HATHAWAY HADN'T been lying. Ivy woke up in the middle of the night shivering despite the thick comforter she'd excavated from her car earlier. As much as she hated to do so, she crawled out of the tent and went to close the windows. At least they were clean now. Once she'd wrestled them closed, she took a moment to stare up at the sky. Even with the lights of Jade Valley shining, she was amazed at how beautiful the starlit sky was. It was as if the number of stars she could see in Louisville had been multiplied a thousandfold.

Of course, it was just the lack of light pollution making it seem that way. She remembered accompanying her grandmother, mother and sisters to what Grandma Cecile called "the old home place" when Ivy was around ten years old. She, Lily and Holly had lain on a grassy hillside near a rickety old shell of a house where Grandma Cecile had grown up. Above them was a blanket of stars so expansive that the only way to describe it was "Wow."

She remembered thinking the stars twinkled like diamonds and that it had been the first time she'd seen the Milky Way.

When a shiver ran along her extremities, Ivy hurried back to the tent and tried in vain to get warm. Even thinking about her new handyman didn't help. Sure, she had sworn off men, but there was no denying the fact that Austin was really good-looking. Tall, lean, dark hair and eyes, with a bit of attractive facial scruff. She'd think of him like fine art in a museum—look but don't touch. And definitely don't try to take it home.

What she was most interested in was how high the estimate for his work was going to be. She'd made it clear that she wanted the building to be safe and solid; otherwise nothing else mattered. But she'd also told him that to shave off some of the cost she was willing to learn how to lend a hand. She'd seen the disbelief in his expression, the doubt that she would be able to do anything useful.

She'd spent her life defying expectations. It made her want to prove him wrong. Plus there was genuine desperation to make this work on her part. There was no plan B.

When it became obvious that she wasn't going to be able to go back to sleep, she exited the tent again. Using a jug of water she'd bought at the same time she'd gotten the tent the day before, she washed her hands and face. After brushing her hair, she headed to the convenience store. It wasn't of the twenty-four-hour kind, but they did open at four in the morning. People evidently started work early in this part of the country.

Though she didn't see anyone nearby and it was only a max of three blocks to the convenience store, she still drove. Small town Wyoming might not be the same as cities, but that didn't mean she felt safe walking alone at night.

"Good morning," the clerk said when Ivy stepped into the brightly lit store. "You're getting an early start."

Ivy had been in Jade Valley only a day, and already she wasn't surprised that someone she'd never met knew her identity. Trudy had told her the previous day that before Ivy arrived at the café, Trudy had already heard she was in town from three different people. Again, it reminded her of the stories Grandma Cecile told of her youth in a small town in the Kentucky part of Appalachia. Only now the speed of gossip was aided by the internet and smartphones.

"Lots to do," Ivy said simply as she walked straight for the restroom.

After she finished, she headed for the freshly brewed coffee. She grabbed some coffee cake to go with her strong brew as well as assorted snacks to get her through until lunch.

"I hear Austin is going to be working for you," the middle-aged woman at the cash register said as Ivy placed her items on the counter.

"Possibly. Depends on how much the bid ends up being."

"You won't find anyone who will do a better job or at a better price." The woman smiled before adding, "And there are worse things to look at."

While the last part was obviously true, Ivy really hoped the first part was as well.

"I've heard good things about his work." Before anything else was said about Austin Hathaway's level of attractiveness, Ivy grabbed her bag of purchases and headed back to her car.

Wanting to eat in a clean environment, she sat in her car in the lighted parking lot until she finished two squares of coffee cake and had consumed half of her large coffee. Once she was fortified with caffeine and sugar, she headed back home to get a jump on her massive to-do list.

By the time the sunrise lit the valley, she had hauled about half of the old boxes from upstairs down to the lower level. Most of the contents were either useless or so deteriorated she couldn't tell what it had once been. One box was full of flyers for a local church bazaar held in 1993. Another had a variety of mildewed matchboxes and half-used candles. It was a wonder some critter hadn't accidentally started a fire and burned down the building.

She started to open the windows on the bottom floor to get some fresh air only to discover they had all been nailed shut.

"Well, that doesn't seem safe," she said to herself.

"What doesn't?"

She yelped as she spun to see Austin standing in the open doorway.

"Sorry," he said, looking genuinely contrite. "I didn't mean to scare you. I seem to keep doing that."

Ivy waved off his apology. "It's okay."

He crossed to where she was standing, and she pointed toward the nails in the window frame.

"Probably to keep vandals and mischievous kids out," he said.

"Still, I'll be replacing those with some proper locks." She looked up at him, realized just how much taller he was than her—probably a full foot. "I'm guessing you have an estimate for me."

"I do." He held out a few sheets of paper folded in half.

She took it, preparing herself for the shock of many zeros.

"Well, here goes. Let's see if I need to sell some plasma."

"I kept things as reasonable as possible without cutting any safety corners."

Was it her imagination or did Austin look a bit nervous? He shifted from one foot to the other then back again.

She opened the paper and started scanning the list of repairs and estimated costs. Trying not to panic, she flipped to the second page, then the third. The final tally made her wish she had a chair to sit down on, but she also realized it could be worse. She'd seen some of the costs of renovating old buildings to turn them into hotels. While her building wouldn't require that kind of treatment, it still needed a lot of work. And good work wasn't free.

"While I didn't expect to have this big of an undertaking when I decided to come here, these numbers look reasonable."

It was quiet, but she still heard the sigh of relief that escaped Austin. Were jobs so hard to come by here that this was make-or-break for him? Worry that her shop wouldn't be able to recoup the cost of the repairs and renovations as well as allow her to pay her normal bills threatened to take up permanent residence in her thoughts. Once again, she refused to let it.

Only positive thoughts. Only positive thoughts. Only positive thoughts.

"When can you start?"

"Right now."

"Oh, well, you definitely come prepared."

"Yes, ma'am."

"Just Ivy."

He nodded. "As I noted on the estimate, I can't do the electrical, but I recommend Rich Tucker. He's very good with all things electrical."

"Considering I know exactly two people here now, I'll trust you on that."

"Okay, I'll get started on things I can do until he can come over."

Austin sounded so businesslike, almost as if he thought one wrong step and she'd fire him before he got started. Hopefully, he'd loosen up as the project got underway.

She left him to his work and returned upstairs. But before she could resume her own work, she had to sit down. With the floor or the closed commode the only options, she went with the latter and massaged her forehead to try to prevent the headache she felt forming. She'd just agreed to spend a sum of money that would drain all of her resources with any income from her store not yet visible on the horizon. She definitely needed to take Trudy up on that offer to waitress before someone else nabbed it.

Ivy grabbed her purse and hurried back downstairs. Austin was unloading a variety of tools and sawhorses in front of the building.

"I have some errands to run. You have my number on the card I gave you yesterday if you need to call me for any reason."

She jogged to her car with the aim of visiting a campground about ten miles out of town. For a modest fee, she could gain access to the bathhouse—a much cheaper option than renting a cabin or a motel room. Because she wasn't going to go apply for a job while grimy.

The campground attendant gave her a strange look when it was apparent Ivy was alone and didn't have an RV or even a pickup truck, but Ivy didn't offer any explanation. She just drove straight to the campsite directly across from the bathhouse. Thankfully, the campground was fully occupied with people sitting in the shade of their RV awnings drinking coffee, lying in hammocks reading books, or cooking over campfires. She tossed out a couple of smiles and waves to those she saw nearby but quickly grabbed her clean clothes and toiletries and went to wash away her hours of work.

It wasn't a fancy bathroom by any stretch of the imagination, but had a shower ever felt so good?

When she arrived at Trudy's Café, the place was packed. Ivy noticed that three tables hadn't been cleared after the diners left, so she started clearing them, depositing the dishes in the bus cart behind the front counter and the napkins and straw wrappers in the trash. Just as she finished clearing two of the three tables, new customers occupied them.

Ivy glanced at the waitress who was busy at the cash register, and the young woman nodded at her.

"What can I get you to drink?" Ivy asked the first couple.

Ivy and Stephanie, the harried waitress, fell into a rhythm of clearing and wiping down tables, taking orders and delivering food to the hungry lunch crowd. Trudy's brisk business renewed Ivy's hope that her own business would flourish too.

When the late morning to early afternoon rush dwindled to a few customers lingering over a late lunch, Trudy emerged from the kitchen and leaned one outstretched arm against the front counter as she looked at Ivy.

"Well, I guess you're hired."

"I haven't even interviewed yet."

"Sure you did, and you seem to know your way around."

"I waitressed to help pay my way through college."

"It shows."

"Thanks for your help," Stephanie said. "There are usually two of us working the midday shift."

"Happy to help. And happy to take the job. Renovations don't magically pay for themselves."

"Is it bad?" Trudy asked.

"It could be worse."

"Which means it also could be better. Well, I'll give you as many midday shifts as you can handle. I've got my early mornings covered by some longtime employees and the evenings by the younger set."

"You're a lifesaver."

Trudy chuckled. "So I've been told. Now, how about we all have some lunch?"

"Thank you, but now it's time for my other job—clearing my new home of years' worth of ick."

"Oh, sounds fun," Stephanie said.

"So much fun." Ivy laughed.

"At least you've got some company," Trudy said.

"Yeah?" Stephanie had obviously somehow managed to miss the gossip about Austin working on the building.

"Austin Hathaway is doing the repair and renovation work."

"He's a good guy. Good-looking too."

It seemed as if everyone thought Austin was the local heartthrob, and the way they referred to him made Ivy think he wasn't romantically attached. If people started to try to match-make, she was going to have to put a stop to it. Her heart and pride still hurt from the betrayal she'd suffered, so she wasn't open to exposing either to a repeat performance.

"If he can make the building habitable and inviting for customers, I'll be happy."

"Well, I'm not sending you off without a meal," Trudy said, and headed toward the kitchen door.

"Really, it's o—"

"Hush now," Trudy said.

"It's no use arguing with her when she wants to feed you," Stephanie said as Trudy disappeared beyond the swinging door.

"So I see. She reminds me of my grandmother."

Grandma Cecile used to send Ivy and her sisters home with enough food after a visit to feed an army platoon. Some people showed their affection with food. Grandma Cecile and Trudy were obviously two of those people.

Gifted with not one but two meals, Ivy drove the short distance home to find Austin sitting on the front stoop. As she approached him, it appeared he was having a simple peanut butter sandwich for lunch.

"Here," she said, extending one of the meals.

"I have lunch," he said, holding up the half-eaten sandwich.

"No offense, but I guarantee this is better."

"You don't have to feed me."

"I'm not. Trudy is. She sent me back with two meals, and I obviously don't have a refrigerator to keep the second one from spoiling."

He hesitated for a moment before he said, "Well, it would be a crime to have Trudy's work go to waste."

"Indeed."

As if they were lifelong friends, Ivy sat on the stoop next to Austin.

"So, how are things going? Please don't tell me you've found any additional problems."

"So far, so good. You'll be happy to know that at least the outside water spigot works out back. We'll have to check the plumbing inside though before it can be used."

"Well, that's a step in the right direction."

Austin opened his lunch container to reveal the roast pork inside.

"You're right. This is better than my sandwich."

"It smelled so good on the way back that I nearly didn't make it here before diving in. I'd already been salivating for the past two hours."

Austin looked over as he took a bite, the obvious question written on his handsome face.

"I might have taken a job waitressing at Trudy's to help pay for all this." She motioned to the building behind them. "To do this right, it's going to eat all of my savings."

Austin was quiet for a moment as he directed his attention across the street at a vacant lot.

"Are you sure you want to do this?"

There was a layer of hesitance in his question, and she could imagine him hoping that it didn't prompt her to back out and cost him some needed weeks of work. The fact he'd asked it anyway told her something about his character—that he didn't want to push her beyond her means. All the positive things she'd heard about him seemed to be true, at least so far, but sometimes people didn't show their true colors until you'd known them awhile.

She nodded and wiped her mouth with a napkin.

"When I saw the contest to win this place, it felt meant to be. Plus there's the fact that I quit my job and moved across the country with all my possessions."

"Not sure I believe in meant to be, but I'll do everything I can to make this place what you want it to be."

"Thank you. I appreciate that." She thought about what he'd said for a moment. "Maybe you're right about there being no meant to be, but there's definitely want to be."

They sat in silence for a couple of minutes while they both ate.

"So why a quilt shop?"

"It was time for a change, and this was something that my grandmother always dreamed of doing but she never got the chance."

"You're a quilter then?"

"I know how. She taught me and my sisters. But I haven't had time to really do much in recent years, what with work and...other things."

Things that would no longer take up her time.

"What about you?" she asked. "Have you been doing construction work since you were young?"

"Here and there. I also run my family's ranch."

"Look at us, a couple of two-jobbers."

Austin smiled a little, and it startled Ivy how much that small change in expression increased his already apparent attractiveness. If he wasn't already in a relationship, it was likely only a matter of time. Because with a small population, she guessed the depth of the dating pool measured on the kiddie end. Unless, of course, he had his own reasons for remaining single.

A newer red pickup pulled up to the curb and parked.

"That's Rich Tucker, the electrician," Austin said.

"Well, this looks like a very relaxed job site," Rich said as he stepped out of his truck.

He wasn't as tall as Austin, nor as good-looking, but it was obvious from his first word that he was more vocal and outgoing.

Ivy closed the take-out container on what was left of her lunch and stood.

"Mr. Tucker, nice to meet you," she said as she extended her hand.

"Please, call me Rich," he said with what was obviously a flirtatious smile.

"Okay, Rich." She retrieved her hand as quickly as possible without being rude and picked up the bag holding her leftovers.

Beside her, Austin stood as well. It gave her an odd sense of security, though she didn't think Rich presented any potential harm.

"I'll show you around," Austin said to Rich.

Ivy accompanied them inside and listened as Austin told Rich what he'd observed during his own visual inspection of the wiring.

"What are you going to do with the building?" Rich asked. "What kind of appliances and electrical needs?"

She told him how she wanted to outfit her living space and then what would be necessary for the business—lights, a few sewing machines for potential classes, heat and air so she could regulate both temperature and humidity levels.

"Okay. I'll get started checking the wear and tear. Any frayed or exposed wires, loose connections and outdated components will be the most obvious hazards."

As he went about his work, taking verbal notes

on his phone about things like voltage levels, circuit load capacity and insulation, she continued to carry the musty boxes down from the upper level. Once she had several on the scraggly front lawn, she started examining the contents. As expected, most of it was total junk.

When she opened the box that had been ridiculously heavy, she half expected to find a cannonball inside. Instead, she was stunned to find a collection of old coins in individual plastic holders. What were the chances any of these were worth something substantial? She sank onto the ground and started looking up some of the coins on a valuation site. Several were worth a few dollars more than face value, which collectively was nice if she could find buyers. Yeah, with all the free time she had.

She pulled out another penny that appeared to be older than the ones she'd examined so far. When she checked the date, a jolt of surprise hit her. Wow, 1909. Maybe this one was worth a little more. She typed the description into the search bar and gasped.

"What's wrong?"

She looked up to see Austin looking at her with concern.

"Look at this," she said, extending the penny to him. "Then read this on my phone and tell me if I'm right in thinking these are the same."

He crouched beside her and first examined the penny, then the description, then the penny again.

"Looks like it's your lucky day." He glanced at the open box filled with coins. "You found this upstairs?"

A sinking realization came over her.

"I can't keep these."

"Why not?"

"It's obvious they were accidentally left behind."

"I don't think they were. John never used this building for anything. He might have planned to at some point, but for years all he's wanted to do is sell it. So all that stuff upstairs was from the previous owners."

"Then this belongs to them."

"I don't think they'll have much use for coins or the money they might bring."

"Why? Are they already rich?"

"No. They're buried in the cemetery on the edge of town."

"Oh."

"When you became the owner of this building, you became the owner of everything in it." Austin tapped the edge of the box. "Including these."

"Well, now I'm going to fantasize that there's enough here to pay for all of your work."

"Maybe there's pirate treasure at the bottom."

Ivy laughed. "I like how you think."

She stood and dusted off the back of her pants, glanced at the box then at the building.

"Let me carry those back upstairs for you," Austin said as he picked up the box much more easily than she had. "I assume that's where you want it."

"Yes, please."

She followed him toward the stairs, thinking about how she hated the idea of leaving the coins here while she worked. But then her shifts at Trudy's would likely coincide with Austin's hours working on the building. And the fact that these coins had sat in that box for years without anyone finding them was a positive sign as well. Still, she'd like to research and catalog them as soon as she could so she could sell them.

But other tasks were more pressing.

She glanced up as they climbed the stairs, aiming to ask Austin when he thought she might have a working bathroom. But the words died in her throat as she caught sight of how nicely his jeans fit. Ivy sucked in a breath and started coughing. She barely averted her eyes before Austin turned and caught her looking.

"Are you okay?"

She waved her hand in front of her nose and mouth as she brought her coughing under control.

"All the dust. I feel like there's so much of it, I could plant a cornfield in it."

Heat swamped her, much more than her physical activity would create. She was not supposed to even be in an emotional place where such a thing was possible. What James had done to her still had the betrayal equivalent of new car smell. She came to Wyoming to focus on herself, on a new business venture, a new life. Not on a new man.

And yet the universe had seen fit to laugh in her face and give her a hot handyman.

Just great.

CHAPTER FOUR

AUSTIN TRIED TO focus on ripping up the floor-boards with water damage below the broken window, but it was hard to tune out Rich's obvious flirting with Ivy. While she was nice, he noticed Ivy was not flirting back. Not that Rich noticed. The man was the best around for electrical work, but he was a bit oblivious to "I'm not interested" signals from women. To Austin's knowledge, Rich was just dense in that department and never crossed the line. If he did, Austin would be the first to drag him out by his collar. He didn't want Ivy to be uncomfortable or to question his judgment in his recommendation of Rich.

"Hey, Rich," he called out to give Ivy a way to exit the conversation.

Rich looked as if he was a smidge perturbed to be interrupted but was smiling by the time he reached Austin.

"You need something?"

"What's the estimate on how long it's going to take you to do the electrical?"

"Luckily it's not as bad as it could have been, so I should be able to wrap it up in about a week." He glanced toward the stairs, which Austin noticed Ivy had taken rather quickly after he'd called Rich over. "Plenty of time to determine what Ivy likes so I can make a good impression when I ask her out."

"You're going to want to abandon that plan."

Rich looked back at Austin. "Wait, are you already making a play?"

"No." The last thing he needed was another woman in his life, least of all one who more than likely would abandon this building and Jade Valley when neither lived up to her dreams.

Dreams too often gave way to reality, so it was best to live in reality to begin with.

"You sure? Seems like you're acting territorial."

"Because I need this job, and I don't want her feeling so uncomfortable that she decides to cancel it and leave."

"Uncomfortable? I didn't do or say anything I shouldn't have."

Rich sounded offended, and Austin didn't want that either.

"Listen, you are the best electrician anywhere near here, but what talent you have with electrical wiring you lack in picking up on women's social cues." Austin placed his hand on Rich's shoulder. "Sorry, buddy, but as they say, she's just not that into you."

"Really?"

Austin nodded.

"Well, that stinks."

"Look at it this way. You got a profitable job ahead of you."

Austin had to smother a laugh when Rich headed out to buy the supplies he needed to get started.

When Ivy didn't come downstairs for a long time, Austin thought perhaps she was hiding. He considered letting her know Rich had left, but right then he heard her descending the stairs again. He glanced over as she reached the bottom, another box in hand, and looked around.

"Rich left a while ago to buy some supplies."

"Oh, okay." She proceeded outside.

When he was finished removing the floorboards that needed to be replaced, he went outside to cut replacements.

"Any more hidden treasures?" he asked as he nodded toward the box in front of her.

"Not unless you count wrinkly flyers about the grand opening of JJ's Boot Shop."

"That place closed when I was in middle school, I think. Didn't last long. About as long as the print shop, the last business in this building."

"Well, that doesn't inspire hope that I'm going to become a successful business owner."

"A lot has changed since then," he said. "More tourists visit now. The fall festival has gotten an overhaul and brings in loads of people."

"That's a bit more hopeful."

The sound of a truck approaching caught Ivy's attention.

"I'm sorry about Rich earlier." Austin needed to clear the air, make sure she understood the situation and wouldn't feel the need to hide every time Rich was around or blame Austin because she had to.

"Was I that obvious?"

"Rich is great at his job, but picking up on subtleties not so much. I told him you weren't interested."

"Thank you. He seems like a nice guy, but I'm not interested in dating anyone."

That made two of them. Even though he didn't like talking about his own reasons, he couldn't help but be curious about hers. She was a very pretty woman, nice, from what he'd seen a hard worker. But she'd also entered a contest to win a building she'd never seen in a state on the other side of the country. She'd made comments about a fresh start. There could be a lot of reasons for that, but his gut told him at least part of it was romantic.

"Chances are others will try to ask you out," he said. "My advice is to make it clear you're not interested in dating."

"But carefully. It's a small town where I'm going to open a business. I don't want to offend people."

"True. But honesty is the best policy, as they say."

"If only everyone believed that."

That wasn't just a blanket statement, because there had been a slight edge to how she'd said it. Bitterness maybe. Perhaps something else, but he wasn't sure. Despite how he'd detected that Rich was making Ivy uncomfortable with his flirting, Austin wouldn't say he was an expert on reading emotions. His history had shown he wasn't. Otherwise, he would have picked up on clues that Grace had been more than frustrated with the situation in which they'd found themselves, that she was going to leave him.

His phone rang, making him realize he had been staring at Ivy. He jerked his gaze away and pulled the phone from the back pocket of his jeans. When he saw "Mom" on the screen, his heart rate accelerated. Was something wrong? That couldn't be how he answered the phone, however. Lately, she'd become more irritable if he hovered, if he offered to help her in any way.

"Hey, Mom." He did his best to keep any worry out of his greeting.

"I just got a call from Dr. Barton's office,"

she said. "They want to change my checkup to tomorrow morning. I told them I might not—"

"It's fine."

"But you just started this new job."

"Really, it's okay." At least he hoped it would be. Ivy didn't seem like the type of person who expected him to adhere to certain hours if he still got the job done in a timely fashion.

Even though it was now certain that his mother would never regain the use of her legs, he insisted that she keep going to the regular checkups so that any postaccident problems could be addressed. And, honestly, the trips to the doctor at least got his mom out of the house and away from the ranch. They allowed her to socialize with other people. He always made sure they stopped at other places as well—the grocery, the post office, the library, Trudy's, wherever he could think of without raising her suspicions. Daisy knew instinctively what he was doing and aided him without saying so. His sister was more grown-up and intuitive than he could have imagined being at her age.

When the call ended, he turned to Ivy. "I'll need to get to work a bit later tomorrow, but I'll stay late." Which meant doing his ranch chores later than he liked, but there was no other option. Daisy could do some of them, but not all. Plus it was her summer vacation, and she deserved to have some time to herself after working hard in school all year in addition to helping him and their mother. She was already largely trapped at home so their mother wasn't alone, so he didn't want to add more to her burden. He didn't want her to grow up to resent him and their mom for robbing her of her youth.

"Everything okay?" Ivy asked.

"Yeah. I just need to take my mom to a medical checkup."

"Sure, take whatever time you need."

"Thanks."

When Rich returned, Ivy didn't disappear upstairs. And Rich had evidently taken what Austin said to heart because he kept exchanges with Ivy on a professionally friendly level. The three of them fell into what felt like a natural rhythm of attacking their own parts of the project. At one point, Ivy was carrying what appeared to be a bunch of old newspapers toward the exit when Rich said, "Come on, baby. You know you want to behave."

Ivy jerked her head in Rich's direction, but he wasn't looking at her.

"He's talking to the wiring," Austin said.

"Huh?"

Austin took a step closer to her and pointed the hammer he was holding toward Rich, who wasn't aware they were talking about him.

"He has the nickname the Electrical Whisperer because he talks to the wiring as he's working."

"Oookay, then."

Austin laughed. "I'm not one to believe in woowoo stuff, but he does have a gift. I've seen him make stuff work that any sane person would have tossed in the trash."

"If it takes woowoo to make this place safe at a price that doesn't force me into bankruptcy, bring on the woowoo."

"SO HOW IS IT? Are you ready to come home yet?"

Ivy heard the hopeful note in her older sister Holly's voice and experienced a moment of guilt. But that wasn't fair. This was her life and she should be able to live it how she wanted. Plus there might be close to eighty miles between Louisville and Lexington, but that still wasn't far enough away from her cheater ex. Any place with a Southern accent of any flavor wasn't far enough. Part of the appeal of moving to Wyoming was that it looked nothing like Kentucky. She'd never experienced waking up and being able to see snowcapped mountains out of her bedroom window.

"It's going great." Ivy deliberately didn't answer the second question because she figured her answer to the first did double duty. "It's like looking at a postcard from my bedroom window."

"Send me pictures. I want to see everything."

Oh no, that wasn't going to happen. Holly was in full protective big sister mode. The minute she saw the state of the Stinson Building, she would be on a plane to Wyoming to drag Ivy back to Kentucky even if she was a grown woman.

"I'm not where I can right now. Plus I'm having some renovations done, so it's a bit of a mess. I'll send you some when it's all done."

"What are you not telling me? Something's wrong, isn't it?"

"Holly, just stop. I appreciate that you care about me, but I can take care of myself. And this is something I want to do. I need to do it, okay?"

She'd told her family all that before she left, several times, but maybe it would sink in more now that she was here, fifteen hundred miles away.

"Fine."

Ivy heard the "But you can always come back home" even though Holly didn't say it out loud.

After a few more minutes of catching up, Holly had to go help a customer in the small floral shop she ran with their mother.

"I want at least one picture before the end of the day," Holly said.

"Yes, Miss Bossy."

As soon as Ivy hung up, she knew exactly what pictures she would send. But first, she needed to wash up so she didn't look like she'd forgotten how to bathe. She placed the small metal tub she'd bought at the discount store under the outdoor spigot and turned on the flow of water. Movement out of the corner of her eye caught her attention. There, sitting under one of the bushes that needed pruning, was a gray tabby cat. Its green eyes watched her with obvious wariness, its body poised to bolt if she moved in a way it didn't like.

"Hello, there. Are you one of my neighbors?"

She'd met several of the neighbors of the two-legged variety. Evangeline Taggert had a small pottery studio next door but not a lot of business, from what Ivy could tell. The lot behind the Stinson Building was residential, and an older gentleman named Reg lived there. Austin had told her to never call the man Reginald because he hated his full name with a fire to rival an erupting volcano.

She wondered if the kitty belonged to Reg or one of the other nearby residents. When she reached up to turn off the flow of water, however, the cat bolted. Either it was skittish by nature or feral. Whichever it was, she carried the water inside then brought a plastic bowl back out to fill with water for the cat. If it kept hanging around, she'd buy some cat food.

She heated some of the water on the camp

stove she'd bought the previous evening along with a huge bag of trail mix and a warm sleeping bag. She told herself that when she had functional heating and air as well as an actual bed, she could use all these purchases to go camping. She imagined that's something a Wyomingite would do, and she was a Wyomingite now.

Once she was clean and had washed her hair, she walked over to the window, opened it and positioned herself for a selfie with the picturesque mountains in the background. She stuck her tongue out and snapped a photo, then sent it to Holly. Before she left for work, she decided to take another photo to post on Instagram. She considered what to say that wouldn't make it seem like she was trying too hard to not be the jilted bride-to-be.

You can't beat this morning view. #newadventures

She closed the camera app and finished getting ready for her shift at Trudy's. Austin hadn't arrived yet, and Rich wasn't due to arrive until early afternoon. Austin had the copy of the building key she'd had made the day before, however, and she just had to hope that no one decided now was the time to see if there was anything worth stealing. She took some comfort from the fact that no one had broken into her obviously packed full car while it sat on the street.

With some time left before her shift started but not enough to do any substantial work, she went to sit on the front stoop and add some things to her online vision board for the quilt shop. She'd just bookmarked another fabric supplier's site when Austin pulled up to the curb, and he wasn't alone.

"Hey," she said when he got out of the truck.

"Hey. I just stopped by to drop off the new window before I take Mom and Daisy home."

Ivy eyed the two people still in the truck. The younger of the two looked too young to be a girlfriend or wife. Was she a much younger sister?

Austin moved to the back of the pickup to grab the window. Ivy got to her feet and walked over to the open truck window.

"Hello, I'm Ivy Lake. Would you like a little tour?"

"We can't—" Austin started right as the teenage girl said, "Yes, please."

Ivy glanced over at Austin in time to see the surprise on his face.

"Daisy, you know—"

"It's okay," his mother said. "Let her look around if Ivy doesn't mind."

Instead of getting out, however, the older woman sat where she was as Daisy scooted out via the driver's side. That's when Ivy noticed the wheelchair in the bed of the truck. She hoped the surprise didn't show on her face.

"I don't mind at all. We'll be right back."

As she accompanied the girl across the street, Ivy noticed that Austin didn't come with them.

"So, your name is Daisy?" she asked as she opened the front door and gestured for the girl to go ahead of her.

"Yes, ma'am. I'm Austin's sister."

"Nice to meet you. And that's cool. We both are named after pretty plants. It's sort of a family thing with me though. My sisters are named Holly and Lily, my mom is Rose and my grandmother's first name was Lavender, even though she went by her middle name, Cecile."

"Those are all pretty names."

"And to add to the whole floral theme, Mom and Holly are florists." Ivy gestured around the lower level. "Pardon the mess. There's obviously still a lot of work to be done, but I think it's going to be awesome when it's finished."

"I've always wanted to see the inside of this building," Daisy said as she walked slowly ahead, looking at the pressed tin ceiling. "I love history."

"I do too. I'm hoping to eventually research the history of this place, maybe put up an exhibit in that corner." Ivy pointed at the front corner to the right of the door.

"I could do that for you. It'd be fun."

"I'm sure you have a lot more fun things to do on your summer break."

"Not really," Daisy said, seeming to deflate a bit. "I do have some Geography Club stuff and I'll do a lot of reading. And ranch chores to help out Mom and Austin."

She'd just met Daisy and already Ivy's heart went out to her. She felt an immediate affection for the girl, a kinship she couldn't yet explain. As she showed her around both floors of the building, an idea started percolating in her head. When they returned to the bottom floor, she halted Daisy before they stepped outside.

"I have a question for you. Before I ask, however, know that your mother and brother will have to approve."

"Okay."

"I can't pay a lot, but what would you say about working here a couple of days a week researching the history of the building, coming up with ideas for the exhibit? I also have some old coins that I need researched and cataloged."

"Yes!"

The girl was so excited that Ivy suddenly wished she'd asked Austin and his mother about the idea first. She would hate it if they said no and crushed Daisy's excitement.

"They'll say yes."

Ivy certainly hoped so.

"DID YOU ASK Ivy for a job?" Austin asked Daisy when his sister brought up the topic during dinner.

"No. All I said was that I liked history and that I could research the building's history for her."

"She must have felt obligated to offer to pay you for the work."

The way Daisy bit her lip told him that he was ruining a potentially fun summer endeavor for her, but he knew from what Ivy had said that she didn't have the money to be hiring yet more people, even if it was for only a couple days a week. Even so, he hated himself for extinguishing his sister's excitement. She was typically so quiet and shy. The way she had hopped out of the truck earlier and chatted with Ivy as if they were the best of friends had surprised him, and now here he was ensuring that Daisy retreated back into her shell.

Hopefully it wouldn't last long, because his keeping the renovation job and not making Ivy feel as if Daisy was taking advantage of her kindness were important. If not for the bills and how it was almost impossible to whittle them down, he wouldn't object to Daisy having a part-time job that she would no doubt love.

"I see no problem with it," their mom said. "Ivy is obviously a grown woman who can make her own decisions."

"Mom—"

"Daisy, can you go feed Pooch?" his mom said, cutting him off.

They all knew that she'd sent Daisy outside to feed their dog so that the adults could discuss the topic without her.

"She's doing this," his mom said as soon as Daisy's footsteps could no longer be heard on the porch.

Austin sighed. He didn't like disagreeing with his mother, but he was trying so hard to keep a roof over their heads and food on the table. But maybe this time, a compromise was the best solution.

"I will talk to Ivy tomorrow to make sure she didn't offer this simply out of kindness."

"So what if she did? You need to learn to let people make their own decisions. Stop trying to be everyone's parent. Daisy may have lost her father, but she still has me."

Austin winced. He didn't think he was overbearing. He loved his sister with his whole heart and wanted only the best for her. It wasn't fair that she'd lost her father like he had. It wasn't fair that he needed her to do more around the ranch and stay with their mom while he was working in town. But there was no one else to do those things, and he couldn't work twenty-four hours a day.

"You may disagree with me, but I need to talk

to Ivy first. Even if she does truly want to have Daisy do the work, her first day doesn't have to be tomorrow."

His mom looked like she wanted to say something further, but she refrained.

After she wheeled herself away from the table and started loading the dishwasher, he stood and headed for the back door. He instinctively knew that his mom was not in the mood for a helping hand. It wasn't the first time he'd had to keep himself from offering to help her and remind himself that her doing normal tasks unaided was a good thing. He had to balance his urge to make things easier for her with not treating her like she was helpless. Often he didn't succeed.

Too many times, like now, he ended up feeling like the bad guy.

He started for the barn to take care of his horse, Merlin, when he spotted Daisy sitting on the ground with her legs crossed, scratching Pooch between his ears. Austin stopped and considered if it was better to talk to his sister or leave her to her thoughts. What more could he say that hadn't already been said? He'd be lucky if she didn't end up hating him before she reached adulthood.

"It's okay," she said, evidently realizing he was standing several feet away.

With a sad sigh, he walked over and sat beside her.

"I'm sorry if I always seem mean."

"You don't." She sounded as if she really meant that, which somehow made him feel worse than if she were angry and sulking like a normal teenager.

He rubbed Pooch's head when the tan mutt— one part shepherd and several parts other unknown breeds—placed his head on Austin's knee as if he detected Austin's inner exhaustion and was trying to offer comfort.

"I'm sorry I caused you and Mom to fight."

"Oh, Daisy. You didn't. I understand you wanting to have more freedom and do things you enjoy during your time off from school. And I understand Mom wanting to let you. I just…" How did he even put into words what he was feeling and have it make sense to someone not quite half his age? Sometimes he felt three times her fourteen years.

"Don't worry about me or Mom," Daisy said. "We'll be okay here while you're away from the ranch."

She sounded so grown-up and responsible that he wanted to cry. He wasn't totally responsible for the current situation, but he'd one hundred percent been the one to destroy her new spark of joy. He felt like the worst brother in the world, more like one of those mean parents who always said no.

The entire situation weighed so heavily on his mind that when he went to bed, he ended up tossing and turning more than sleeping. When he woke up a little after four in the morning, and it became obvious that he wasn't going to be able to go back to sleep, he got up and dressed. Might as well get his ranch work done and head to Ivy's early.

When he arrived not long after sunrise, he planned to sit in his truck while he drank his coffee until he made sure Ivy was awake. But to his surprise, she was already outside clearing overgrown shrubbery away from the front of the building.

"And here I thought I was getting an early start," he said as he crossed the street.

She made a circular motion toward her head. "Too many ideas floating around up here for me to sleep."

He could relate.

Ivy pointed at the area she'd already cleared, the pile of brush off to the side the result. "I'm going to add something to your to-do list, and I'd like to move it to the top of the list. Can you add a wheelchair ramp right here and make the entry into the store accessible?"

"Ivy—"

"I'm going to stop you right there. Yes, seeing your mother's wheelchair made me think of this,

but it's a necessity anyway. Even without legal requirements, I want everyone to be able to access
my store. And if your mom would like to come
with Daisy, she should be able to."

Austin stared at Ivy and something moved in
the area of his heart. When he realized what was
happening, he looked away. She was simply a
kind person temporarily in his life, nothing more.
What he was feeling was just appreciation for
that kindness.

"About Daisy—I talked with her last night and
she understands that if you were just being kind
to her in offering to let her work here, then you're
not obligated. I know that you're being careful
with the expenses of getting this place ready to
live in and operate as a business."

He looked back at her to see her staring at him
as if she couldn't believe the words coming out
of his mouth.

"Did you tell Daisy she couldn't work for me?"

"Not exactly. I just told her that you might
have seen her excitement and misinterpreted it
as her asking for a job."

Ivy crossed her arms, and he'd swear her expression changed to one that made him feel as
if he was about to get a scolding.

"Do I seem like a person who can't make ra-
tional decisions?"

"That's not what I meant." Why couldn't he stop saying the wrong things at the wrong times?

"Good to hear. I didn't offer Daisy the job because I felt obligated. They are tasks that right now I don't have time to do and ones she seemed genuinely interested in."

"If you're sure."

"I am. Now, on to the ramp." She motioned behind her. "Work up an estimate, and I'll go ahead and give you the money to get the supplies you need."

"Thank you."

"No need to thank me. What helps your mother will help others. And what helps Daisy will help me. It's a win-win-win-win."

Ivy returned to clearing out the sad, forgotten shrubs as he started taking measurements and jotting down the supplies he'd need from the hardware store. He caught himself glancing toward Ivy more than he should. He noticed she was making a pile of small, flat stones she'd found once the bushes were cleared away.

"Planning on going rock skipping?" he asked.

"What?" She noticed he was pointing at the little mound of rocks. "Oh, no. I paint little pictures and sayings on them and leave them in random places for people to find."

"Okay." He drew out the word because he'd never heard of such a hobby.

"It's fun. When people find them, they post pictures. Sometimes they'll take them and put them somewhere else for someone else to find, or they paint their own and replace the original. You should try it sometime. It's relaxing and nice knowing it'll make someone smile."

He hadn't known Ivy long and didn't know her well, but already he was confident that she was genuinely one of the nicest people he'd ever met.

"I guess the world could always use more reasons to smile."

A flicker of something that looked like sadness passed over her expression for a moment before she smiled again. "Indeed."

Rich pulled up and parked, drawing their attention. The three of them once again fell into the rhythm of their own parts of the project. Rich did his talking to the wiring thing as he replaced what needed to be replaced. Ivy continued weeding and brush removal until it was time for her to get ready for her shift at Trudy's. And Austin headed to buy more lumber and concrete mix as well as order a handrail for the new ramp. Before he exited his truck outside the hardware store, however, he texted Daisy.

You can start work tomorrow.

He had just stepped into the store when she texted back.

Thank you! This was followed by a huge smiling emoji.

It lifted some of the burden off his heart that he'd made his sister happy. Now if he could just figure out how to do the same for his mother. She'd lost so much, endured more than her share of heartache. He knew she needed to move on and she did her best, but grief still sat on her shoulders like an invisible weight. She had managed to start life anew after Austin's dad died, had been happy in her second marriage and had a daughter to join her son. But how could she move on from losing a second husband when her paralysis would remind her every day for the rest of her life?

"Hey, Austin." The sound of a familiar voice drew him out of his heavy thoughts.

"How's it going, Isaac?"

"Can't complain."

Isaac Lewis had been his dad's best friend, and he'd taken Austin fishing several times after his father's death. He also happened to be a good plumber.

"You have some time today?" Austin asked.

"Sure. This have to do with the job you're doing on the Stinson Building?"

"It does." He explained how Ivy needed operational indoor plumbing and restroom facilities.

"As luck would have it, I just had a job fall

through. Instead of renovating their bathrooms, the Pilsons have decided to get divorced instead."

Sadly, disagreements about renovations and money had likely ended more marriages than that of the Pilsons.

"I met Ivy yesterday when I was in Trudy's. She's a little ray of sunshine, isn't she?"

"She's nice." Yes, a ray of sunshine was a good way to describe Ivy, but he wasn't going to give any potential matchmakers—and there were plenty in a town the size of Jade Valley—any ideas. Even if he admitted to himself that she was attractive and had he met her before he had met Grace, maybe he would even ask her out. But having your wife abandon you soured you on romantic relationships.

Isaac chuckled, but Austin chose to ignore the potential implication of that chuckle. Instead, he invited the older man to come over to the job site with him after Austin finished buying what he needed to build the ramp.

Twenty minutes later, Isaac was staring at the area that was supposed to be a bathroom on the upper floor of the Stinson Building.

"Well, nothing like starting from scratch," he said.

"How long do you think it'll take?"

"Miss Ivy will have a fine new bathroom by the end of the week. I can add plumbing for and install a kitchen sink too, if she wants."

"Really?" Even for Isaac, that seemed like a fast turnaround.

"Yes, I'm just that good."

Austin laughed.

"You've got the Electrical Whisperer downstairs, the plumbing genius upstairs, and you're the hardworking jack-of-all-trades. We'll turn this place around so fast, they'll write songs about us."

"I like the sound of that," Rich called out from the first floor.

Austin snorted then gestured dramatically toward the bathroom space. "By all means, work your toilet magic."

As Austin descended the stairs, he realized how much his mood had lightened. Other than worrying about his mom, everything else seemed to be going well. But he was still hesitant to believe it would last, worried that if he let down his guard it would invite bad luck back into his life.

CHAPTER FIVE

TRUDY'S WAS HOPPING as if there was nowhere else in town to eat. But a quick look across the street showed that Alma's was equally as busy. Both places were full of the tourists who were temporarily stranded by their bus breaking down at the edge of town. Considering they'd had to walk about a quarter of a mile to get to the business area of Jade Valley, the group of women were in good spirits.

"So where are y'all from?" Ivy asked the ladies at the table where she was refilling water glasses.

"Oh, honey, I have to ask you that instead," one of the older ladies said. "I haven't heard a Southern accent live in a long time."

"I'm from Kentucky."

"Tennessee, though it's been forty years since I lived there. Everyone still tells me I have my accent though."

"I can hear it, though maybe it's softened a little bit."

"You, however, must be a recent transplant."

"I am. Less than a month."

"I came out to Denver for college and never went back. What brought you?" The woman leaned toward Ivy and lowered her voice a little. "A hot cowboy? That's what got me."

Ivy laughed a little and was startled when Austin appeared in her thoughts.

"Just ready for a change." She hurried away from the table before the ladies could ask any further questions that she didn't want to answer.

As she and Fiona, another waitress who worked on the days when Stephanie was off, were kept running taking orders, delivering food to tables and making sure no one ran out of their chosen beverage, she learned the ladies had all been in a sorority together back in the early 1980s. Now they lived in all parts of the country and even in several international locales, but every two years they gathered back in Denver to embark on a week of adventures together. And this year's agenda was the Grand Teton and Yellowstone national parks. Now that their trip had experienced a setback, they were making plans to explore all the shops in Jade Valley and eat themselves silly.

"You will want to make sure to save room for dessert. Trudy is famous for her pies. We have five different flavors available today," she told the ladies at another table.

When one of the women expressed concern about gaining weight, another laughed and said, "You know calories don't count on vacation. I distinctly remember telling you that during our trip to Sedona last year."

This caused everyone at the table to laugh, and Ivy laughed right along with them. It felt good to do so, especially since the topic of conversation at another table was the upcoming marriage of a daughter.

Ivy had done a pretty good job of keeping thoughts of James and his betrayal at bay, so much so that she was proud of herself. Being so far away from Louisville, with surroundings that looked nothing like Kentucky, helped in that regard. So did working from the time she got up until she collapsed in her sleeping bag at night. She'd be glad to stop having to sleep on the floor, but at least she wasn't cold anymore and she'd cleared enough dust out of the top floor that she spent less time sneezing.

At the end of her shift, Ivy discovered that she'd done even better with tips than she'd thought. Fiona had as well.

"Buses full of generous ladies need to break down at the edge of town every day," Fiona said.

Even though she'd tried to push thoughts of James away, that conversation about the upcoming wedding stuck with her. If things had gone as planned, she'd be making her own wedding plans. She'd already been planning the honeymoon trip to Italy. His betrayal had robbed her of so much, including that dream vacation. Maybe someday her business would be so successful that she'd take a solo trip.

"You okay?" Fiona asked.

"Yeah, fine. Just remembered something I need to do for the renovation."

Find a way to excise all memories of James and the moment when he'd turned her world upside down.

Ivy tried to rid herself of the gloomy mood by buying a box of the little cherry and cream cheese tarts Trudy had made before she headed home. She imagined drowning her sorrows by stuffing her face with all of them, but in truth she'd probably share them with Austin and Rich. That would be a much better decision for her waistline.

When she reached her place, there was a third truck parked outside. Maybe it was someone Austin or Rich knew, perhaps someone delivering supplies they needed. But when she stepped inside, she noticed an older gentleman she'd met at Trudy's. What was his name? She'd met so many people that it was becoming difficult to keep all the names straight. She needed a flow chart to keep track of who was related to whom, who owned what businesses, who sided with

Trudy and who sided with Alma in the mysterious feud she'd learned about from her coworkers.

"Hey," Austin said when he noticed her. "This is Isaac Lewis. He's helping out with the plumbing."

"We've met," Ivy said as she shook Isaac's hand.

"Good to see you again."

"Isaac said you should have a functioning bathroom sooner than if I do it myself," Austin said.

"That's the best thing I've heard all day, and I had a customer ask me if I'd been Miss Wyoming a couple of years ago."

Granted, the young man who might have been twenty was flirting, but still it had been nice to hear. Being cheated on didn't do wonders for a girl's self-esteem, even if she knew it wasn't her fault.

"In fact, indoor plumbing on the horizon is worthy of a celebration." She opened the box of tarts, and she had to laugh when Rich appeared from wherever he'd been as if answering a siren's call.

"Never get between Rich and sweets. You may lose an eye," Austin said.

Ivy didn't know why that struck her as hilarious, but she laughed so much she snorted. Maybe it was because she was normally a person who easily found humor, but the past few weeks had not offered much that was worthy of laughter. That a good-looking handyman, an electrical whisperer and a plumber would be what brought laughter back was unexpected but oddly on brand for her new hometown.

The four of them seemed to instinctively stay out of each other's way as they made progress toward their individual but interconnected goals. In her continued examination of deteriorating boxes, she found everything from old, musty hymnals to what looked to be some grandma's varied collection of vintage buttons. The washing and sorting of the latter, she added to Daisy's task list.

"It's amazing the amount of junk that's been stored up here," Isaac said after he hauled out the toilet, which he'd said wasn't going to work in the space allotted—probably the reason it had been sitting in the middle of the room.

"It does seem like Jade Valley's collective junk drawer." And yet it had sort of become fun to discover what all was left behind, like a treasure hunt.

As she carried a box of various and sundry useless items outside to the pile that Austin said he'd haul away for her, she noticed he'd made amazing progress with the ramp. He'd been building the wooden form for it when she returned from her shift at Trudy's. While she'd been upstairs working, he'd mixed and poured the concrete. Now he smoothed the surface.

"Looks great," she said after dropping the box beside the others. "How long before it's usable?"

"It should cure for about a week."

"That long?"

"Maybe a little less, but I'd rather go the full week to make sure."

She nodded. "After that, your mom can accompany Daisy if she wants to."

Austin straightened and wiped the sweat off his forehead. Ivy's heart skipped a little bit. A man who was that dirty and sweaty shouldn't look that good, but he did.

"I appreciate it. I don't know that she'll want to though."

"Well, it's a standing offer." She got the feeling there was tension surrounding the situation with his mother, but she didn't know him well enough to ask. There was a delicate balance between getting to know people and intruding.

"I'm glad Daisy is going to be helping me out though." She told him about the box of buttons and that she was considering how to incorporate them into the store. "Depending on what we find in that box, I might do some sort of display."

"I'm sure you'll think of something. Do you know what you're going to call the place yet?"

"Not one hundred percent. I've thought about

Cecile's because it was my grandmother's dream to have a place like this, but that might also confuse people."

"Maybe just call it Quilters' Dream."

The rightness of that name lit up Ivy's brain like a college football stadium on game night.

"I love that. It fits perfectly." She looked up at the front of the building. "The quilt shop was Grandma Cecile's dream, and this building is my new dream."

"What was the old one?"

The question surprised Ivy, but when she looked at Austin, it appeared it had surprised him even more.

"Sorry, I don't know why I asked that," he said. "That's none of my business."

"It's okay. We all say things we don't mean to sometimes." She sighed. "But I'm not ready to talk about it."

The betrayal was too fresh, too raw, too embarrassing. She wanted to leave everything about it back in Louisville. This was her new start, the new stage of her life that was free of James. Ivy was determined to not let him taint it.

She noticed the look on Austin's face as he lowered his gaze to the concrete trowel in his hands. He looked as if a few more bricks had just been added to a load he always seemed to carry on his shoulders.

"Austin," she said, then waited for him to meet her gaze. "Don't beat yourself up over it. Just because I don't want to talk about it doesn't mean you have to feel bad. Curiosity is natural, especially when someone enters a contest to win a building, then picks up and moves across the country alone to start a new career. Heck, I'd be darn curious if it was someone else and found out someone who used to do advertising for a hotel chain was going to pivot and open a quilt shop. I mean, one of these things is not like the other."

Despite what she'd said, the oddest urge to just spill everything overcame her, along with the feeling that Austin would be a good listener. But she suspected he had enough going on in his own life without hearing about someone else's woes. As he was obviously curious about her reasons for coming to Jade Valley, she wondered about him as well. Why did he work so hard, barely taking a break? Did the fact his mother used a wheelchair have anything to do with the way he seemed as if he was always ready for the other shoe to drop?

It reminded her that she was far from the only person going through a difficult time. There were so many others navigating far worse. Maybe keeping things in perspective would help her heal, to be able to talk about what happened without feeling as if she might fall apart.

AUSTIN CAME BACK in from his early morning ride to check on the herd to find the kitchen table filled with a larger breakfast than normal. Daisy turned from the stove, wearing their mother's strawberry-patterned apron, a plate of crisp bacon in her hand.

"What's all this?" he asked.

"It's her first day of her first job," his mom said as she retrieved milk from the refrigerator. "We're celebrating."

Austin noticed that Daisy seemed a little nervous, but he had a gut feeling it had more to do with her thinking he might change his mind last minute rather than worrying about the actual job.

"That's a good idea, though this seems like enough for three meals."

"We can take some leftovers for lunch," Daisy said.

Again, he could tell there was more to what she said. He knew her well enough to figure she had said that to make sure he knew that he didn't have to worry about buying her lunch in town. Not for the first time, he hoped that when Daisy grew up, she got an incredible job that allowed her to do all the things she wanted to without having to worry about how much they cost. He was ashamed he couldn't give that to her, but if this job with Ivy set Daisy on that path, then it was a good thing.

As they ate, they talked about what he'd been doing on the building so far. He didn't mention the ramp because he was still trying to think about how he could convince his mom to come into town with him and Daisy on the days they were both working. He knew she could mostly take care of herself, but he worried about her mental state if she had too much time alone. Losses hurt the most when you were by yourself with nothing but time to think.

"It sounds like it'll be a nice place," his mom said.

"I bet Ivy would like to see the quilts Grandma Wilkes made," Daisy said while bringing a forkful of scrambled eggs to her mouth.

"I'm sure she's much more interested in those fancy art quilts."

"I don't know," Austin said, seeing a potential opening for getting his mom interested in something, maybe a reason for her to accompany them to town the next week. "Ivy seems to have an affinity for older stuff—the building, those old coins and buttons Daisy is going to be researching and organizing."

His mom made a noncommittal answer, and he and Daisy shared a conspiratorial glance. She was a smart kid, so she no doubt knew exactly what he was doing. But they both knew when enough had been said, when anything further would have the opposite of the desired effect.

Once he and Daisy were in the truck and on the way to town, he glanced over and saw she was reading a book, a common occurrence with his brainy little sister.

"What are you reading?"

She read out the title, about an expedition to the South Pole.

"That's not one of the places you want to go, is it?"

She shrugged. "I don't know, maybe. But my list has a lot of other places on it before Antarctica."

For him, it got plenty cold during a Wyoming winter. He couldn't imagine wanting to go to the literal ends of the earth where it was even more brutally cold. Though he worried about where she might travel someday and whether she'd be safe, he did his best to keep those worries to himself. After what she'd lost, she deserved to chase her dream unimpeded.

Thinking about dreams brought his thoughts back to Ivy. Though she'd been her usual kind self about his stupid question the day before, he still felt guilty for bringing up her reason for moving to Wyoming. It was even more obvious by her answer that she hadn't made the drastic change in her life simply because of a sense of adventure. Had she lost someone too?

Normally, he didn't bother wondering too much about other people's personal lives. He didn't have time for it, for one thing. But ever since he'd met Ivy, she'd sparked his curiosity. Surely he wasn't the only one though. It wasn't every day that someone up and moved across the country to Jade Valley, especially someone with no ties to the town or even the state.

When he parked in front of Ivy's place, Daisy was quick to set aside her book and hop out of the truck. He smiled at her enthusiasm for tasks that others would find tedious. But Daisy had always liked things that most of her classmates didn't, and for the most part she didn't seem to mind being different. She lived in her head most of the time.

At least that's what he assumed was going on with her. The unexpected excitement over this new job and how easily she seemed to talk with Ivy right from the moment they met made him wonder if he'd missed something. Was he so busy ranching and grabbing any other work he could get that he wasn't seeing things that were right in front of him? He made a promise to himself to set aside some brother-sister time so they could talk and do something together that was fun rather than work.

All he seemed to do was work. Part of it was necessity, but truthfully part of it was also so he didn't have time to think about Grace and how she really hadn't been in their marriage for better or worse.

Because he'd had a lot of practice doing so, he shoved those thoughts away again and got out of the truck to tackle another day of work.

As he got started scraping away the old paint around the windows, which thankfully and to his surprise was not lead-based, he caught himself looking in Ivy's direction more times than he cared to admit. He tried to tell himself it was to check on how Daisy was doing, but that was a lie. Then he'd tell his brain it was simply because she was nicer to look at than Rich or Isaac, which was both true and another lie.

He was actually glad when she headed to work at Trudy's, and he deliberately shifted to the other side of the building so he wouldn't be tempted to watch her walk up the street.

"Am I detecting a bit of interest?" Isaac asked, startling Austin with his nearness.

"No," he said simply.

Isaac chuckled. "Just so you know, that wasn't very convincing."

Austin looked over at Isaac. "You know what happened and why I have zero interest in another relationship."

Why did that statement, which had always felt absolutely true, feel as if it was a little shakier in the truth department now?

"Yes, you got a raw deal with Grace. But that doesn't mean you have to be alone the rest of your life."

"I'm not alone. I have Mom and Daisy and plenty of work to fill my days."

"Not the same thing, boy. Not the same thing at all."

As Isaac walked away, Austin felt like kicking himself again. Isaac had lost his wife, Birdie, two years before to a brain aneurysm. He'd suffered the type of sudden loss that didn't even allow for a goodbye, the same way Austin, Daisy and his mom had. Not that it was any less horrible, but at least Austin had the chance to say his goodbyes to his father as the cancer slowly took him away.

Isaac was such a jovial guy that it was easy to forget that he still grieved Birdie's loss.

Knowing nothing he could say would change that grief, Austin placed the paint scraper back on the windowsill. If only getting rid of sad memories was as easy as peeling off old paint.

When he later stopped to grab a cold bottle of water from the cooler at the front of the building, he noticed a look on Daisy's face that made him pause.

"What's wrong?"

"Am I seeing this correctly?"

He realized that she didn't look distressed but rather stunned. Stepping up beside her, he saw she'd pulled up details on an old penny she was holding in her hand. Austin leaned down so he could see what had surprised her so much.

No wonder she was stunned.

"Would someone really pay that?" she asked in disbelief.

"Maybe. People pay surprising amounts for collectibles."

Austin looked toward the open door and windows as if thieves might suddenly leap inside and make off with the valuable coin.

"Log it like the rest you've been doing. And when Ivy gets back, you're going to make her day."

Daisy's wide smile rivaled the sun. How long had it been since he'd seen her smile like that?

Even though she was excited, he could tell she was also nervous—so much so that when she needed to go to the convenience store to use the restroom, she made him promise to not leave the room where the coins were spread out on the old countertop left over from the Stinson Building's beginnings as a grocery.

When she returned, she held the orange soda she liked in one hand and his favorite grape in the other. Though it was not out of character for her, he still felt as if this was her once again thanking him for allowing her to take the job. Feeling a rush of affection for his sister, he put his arm around her shoulders and gave her a quick hug.

"That's enough," he said. "Keep your money for yourself."

When he spotted Ivy walking down the street a few hours later, he was glad that both Rich and Isaac were temporarily gone to buy more supplies. He trusted both men, but still the fewer people who knew about the value of what Ivy had lucked into the better.

"You ready to make someone's day?" he asked Daisy.

"Is she here?"

He nodded.

Daisy hopped up from where she'd been deep into her work of continuing to research the collection of coins, grabbing her phone and the miraculous penny.

By the time Ivy stepped into the building, Daisy was practically vibrating with excitement. Ivy noticed both of them staring at her and stopped in her tracks.

"Is something wrong?"

"The opposite," he said, then motioned toward Daisy, who rushed forward to show Ivy what she'd found.

Even more than when Ivy had found the previous valuable coin, she appeared shocked.

"I… I can't believe it." She looked between the coin and the listing on Daisy's phone several more times, then up at Austin, and finally at Daisy. And then she squealed and pulled Daisy into her arms.

As the two of them jumped up and down, moving in a circle, Austin laughed. Then, to his surprise, Ivy reached out and pulled him into a celebratory group hug. Her arm felt so tiny around his waist. She seemed even shorter while standing this close to her.

He realized just how long it had been since he'd been hugged. And how much he'd missed it.

CHAPTER SIX

TRYING TO FOCUS on clearing out the last of the upstairs junk after discovering she owned a penny potentially worth ten thousand dollars was like trying to sleep with a tornado siren blaring next to her ear. In other words, impossible. Hiding her excitement from Isaac and Rich when they returned from their errands proved difficult, and she kept checking the little zip-up pocket in her Capri pants to make sure the two really valuable coins were still there. She wasn't about to walk away from them until she could hopefully sell them.

"What do you plan to do?" Austin asked her as she dusted her hands after carrying a broken chair out to the front lawn.

"Get rid of them as soon as possible. The fear of losing them will make me a nervous wreck."

"Daisy looked up rare coin dealers, and there's one in Cheyenne. She's hurrying to get through the rest of the collection so you'll know everything you have."

Ivy glanced toward the open front door.

"She's a great kid, very hardworking."

"Yeah, she is."

"She reminds me of myself when I was her age. I wasn't as quiet, but I was bookish and loved history. It's part of what attracted me to my previous job."

"I thought you worked at a hotel."

"No, I worked for a hotel chain. We took old buildings and renovated them into boutique hotels. One was an old textile mill. Another was a former distillery. A small college that closed. Even a former Thoroughbred racing stable. When I left, the owner was considering buying an old prison."

Austin shook his head. "Who would want to sleep in a prison?"

"You'd be surprised. People like unique experiences."

"I guess." He motioned toward the front door. "Daisy's reading a book about the South Pole for her geography club. When I asked if she'd ever want to go there, she said maybe."

"That's adventurous."

"A little too adventurous for my comfort, but when she grows up I want her to be able to go and live the life she wants, travel wherever she's drawn to. She's had a curiosity about the world since before she could even verbalize it. Mom has a picture of her sitting in front of the TV when she was two with this look of awe on her little face. Her dad was watching a documentary about the Zambezi River. I had to look it up because I had no clue where it was."

She hesitated asking the question that sprang to mind, but she'd been growing more and more curious about Austin. Even if she wasn't looking for romance, she couldn't seem to prevent her eyes from wandering to him when he was nearby. There was no denying he was an attractive man. His work ethic and how he took care of his family only added to that attractiveness.

"You said 'her dad,'" she ventured carefully.

"We had different fathers."

The fact that he used the past tense caused sadness in her heart. She didn't ask anything further, especially when Daisy stepped outside.

Austin shifted his attention to his sister. "Ready to go?"

"Yeah." But instead of heading toward the truck, she crossed the yard to Ivy and extended a notebook to her. "I should be able to finish with the coins in the morning."

"Wow, you're fast."

"It's interesting." She glanced around. "And exciting."

Ivy smiled. "So exciting. Thank you for your hard work."

As the two of them headed off down the street

with Austin behind the wheel, Ivy realized that having Austin and Daisy around made her happy. Not long ago she couldn't even imagine being happy again. The life she'd planned for herself had been pulled out from under her. Maybe that was one of the reasons she felt so comfortable with Austin and Daisy. From what she'd gathered, they'd had their lives yanked in cruel directions too.

She heard a light chuckle and jerked her attention away from Austin's truck turning the corner onto Main Street. Isaac stood at the top of the steps leading into the building, an amused look on his face as if he was privy to a joke that no one else had heard. She suspected she knew the direction of his thoughts and had to figure out a way to change that direction.

"How goes the bathroom?"

He smiled, signaling that he knew very well what she was doing but didn't call her out on it.

"Good. Before you know it, you'll have such an awesome bathroom that you can charge for tours."

Ivy snorted a little at that.

"I'll settle for functional."

"There might be a slight delay in getting a couple of the items I ordered. I'll know for sure soon."

"Okay."

After everyone had left for the day, Ivy went out

back to fetch a bucket of water from the spigot. She spotted the cat again, in almost the same spot. She'd asked both Reg and Evangeline about the cat, and both had said they suspected it was a stray.

"Well, hello there. Nice to see you again."

The cat just stared at her. Ivy wasn't sure if she was imagining it, but the cat seemed slightly less likely to bolt than the last time. Maybe it appreciated the water Ivy had set out for it.

"I've got a job for you too," she said. "You see any mice or rats, you take care of them. In exchange, I'll buy you the good cat food."

The cat responded by keeping its distance. But it didn't run away. Instead, it settled a bit more comfortably and began to lick its paws.

"I need a bath too." She had never looked so forward to a long, hot shower in her life.

Today's find in the coin box, however, made her breathe a bit more easily about the cost of her new bathrooms—the one in her home and the much smaller one for customers downstairs. She took the coin out of her pocket and turned it over and over, encased in its plastic holder. How was it possible that someone would pay thousands of dollars for a penny? She understood the concept of rarity equaling value, but it was still hard to wrap her mind around.

A sudden breeze cooled her skin. She wondered how she would fare during her first Wyoming winter. Even though she'd never been to the state before moving there, she knew that it would be a new type of cold. It was kind of funny she was the one who moved there when it was her younger sister, Lily, who was the fan of winter weather. Lily spent her days working in a hospital, where people often suffered and sometimes died. She said that seeing that made her really want to live, and so her vacations typically involved snowboarding or skiing in the winter, white-water rafting or hiking in the warmer months. The summer after she graduated from college, she had through-hiked the nearly twenty-two hundred miles of the Appalachian Trail with friends from her college hiking club.

With all that adventure in her personality, Lily had been the one to worry least about Ivy heading off across the country to start a new life. The two things her younger sister had said were that she simply hoped Ivy wasn't doing it too soon after her broken engagement and that she'd miss being able to just drive up to Louisville to see her.

Ivy missed her sisters and her mom too, as well as good friends she'd made while living in Louisville. But she needed the change at a soul-deep level. And if she had waited, she might have let common sense overrule taking a leap of faith.

She looked up at the impossibly blue sky. So far, she liked the leap of faith.

BY THE TIME another week of work passed, Austin was shocked at how much progress had been made, even though he'd taken part in it. True to his word, Isaac had completed the upstairs bathroom except for a couple of small items that were on back order. Austin and Daisy had laughed at the squeal of excitement when it had been revealed to Ivy.

"Sounds like she likes it," Austin had said.

"She's probably happy to not have to use public restrooms anymore. She said she's been to every business in town."

True. But based on things Ivy had said in passing, he knew she was most looking forward to having ready access to a shower.

He jerked his attention back to the sanding of the floorboards because he did not need to think about Ivy in the shower.

Rich hadn't arrived for the day, and Isaac left to do an emergency plumbing call. Since it was a day off work from Trudy's for Ivy, she joined Austin and Lily outside in the shade to have lunch. Instead of eating her sandwich, however, Ivy leaned back on her hands, lifted her face to the sky and closed her eyes.

"This weather is perfect," she said. "I know I'll likely be grumpy in the winter, but for now it's fabulous. It's ninety-three degrees back in Kentucky right now, with high humidity."

"That sounds miserable," he said, doing his best to not pay attention to how she looked beautiful even dressed in a worn T-shirt and shorts, with tendrils of her hair having escaped from her ponytail. He absolutely could not look at her legs. They were in danger of reminding him of how alone he'd been since Grace walked out on him without a word of warning.

It didn't help that he liked everything he'd observed about Ivy so far. He'd tossed aside his initial thought that maybe she wasn't that smart if she gave up a good job to move across the country into an old building that almost wasn't livable. She'd proven that she was actually smart as well as a hard worker and kind. Now he couldn't help but wonder what had driven her to make such a drastic change, which was the exact opposite of how he'd reacted in the wake of major upheaval in his life. He'd dug in his heels, put his head down and worked harder at the same things he'd always done.

The things that had driven Grace away.

"Now that the ramp is ready, you can bring your mom here," Ivy said, yanking his attention away from the past.

"Maybe." He sensed Ivy looking at him in the wake of his simple reply, but he pretended not to notice.

"Mom doesn't like to go places anymore," Daisy said.

"Daisy," he warned.

"It's not a secret," his sister said, surprising him by not immediately going quiet. She shifted her attention to Ivy. "Mom is still sad about what happened to Dad and her legs."

"Oh, I'm sorry to hear that. But it's understandable." She paused for a moment. "I don't mean to tell you how to handle your private family matters, but I'll share one thing. My mom said that the thing that saved her after my dad left was staying busy. My grandma Cecile, Mom's friends, they refused to let her stay alone too much. They made sure to provide her with things to do until Mom was ready to take those steps on her own."

"Mom has been through a lot, more than her share," Austin said.

"Which means she's in more danger of succumbing to depression." Ivy placed one of her hands on Daisy's knee and smiled. Then she met Austin's eyes. "I'm sorry if I'm stepping across a line, but I know from experience that being too alone with one's thoughts for too long isn't a good thing. It's not a path to healing."

Was she right? Had they given their mom enough time to grieve on her own? If they continued to do so, were they doing her more harm than good? He hated that there were no easy answers because everyone handled grief differently and healed at different paces. But what if his mom wasn't actually healing? What if she had suffered so much that there was no more healing in her?

"Tell me about your mom," Ivy suddenly said. "What things does she like?"

"She's always just worked being a mom, on the ranch, and then helping Daisy's dad run his river rafting business," he said.

"She likes art."

Austin looked at Daisy, wondering why she would say that. "Since when?"

"Since always. Didn't you notice how she used to doodle all the time?"

"Lots of people doodle."

"She's also the one who collected all that driftwood that was out in front of the office."

It took him a moment to remember what Daisy was talking about—a bunch of differently shaped pieces of driftwood that had been assembled to look like a white-water raft.

"I didn't know she did that. Why didn't she ever say anything about it?"

"She probably didn't think it was worth mentioning, but I thought it was cool."

Austin felt like a pitiful son. How had he lived three decades and never realized his mother had an artistic streak? He suspected that she never mentioned it because it wasn't practical and he, like his father, was of the practical mindset.

His appetite gone, he placed the rest of his sandwich in front of Daisy and got up.

"You're done?" Daisy asked.

"I'm still full from breakfast." He wasn't sure why he lied. Maybe it was so Daisy and Ivy didn't attribute his lack of appetite to the conversation they'd been having. "I want to finish sanding the bottom level floor today."

He turned and went back into the building, his mind trying to remember all the times his mother may have expressed a personal interest that he hadn't even noticed. In all his efforts to be a good son, had he been a bad one instead?

IVY FELT TERRIBLE as she watched Austin walk back inside. Why had she pushed? Why had she asked such personal questions?

"It's not your fault," Daisy said.

"What?"

"I can tell from the look on your face that you think his mood shift was your fault. It's not."

"I shouldn't have offered my unsolicited opinion."

"It's…kind of good to actually talk about stuff." Daisy picked the edges of her bread off. It wasn't that she didn't like it because Ivy had seen her eat some a few minutes ago. It was a fidget as memories likely washed over her.

Ivy reached over and took one of Daisy's hands in hers but didn't say anything. It was silent support, telling Daisy she didn't have to say anything but that if she wanted to, Ivy would listen.

Daisy looked toward the front door of the building, as if checking whether her brother was within earshot.

"He's always so busy working, taking care of me and Mom. He's carrying the load of five people, two of them who aren't here anymore."

Ivy realized that Austin wasn't the only one carrying more than their share. From what she'd seen of the siblings, Daisy never complained. She seemed to keep everything inside. Was it so she didn't add to her brother's worries?

"You probably have figured this out already, but Mom was paralyzed in the accident that..." She trailed off, obviously finding it difficult to say the words. "My dad didn't make it."

"I'm so sorry, Daisy. No one should have to go through what you have. What your mother has. I can't imagine."

To lose not only one husband but two seemed cruel enough, but to be paralyzed as well was just too much. It was no wonder she suffered from at least some level of depression. Honestly, it would be more surprising if she didn't.

"She tries, I know she does, but she seems to just want to be alone a lot."

Ivy thought about how she'd hidden in her apartment eating seemingly endless amounts of junk food and ice cream after James's betrayal had been revealed. She'd felt dreadful and didn't want to see anyone or anyone to see her. How much worse must it be for Mrs. Chapman? At least that was what she assumed Daisy's mom went by, that she had taken her second husband's name.

"Do you think your mom will come with you two the next time you come to work?"

Daisy shrugged, her sandwich now totally abandoned. "I don't know, but I'll try."

"No pressure." Ivy considered if she should say anything else or let things be.

"Do you really think forcing her out of the house will help?"

Ivy didn't want to make a misstep that would hurt Daisy, Austin or their mother. But her gut instincts told her that the answer to Daisy's question was yes.

"At the very least, I don't think it will hurt."

Her instincts had failed her before, so she prayed that they didn't again. If they did, this time she wouldn't be the only person to get hurt.

AUSTIN'S NERVES VIBRATED just below the surface all the way into town two days later, afraid that

TRISH MILBURN

at any moment his mom would change her mind
and ask him to turn around and take her home.
He could tell that Daisy's thoughts were running
along the same lines. Instead of reading a book
this morning, she kept chattering away about Ivy,
the building, the coins, funny things that Rich
or Isaac had said.

"Ivy certainly sounds like she has a lot of big
plans," his mother said.

Austin could tell from her tone that she wasn't
sure all those lofty plans would materialize. He
understood that line of thinking because he'd
felt the same not that long ago, but gradually
he'd started to believe that Ivy could accomplish
anything. He still caught glimpses of sadness in
her, and he guessed they had something to do
with why she'd moved to Jade Valley. But they
never lingered long as she thought of some new
thing she wanted to add to her future store, as
she stopped work to chat with any local resident
who walked through the front door curious about
the building's renovation and its new owner, as
she laughed at Rich's recounting of a recent disastrous date he'd gone on.

During that last one, however, he'd noticed that
her laughter wasn't as bright and full as usual. It
led him to believe even more that whatever had
driven her to Wyoming had indeed been romantic disappointment. He'd caught himself grip-

ping his hammer more tightly as he worked on a simpler wooden ramp to give access to the back door of the building. He didn't like the idea of her being hurt. He knew what it felt like and wouldn't wish it on anyone.

Maybe she'd been the one to end things though, and her clean break had included a change in venue and career.

"She does," he said, bringing himself back to the present and what his mother had said. "She's a hard worker, so I won't be surprised if she accomplishes everything she sets out to do."

"I thought you said she probably wouldn't last."

He hadn't remembered saying that in front of her, but evidently he had.

"That's what I figured at first. But no matter how many things that Isaac, Rich and I have found that have to be fixed or replaced, she's asked about the best combination of quality, safety and price then let us do our work. Early on I suspected the next bump in the road would send her back to Kentucky, but she's still here."

Granted, finding two really valuable coins helped her financial outlook, if she could find a buyer. He hoped she could off-load those coins soon because he worried about her walking around with them—either that she would lose them or, unrealistically, that someone would figure out she had them and take them from her by force. He didn't even like the idea of her taking them to a coin shop by herself.

When they reached Ivy's, she was already outside power washing the exterior of the building now that he'd completed the exterior painting of the window frames and doors.

"Looks like she's an early riser," his mom said, a hint of respect in her voice.

"She said that she's lived in the Eastern Time Zone her entire life, so her body is still operating two hours ahead of the time here," Daisy said.

Ivy noticed them and turned off the sprayer.

"Welcome," she said to his mom as she approached the truck. "I hope you like doughnuts. I might have gone a little overboard at the bakery this morning."

"You didn't have to do that," Austin said.

"Does anyone ever *have* to buy doughnuts?"

He smiled a little at that. "No, I guess not."

"I've been known to enjoy a doughnut now and then," his mom said, surprising him with the slight lilt of amusement in her voice. "Especially if there's jelly filling involved."

"Then you're in luck," Ivy said as she led the way to the front of the building.

Austin pushed his mom's wheelchair up the newly constructed ramp and into the building.

"It still obviously needs a lot of work," Ivy said as she gestured at their surroundings. "But at least it doesn't look like a dust storm just blew through anymore. And I've finally stopped sneezing."

Austin watched as his mom looked up at the ceiling, at every corner of the room.

"I haven't been inside here in probably twenty years. It was a used bookstore then, but that only lasted maybe six months."

"Sounds like this building has housed a lot of different businesses over the years."

"Yeah, always been one of those places where nothing lasts long."

Austin winced. Even though his mom didn't mean any offense, he hoped Ivy didn't take the comment as such.

"Well, I intend to end that trend."

His mom looked at Ivy, as if trying to read whether she really meant those words. He thought he saw Ivy fidget a bit under his mom's gaze.

"I hope you do," his mom finally said.

It said a lot about the dark place his mom had been since the accident that a simple comment like that, or the fact that she seemed to enjoy her powdered doughnut filled with raspberry jelly, brought him hope that she might be turning the corner.

"Are there any left for me?" Isaac asked as he stepped in the door a few minutes later.

"There's plenty for everyone," Ivy said, also

pouring him a cup of coffee from her pump thermos.

Isaac took a cruller and pulled up an over-turned five-gallon bucket to sit next to Austin's mom. "Good to see you, Melissa."

Austin hated that the two of them were in the same boat now, widowed and still grieving. At least his mom had him and Daisy at home. Isaac had to live in his house alone. Austin made a mental note to invite him over for dinner some-time soon. Maybe he could barbecue. It had been quite a while since he'd fired up the grill.

Daisy looked over at him and pointed at the box of doughnuts at the same time she wiped chocolate icing away from the edge of her mouth. She looked so much like she had as a little girl that he couldn't help but smile.

"You're not allowed to watch your figure if the rest of us are tossing ours to the wind for today," Ivy said.

His skin heated at her mentioning his figure, and he tried not to think about hers even though he'd definitely noticed it. Wanting to hurry and banish those types of thoughts, he practically in-haled his plain glazed doughnut then got to work applying grout to the places in the brick walls that had chipped away with time. He'd asked Ivy if she wanted the walls painted, but she said she liked the look of the bare, authentic brick.

"Covering it is like pretending the past didn't happen," she'd said.

There were times he wished the past hadn't happened, but that wasn't how the march of time worked. You had to make your way through the bad along with the good.

If only there hadn't been so much bad.

As he worked, he caught pieces of the conversation between Ivy, Daisy, his mom and Isaac. Even though his mom was the quietest, she did occasionally offer her thoughts on what items would sell best in the store, her memories of the Stinson Building and all the businesses she could remember being housed in it.

When he took a break to get a drink of water, Ivy came up to him, wrapped her hand around his upper arm and propelled him outside.

"What's wrong?" he asked once they were down the steps and around the edge of the building.

"What's wrong is that you are watching your mother like a hawk. She's not a child about to toddle into an open fireplace."

"Excuse me?"

Ivy looked toward the open windows before speaking again, her voice lowered. "You're hovering. I know she's your mom and you're worried about her—I totally get that. And I'm sorry, yet again, if I'm overstepping. But I think maybe you are too overprotective, and maybe you should work outside for a while."

Austin almost told Ivy that, yes, she was overstepping, that he knew how to take care of his mother. But something stopped him. Had he really been taking good care of his mom? Yes, he worked hard to provide for their family. He drove her to doctor appointments. Did all the things she no longer could around the ranch. But none of that had seemed to help bring her out of the depression that she sometimes tried to hide, tried to deny, but sometimes couldn't. Maybe he wasn't equipped with what it took to help his mom heal emotionally.

Unlike himself, he felt the urge to cry wash over him.

"Austin?" The concern in Ivy's voice caused his irritation at her to evaporate.

"Maybe you're right."

Ivy surprised him further by taking his hands in hers.

"Look at me."

He exhaled then complied. The compassion he saw in her eyes moved something inside him, something that he was afraid to even attempt to name.

"I haven't known you long, but it's obvious you love your mother and Daisy. And that you'd do anything for them. But sometimes that leads to doing too much of one thing and not enough of another. That's not a criticism. It's just a fact of how humans operate." She hesitated, looked down at their joined hands as if them touching was nothing out of the ordinary. Maybe to her it wasn't, was just something she did when she was trying to be helpful.

He wanted to ask her if she was giving this advice because of personal experience, but he reminded himself that some things were private and should stay that way unless the affected party chose to share the details. He certainly didn't want to go around admitting that his wife had left him, that she'd forced him to make an impossible choice that had led to her leaving.

Austin didn't know what to say so just nodded. Then, wanting to rid himself of the twitchy feeling having her hold his hands caused, he retrieved them and turned toward the water sprayer.

"If you close the windows when you go inside, I'll take care of the sections you haven't washed yet."

He still hadn't moved when Ivy appeared at the window to close it. He looked up at her, and she gave him a reassuring smile before pushing the windows closed. As he set to spraying the dirt and debris of time off the exterior of the building, he couldn't get the sight of that smile or the feel of Ivy's small hands out of his mind.

CHAPTER SEVEN

IVY SAT DOWN beside Austin and Daisy's mom, who had told her to call her Melissa, and stared at the large space on the wall between the two sets of windows.

"I keep trying to think of something to eventually put there that would be eye-catching but fit the theme of the store," Ivy said. "I thought about a quilt, but that seems too obvious."

"Maybe a painting? Eileen Parker at the art gallery could probably put you in touch with someone. I heard that Maya Pine's husband is a painter. Maya runs the local news site since we don't have a newspaper anymore."

"Hmm, maybe." Ivy tilted her head sideways. "It would be cool to have something crafty, but I'm afraid that's not where my talent lies."

"I don't know. You seem to have a lot of ideas about how you want this place to look."

"I do, but you'll notice none of it involves me and a glue gun. I'd probably glue my fingers together."

There it was—a hint of a smile. Even though she was only getting to know Melissa, it felt monumental, like the sun peeking out from behind the clouds after two weeks of endless rain and flooding.

"Have you always liked old buildings?" Melissa asked.

"I have. I remember going to places like Fort Boonesborough, the Mary Todd Lincoln House and Federal Hill, which is better known as My Old Kentucky Home. That's the name of the song they sing before the Kentucky Derby."

"I guess you grew up around different types of horses than we have here."

"There are lots of Thoroughbred farms, true, but they weren't really part of my world."

"Rich people horses."

"Exactly."

They chatted some more about Ivy's growing-up years in Lexington, her time at the University of Kentucky, how her roommate had helped her land the job with the hotel chain after college.

"Daisy has talked a lot about the places that were turned into hotels. It sounds…interesting."

Ivy got the feeling Melissa hesitated on that last word because it surprised her. Maybe she hadn't been interested in anything for quite a while.

"I like seeing forgotten things given new life.

Jade Valley reminds me a lot of some of the old downtown areas that have been refurbished and rejuvenated with new businesses. So many downtowns have died because of bypasses and box stores. I understand that times have changed, but just because something is old or has outlived its original use doesn't mean it should be abandoned."

Ivy considered her next words carefully, wanting to be subtle enough that it wasn't obvious what she was doing but not so subtle that the message she intended would be missed altogether.

"I guess life is like that too. My mom didn't know what to do with herself when my dad left. It was a kind of out-of-the-blue thing. But my grandma Cecile was a 'pick yourself up and dust yourself off' sort and gave Mom a bit of a kick in the pants. Grandma gave her the money to buy the florist business where she worked when the owner wanted to retire. She and my sister Holly still run it. I didn't figure out until I was an adult that Grandma had given Mom the money she'd saved for years to open a quilt shop." Ivy felt suddenly teary recounting the story, but she blinked several times to clear her vision. "That's why I'm going to make this shop work, to fulfill the dream she was never able to."

"That's a good way to honor her."

Figuring she'd said enough that she hoped would help Melissa, Ivy shifted the conversation a bit.

"I wish I had her creativeness though." She kicked the box of buttons that sat next to her foot. "Like she would know what to do with all these buttons. I can't stand the idea of throwing them away, but none of them match. I thought maybe displaying them in canning jars." She looked over at Melissa. "If you happen to get any ideas, I'm all ears."

Daisy returned from her trip to Little Italy to pick up the pizzas Ivy had ordered for lunch.

"Oh good, I'm starving," Isaac said as he appeared at the bottom of the stairs.

"Are you part bloodhound?" Ivy asked.

Beside her, Melissa actually huffed out a little laugh. Ivy noticed Daisy's shocked expression, one she quickly hid. The girl was easy to read. It was obvious that it had been a long time since she'd heard her mother laugh, but she'd hidden her shock so Melissa wouldn't realize that she'd just taken a big step in her healing process. Ivy wished Austin could have witnessed it. Maybe if he had, it would help lift some of the burden he so obviously bore.

Even though he surely had seen Daisy arrive with the pizzas, Austin didn't come inside. Did he honestly think she'd banished him even from lunch? Before she could get up to tell him to come inside, however, Isaac went to the window, opened it and yelled, "Get in here and eat, boy."

Ivy pressed her lips together to keep from laughing at the idea that Austin was a boy. Anyone with any sense could see he was a full-grown man and a handsome one at that. Chances were he'd meet an equally attractive woman at some point, get married and have at least a couple cute kids who would grow up on a ranch under the wide Wyoming sky, learning a strong work ethic from their father.

An uncomfortable tightness in her chest had her standing. She needed to be alone long enough to get rid of that feeling she knew all too well now. It visited her in the middle of the night as she lay in her sleeping bag, listening to the still surprising silence of the world around her. It caught her unaware when she saw a couple walking down Main Street hand in hand or when a customer in Trudy's was accompanied by an adorable baby.

She'd come to think of the tight feeling as the two Ls—loneliness and loss. Even though she was surrounded by people all day, every day, could even laugh and look forward, at night the reality of what had happened and the fact that she was really alone in her new journey would hit her full force. During the day she could mostly keep it at bay, but at night the truth would not be denied. Despite her determination to move past it and telling herself that James was not worth her tears, they sometimes came anyway. And now they threatened again.

"I'll be right back." She hurried up the stairs and walked straight to the windows at the front of the building. When she was feeling down, sometimes the incredible view of the mountains helped to lift her mood. She'd stare at them, marvel at the forces that made them, take deep breaths, and the tight knot in her chest would gradually ease.

This, however, was the first time the feeling had been this strong when she was around others. Did that mean that instead of getting past the pain of James's betrayal, it was getting worse? She'd thought she was doing remarkably well in her first days in Jade Valley, but maybe it had been a temporary reprieve. Had running away from Kentucky been avoidance instead of a positive step in her own healing?

Who was she to try to guide others on a healing path when her own grief was so fresh?

No. You helped others even when you were hurting.

Maybe through helping others heal, she'd end up healing herself. And if not, she'd still put some good out there into the world. Grandma Cecile had always told her that people should do something good every day, whether that was something as huge as hiding Jews from the Nazis in their attic or as simple as holding a door open for someone at the store.

"Even if all you can do is smile at someone, you never know if that might be the thing that gets them through their tough day," she'd said.

Ivy had taken that mindset to heart. Some days were just more difficult than others. When she'd been struggling so much with an economics class in college that she'd been on the verge of tears all semester. When someone had stolen her little car out of her apartment's parking lot and it had been found across the river in Indiana stripped to uselessness. Definitely when her father had decided to leave.

And that moment in that hotel ballroom when it had become obvious that James was not the man she had thought him to be. That he did not love her like he had claimed.

Ivy deliberately thought of Grandma Cecile and how strong of a woman she'd been. She actually smiled when she thought of what her tiny grandma would have likely done to James if she'd been the one in Ivy's position. Instead of running away, she imagined her grandmother climbing onto the top of one of those gorgeously appointed tables and announcing to everyone present that the engagement was off because James was a liar and a cheat, but that everyone should go ahead and drink and eat because James was footing the bill. Then she would have descended from the tabletop and kicked James in a certain place with such force that it would remain a memory for the rest of his days. Only then would she have turned and left the ballroom.

Grandma Cecile had been much cooler than Ivy.

Ivy realized she was sitting somewhere in between Grandma Cecile and Melissa—sad about what might have been, what she'd lost, and determined to not let it control her and keep her pressed down with that sadness.

She took a long, deep breath as she stared at one of the snowcapped mountains then let it out just as slowly. Determined to make the rest of the day positive, she turned and followed the smell of bread, pepperoni and sausage.

By the end of the day, her blue moment from earlier had drifted away like the puffy white pappus of a dandelion. Instead of dwelling on what might have been when she settled in for the night, she pulled out her phone and went to her favorite fabric site. She scrolled through the newest designs and bookmarked some really beautiful ones. A striking blue that reminded her of home caught her eye. When she magnified the design, she almost laughed because they were cute little dandelion puffs like the ones she'd just pictured in her mind. It felt like a sign that she was meant to have this fabric as a symbol of letting the past go. She wouldn't order it for quilts but rather for a dress to wear to the grand opening of the store.

Fearing it might be sold out before then, she went ahead and placed an order. That gave her another thought, and she searched for the perfect fabric to make Daisy a dress too. It didn't take long to find one that had compasses and maps, great for a girl who loved geography and wanted to travel the world.

Her shopping done for the night, she set her phone aside and curled into the sleeping bag. Not even a minute passed before a sound had her sitting up and her ears straining. When she realized it was someone trying to open the front door, her heart started hammering. She scurried out of the sleeping bag and crossed to the window. It was too dark to see much, but someone was definitely on her front stoop. She heard voices though she couldn't make out the words.

With her hands shaking so much that she almost dropped her phone, she called 911.

The good thing about living in a small town was that when you called 911, it didn't take the police long to arrive. But whoever had been trying to break in must have seen the patrol vehicle before she did because two figures went racing down the street. In the next moment, the night came alive with a siren and the bar lights atop the sheriff's department SUV. Whoever had responded to her call hit the accelerator and rocketed down the street after the prowlers.

Ivy turned on the light and looked around for anything she could use as a weapon. Her gaze landed on a length of pipe that Isaac had removed from the upstairs bathroom. She grabbed it and held it at the ready as she descended the stairs and flicked on the overhead lights to the main level.

Everything looked as it had when she went to bed. With her heart still thumping like a chased rabbit's, she crossed to the front door. She relaxed a fraction when she found it both still locked and the windows intact. Even so, she knew there was no way she was going to be able to sleep now.

She thought of the valuable coins upstairs and how she really needed to make plans to get rid of them.

Trying to get her nerves to calm down, she paced the floor that was due to receive the first coating of new polyurethane tomorrow. She glanced at the old wood and glass display cases that she'd cleaned and that Austin and Rich had pushed up against the wall after Rich had finished the last of his electrical work and declared her wiring updated and safe. She'd still have to pass an inspection, but she had confidence in Rich's work. What Austin had said about Rich being the absolute best electrician in the area, possibly the state, she now believed.

Thus why he was in high demand. He had a dozen jobs come his way while he was working on her building.

Isaac had just put the finishing touches on the upstairs bathroom too, and had moved on to finishing the downstairs bathroom.

Suddenly the idea of living alone in the building made her doubt the sanity of the move again.

The sound of a vehicle outside propelled her to the front window. She watched as an officer got out of his vehicle and approached her front door. She opened it before he even had to knock.

"Good evening, ma'am," the deputy said. A glance at his nameplate revealed his identity as J. Langston. "Can you tell me exactly what happened?"

She gave him the short rundown of events. "I take it this means you didn't catch them."

"No, ma'am. I'm going to sit outside for a while unless I get another call. If I have to leave, don't hesitate to call 911 again if they come back."

Despite her telling him that the door had still been locked, he requested to do a thorough search inside to make sure. Once he was satisfied that no one else was inside, he retreated to his vehicle. Even though she knew he was outside now, keeping an eye on her property, she still stayed up and made a list of the things she wanted to look for at the community rummage sale that weekend. She'd heard the proceeds were going to help fund various projects—the repainting of the Welcome to Jade Valley signs on both ends of town, stocking and running the local food bank, and a fund that helped pay the expenses of residents who had to go to Casper and Cheyenne for specialized medical care such as cancer treatments.

If she didn't forge ahead with her plans, the little voice in her head that liked to whisper that she'd made another mistake might grow louder. If she didn't continue working to make this building not only her business but also her home, she risked having the fear she'd experienced at the sound of someone trying to break in eclipse the joy she felt with each step made toward opening the store.

As the night dragged on, she shifted from planning for her living space to reading about all the legalities and tax filing requirements for the State of Wyoming. The latter was what finally started making her drowsy. She leaned back in the chair and focused on the splotchy ceiling that Austin would be painting soon. She loved the texture of the tin tiles, but since she was keeping the dark brick walls she wanted the ceiling to be what reflected the light from the windows. Customers were more likely to browse and buy in a bright, airy store than one that felt dark and gloomy.

She looked around the room, taking in everything Austin had done so far. Even though they had a good ways to go, it already looked like a completely different space. To be honest, part of her dreaded the day when all the work was done and Austin would no longer be a fixture in her life. And she had to admit that it was at least partially because he was so attractive. That admission had surprised her when she first realized the truth of it. Fresh off James's betrayal, she wasn't looking for someone to replace him. But like candy helped cover the bitter taste of medicine, eye candy helped ease the bitter pain of betrayal.

It was more than that though. Yes, Austin was handsome, seemed more so every day if she was being honest, but who he was as a person was also attractive. Ivy wanted to know more about him, but she was careful in what she asked—of him, Daisy or his mother. She didn't want any of them getting the wrong idea.

Getting to know all the layers of Austin felt like waiting for water and wind to erode away a rock. But maybe somewhere inside that rock was the surprise of an amethyst geode.

Ivy shook her head at her fanciful thinking. It

was a sign her brain was overtired and needed rest, and there was no sleeping in tomorrow.

She dragged herself up out of the chair and went to glance out the window. Deputy Langston was still sitting outside, so she felt safe enough to turn out the light and head back upstairs. Once again she crawled into her sleeping bag, but despite her fatigue it still took a long time for the tension in her body to relax. She noticed every little sound, strained to hear if Deputy Langston drove away.

Ivy exhaled in frustration as she stared at the top of her tent. She forced herself to close her eyes and think of things that had nothing to do with prowlers. The types of treats she'd have at the grand opening of the store. How her mother had texted her to share a story of a ninety-seven-year-old man who had come into the floral shop to buy a dozen pink roses for his ninety-five-year-old wife for their seventieth anniversary. The fact that she'd given the stray cat the name Sprinkles and each day he seemed to become a bit more used to her and move a little closer.

Her thoughts started drifting as sleep inched up on her. An image of Austin, laughing at something Rich had said, made her smile. What a nice image to see before finally slipping into dreamland.

AUSTIN MADE IT a point to not watch his mom too closely when she came with him and Daisy, but even so he was seeing evidence that Ivy had been right about getting her out of the house. His mom chatted with locals who came by to meet Ivy—Sunny Wheeler, who was excited by the idea of having the quilt shop open in time for the fall festival; Maya Pine, who interviewed Ivy for the local news site about her plans; even Sheriff Angie Lee, who had chatted briefly with Ivy outside.

He overheard his mom sharing more details about all the businesses she could remember occupying the Stinson Building. He'd been startled to learn that she and his father had shared their first kiss out behind the building when they were supposed to be at the library studying for an English exam.

"Mom!"

"What?" she'd asked as she looked at him. "It's a perfectly normal thing for teenagers to do. As long as they don't go too far." This last bit she said with her gaze fixed on Daisy.

"Don't look at me," Daisy said. "There are exactly zero boys here I'm interested in."

Even though he thought Daisy a bit too young to date yet, let alone kiss anyone, her answer also made him a bit sad. Daisy would probably meet someone and fall in love during one of her future far-flung travels and make it less likely she'd ever live in Jade Valley after she graduated and went off to college. He wouldn't hold her back, wouldn't trap her somewhere she couldn't achieve her dreams, but it would still make him sad.

He placed the paint roller he'd been using on the ceiling back in the pan and rubbed his neck. A glance down revealed his mother was at the front door staring outside at something. Needing a break from having all the blood drain from his arm as he painted above his head, he descended the ladder to see what had drawn her attention. Ivy was at work and Daisy was at the library looking up old documents about the Stinson Building, so it wasn't either of them. And the last time he'd looked down, his mom had been sorting buttons into jars by color.

"What's so interesting out here?" he asked as he approached her.

She pointed toward the pile of junk he would be hauling off soon.

"Can you cut that piece of plywood into a square that will fit between those windows?" She pointed at the wall space between the two sets of windows on the left side of the building.

"Sure. What are you planning?" He thought about how Daisy had mentioned that their mother was artistic and crafty. Was she actually going to put that to use?

"Maybe nothing. Maybe something."

He latched on to that "maybe something" and retrieved the piece of thick plywood, cut it to her specifications and then gave it two coats of the white paint he was using on the ceiling.

"It should be dry by tomorrow." Even though Daisy and his mom didn't typically come to work with him every day, he wasn't going to remind her of that. If bringing his mom with him every day helped her become more like her old self, he would lift her and her wheelchair in and out of the truck however many times it took.

When Daisy returned from the library, she pulled him aside.

"I know why the sheriff came by earlier. Someone tried to break in here last night."

"What?" Fear shot through him, even though he knew Ivy was safe. "Where did you hear that?"

"At the library. Someone saw a sheriff's department vehicle sitting outside late last night, with all the lights in the building on. Well, you know how nothing is a secret in this town other than why Trudy and Alma don't like each other."

He knew he didn't like Ivy staying here alone. It would be the same for any woman living alone, he told himself.

Only that wasn't exactly true, was it? He didn't

worry about Trudy all the time. Or Mrs. Miller, his former English teacher, whose husband was a patient in the nursing home. There were likely dozens of people who lived alone all over the county, ones who were even more in danger of a home invasion than someone who lived only four blocks away from the sheriff's department.

He tried not to assign too much meaning to his concern but wasn't entirely successful.

When Ivy returned from her shift at Trudy's, one look told him she didn't get enough rest the night before. She should probably go take a nap, but he knew her well enough by now to know she wouldn't.

He waited until she went outside to get something out of her car to ask her about what had happened the night before.

"How did you know…? Never mind, small town. Everything is fine. Sheriff Lee told me they caught the kids, two teenagers, not even from here. They'd evidently vandalized some older buildings in the next county over as part of some online trend. Unlucky for them, one of those buildings is owned by a big shot attorney in Portland who isn't inclined to go easy on them. With all the evidence they posted themselves, I think they are toast."

"Still, it could happen again. Aren't you scared here alone?"

"I won't lie and say I slept well after what happened, but I don't think Jade Valley has crime run amok."

He wanted to tell her to…he wasn't even sure what. Telling her to abandon her new home was a bridge too far. An alarm system maybe? He glanced toward the open front door and straight back through the first floor to the bottom of the stairs.

"I can enclose the top of the stairs with a wall and a door you can lock instead of your living space just being open to the bottom floor. It'd be an extra layer of protection."

Austin expected her to shoot down the idea, but she appeared to be considering it.

"I actually like that idea, even without the security concerns. Keep my work and home space more separate."

"Maybe you should get a safety-deposit box at the bank for the coins."

"I've already got an appointment to take them to a dealer in Cheyenne."

"I'll go with you."

She looked up at him. "Actually, I would appreciate that. It didn't bother me to drive cross-country, but having something worth that much with me makes me nervous. I'll pay for your time, of course."

"No, it's not work."

"I'm not going to take away from your work hours and not pay you."

"Fine." He wasn't going to accept pay for ensuring her safety, but she didn't have to know that until the trip was over. And he wasn't going to assign more meaning to his offer than was there.

"When is your appointment?"

"Not until next Monday, so plenty of time to finish that ceiling." Ivy smiled widely, and he found himself smiling back. It seemed the longer he was around her, the easier it was to smile. But, again, he told himself there were no romantic thoughts attached to that realization. She had that effect on everyone. Isaac and Rich had laughed at something she said on numerous occasions. Daisy seemed to come out of her introverted shell and shine brightly when around Ivy. It made him wonder if she was content with a brother who was so much older than she was, or if she had longed for a sister.

And then there was his mom. She was beginning to show an interest in life again beyond simply getting from one day to the next.

"What's that for?" Ivy asked as she pointed toward the piece of plywood he'd painted.

"I don't know. Mom seems to have something in mind. She wanted it cut to fit between the two sets of windows on the left wall."

"Oh. We were talking about what I should

hang there. To be honest, I was hoping it might spark something in her. Daisy saying that your mom was crafty and artistic made me think it was worth a try."

"Why do you do that?"

Ivy looked up at him with a confused expression. "What?"

"You seem to try so hard to help everyone around you, people you barely even know."

"Don't you think there should be more of that in the world?"

"Well, yeah, probably."

"Both my grandma Cecile and my mom have always said that there are plenty of people in the world who don't care about others, but there can never be too many who do."

"And you've taken that to heart."

"I have. Also, it works wonders when you feel awful yourself."

"Do you feel awful?"

"Not in this moment, no."

Which seemed to say that at some point she had, and perhaps recently. Maybe it was even what drove her to Wyoming.

"Thank you," he said, nodding toward the building where his mom and sister had their heads bent over some task. "For caring about them."

"It's not just them, you know."

His heart gave an extra *ba-bump* against his

rib cage, and he had to remind it that he was single and going to stay that way. Even so, he didn't know how to respond.

"Everyone has been kind to me, welcoming me to town, offering to help in any way they can," Ivy said.

Of course she meant the citizens of Jade Valley as a whole. He'd heard how nice she was and how well she fit into the community from Trudy to Maya Pine to the old guys who sat on the town square after they'd had their breakfast at Trudy's or Alma's each morning.

"She's a cute little thing," one of the men had said when a gaggle of them had wandered down to check out what was going on at the Stinson Building one morning.

"I bet someone snaps her up within a month," another had added.

"She's not a prize to be won," Austin had said, which had earned him a round of laughs and elbowing between the old guys, as if they were privy to information he was simply too young to know.

He'd managed to resist saying what he thought—that they were living in the past. No wonder their wives kicked them out of the house each morning. They probably had to in order to have some peace and quiet or get something done without their husbands underfoot. He imagined the wives calling each other and saying in exasperation, "You'll never guess what that old fool said this morning."

The retirees were good people, would help anyone who needed it, but they could benefit from some updating of their views on women and relationships. If anyone ever talked about Daisy that way in front of him, he'd drag the guy by the ear to the river and toss him in for a nice, cold swim.

"Do you think we can find a door that fits with the age of the building?" Ivy asked, yanking him out of his thoughts and back to the earlier part of their conversation.

"You're going to the rummage sale this weekend, right?"

She nodded.

"There's always the unexpected there, so I'd check there first. If not, then we can check Fizzy's place."

"Fizzy?"

"He owns a junk and salvage place several miles outside of town. I've heard from Daisy that it would take days to finish visiting the Smithsonian. Well, Fizzy's is kind of like that. I wouldn't be surprised if there's a portal to another world in there somewhere."

Ivy laughed. "Well, this I've gotta see."

Why did Austin suddenly want to take her on a tour of the bizarre landscape of Fizzy's, where seeing a Japanese lantern, a chain saw carving of

Bigfoot and a ten-foot-tall pile of cigar boxes while standing in one spot wouldn't be unheard-of?

Because she made him feel lighter inside. Like when he was talking to and laughing with her he could set aside his burdens and simply enjoy life.

He suddenly dreaded when this renovation job would come to an end, and not just for monetary reasons.

CHAPTER EIGHT

THROUGHOUT HER LIFE, Ivy had been to yard sales, garage sales, estate sales and more than a few thrift stores. None of those compared to the Jade Valley Rummage Sale. Covering the yard of the Methodist church and the adjacent field, the offerings were a combination of items cleaned out of people's closets and garages, actual antiques, and a junker's paradise.

"Is Fizzy here?"

Austin actually laughed at her question. "That would require Fizzy to make more effort than he's accustomed to making. He's more of a 'stack it high and they will come' sort."

Even without Fizzy's contribution, Ivy was certain she would end the day with a lot of furnishings for her new home.

She was also probably going to be, as her grandma Cecile used to say, "fuller than a tick on a dog." Because the air was filled with the scents of grilling meat and deep-fried dough. Her mouth watered at the sight of fresh-squeezed lemonade being sold by the high school basketball team and a large variety of cookies made by the local garden club.

"This is like a yard sale on steroids meets the county fair," she said.

"Melissa!" one of the garden club ladies called out, all smiles and waves as she spotted Austin's mom.

Melissa had said she could stay back at Ivy's place, working on whatever she had up her sleeve for the wall, but Ivy had said, "I think the whole town turned out and we've all been working hard, so today we should go have some fun."

Ivy used her best "pretty please" face, and Melissa smiled and relented. After Melissa indicated it was okay for Ivy to take the handles of her wheelchair, Ivy called back for Austin and Daisy to lock up on their way out.

"It's so good to see you," the thin woman with hair dyed bright red said as she came out from behind the cookie table.

"You too, Suzanne."

Ivy was glad to see that despite her initial hesitance to come, Melissa seemed more open and willing to chat than when she'd first met her.

"Do you want to go around with us or stay to visit with your friends?" Ivy asked.

"You all go on." That she didn't appear to be saying that because she thought it was a burden for her to accompany them was another step in the right direction.

Ivy and Austin had only managed to get as far as the funnel cake truck before Daisy ran into her friend Candace and they were off as well.

"Looks like you're stuck with just me," Austin said.

"Oh, the horror," she said, with a dramatic back of her hand to her forehead.

Austin snorted at her display.

The truth was she didn't mind walking along the rows of offerings beside him, sharing fried dough covered in powdered sugar. She considered him a friend now, though there were no "Hey, let's be friends" statements like when you were a kid. As she'd tried to go to sleep the night before, her thoughts had kept drifting to him and how concerned he'd been about her safety following the attempted break-in. After how things had ended with James, it was nice to be around a guy who seemed as genuine as the first day of summer was long.

But she'd thought James was a stand-up and honest guy too, hadn't she?

She shoved thoughts of James aside, determined to enjoy this day and find the perfect items for her new home.

As if she'd summoned it, she spotted a metal bed frame two rows over. She practically leaped over people to get to it, trusting Austin to follow. By the time she reached the seller, however, she'd remembered to wear an only slightly interested expression.

"How much for this bed frame?" she asked.

When the man quoted a price, she winced. Not because it was a terrible price but because she knew it could be better. As she went back and forth with the guy, Austin stood beside her, saying nothing. Only when the owner of the bed frame stepped away to aid another customer did Austin lean close and say, "You do remember this is a charity event, right?"

For a moment his words didn't register, only the shivers that ran over her entire body at the sound of his lowered voice so close to her ear.

"I…yeah, I know."

The combination of his reminder of how the funds were going to be used and the need to move on had her agreeing on a price if the owner threw in a stained-glass lamp. The deal was struck, money paid and Ivy's name affixed to the items for later pickup.

She told herself that allowing such feelings for Austin to find a place to settle within her so soon after the end of her engagement was a very bad idea. This new life of hers was supposed to be forged alone.

When Austin was recruited to help a couple

other guys load up a truck with heavy furniture, Ivy watched the shape of his biceps as he lifted. She caught herself smiling and shook her head, turning away to continue shopping.

"It's good to see Austin with someone again," a woman she didn't recognize said. She patted Ivy on the shoulder in the way of kindhearted strangers before moving along.

Ivy wanted to call her back and tell her that she and Austin were friends, nothing more, but it was too late. The middle-aged woman was swallowed by the increasing crowd. Ivy hoped erroneous rumors didn't start circulating. It was a widely known truth that gossip was the fuel on which small towns ran.

But as she moved from booth to booth, purchasing the items that would make her living space more like a home, she kept wondering about the person in Austin's past. She did her best to push away those thoughts and why she might be fixating on them by handing over money for some pretty teal curtains with rustic white rods, a couple of handmade quilts, an antique chest of drawers that matched the curtains remarkably well, a shower curtain with happy faces all over it, a folding chalkboard sign to use outside the store once it was open, and various other odds and ends.

Figuring she'd done enough shopping for the

time being, she purchased a cold lemonade and went to sit on a circular bench that had been built around the base of an oak tree next to the church. That's where Trudy found her and parked herself next to her.

"I'm not used to seeing you outside of the café," Ivy said.

"I never miss this sale. Josephine can handle the kitchen just fine."

Josephine was a sweet woman who was even shorter than Ivy's five foot three. She'd come to the US twenty years ago from Mexico to do migrant farm work and had finally earned her US citizenship five years ago. And she made a marbled tres leches cake that was quite possibly the best dessert Ivy had ever tasted, not that she would say that in front of Trudy, who had quite the fine hand with desserts herself.

"One year I found a plate to replace one in a set I'd inherited from my mother," Trudy said. "I'd had that dinnerware set, minus the one broken plate, for thirty years. A couple of years ago, I was the first one to arrive and I got basically a new TV, a huge one, for ten dollars. Now I can pop some popcorn, sit in my recliner and feel like I'm at the movie theater."

Ivy laughed at that mental image. "I might be a little jealous."

"Since you're sitting down, I assume you've done a fair amount of shopping already."

"Enough that I hope I get good tips next week." And the potential buyer for the two valuable coins actually came through. She'd been careful not to sound desperate to get rid of them when talking to the dealer. When he'd said he thought he knew someone who would be interested, she'd told him that she didn't want to make the three-hundred-mile drive unless the buyer was serious, that she could arrange to sell it elsewhere.

She'd witnessed some expert bargaining tactics utilized by Mr. Sterling when he'd been trying to purchase properties to turn into hotels, and she put them to good use from time to time.

Ivy spotted the woman who had made the comment about Austin earlier.

"Who is that lady in the pink top looking at the bakeware?"

Trudy looked where Ivy indicated. "That's Ann Fleming. She's the principal at the elementary school. Why?"

Ivy knew she had to tread carefully, so as not to give Trudy the wrong idea.

"She came up to me and told me it was good to see Austin with someone again, but she moved away before I could correct her assumption."

Trudy made a sound that indicated she'd heard

her but was uncharacteristically quiet. Ivy glanced over at her.

"So you don't know he was married before?"

That revelation startled Ivy, but she did her best not to show it. "No. Why would I?"

"I thought the two of you had gotten close."

"We're friends."

There was that "mmm" sound again, and it was enough that Ivy knew she had to reveal a bit about herself.

"I just got out of a long-term relationship, so the last thing I'm looking for is another one." Sure, she'd begun to appreciate the shape of Austin's body, the way her heart felt happy when he smiled, but that didn't mean she wanted to date him. The painful sting from James's betrayal still lingered. You didn't simply jump from an engagement to dating someone new. At least she didn't. The casual dater in her family was Lily.

"That's understandable. But you never know what life has in store for you."

"I hope it has a successful business in store for me."

"Of course. But a happy life isn't made up of just one thing."

"Right now, one thing is all I can handle." Sure, she was making friends, working at Trudy's and gradually getting more involved in the community, but those were not Big Things. Renovating an old building, starting a business with no guarantee it would succeed, rebuilding her life—those *were* Big Things. A romantic relationship fell into that category as well, and that space needed to stay vacant—at least until it wasn't battered and bruised and broken anymore.

Ivy deliberately engaged in conversation with everyone she knew, introduced herself to others, shopped a bit more, and ate a mouthwatering burger and delicious seasoned fries. She caught sight of Austin a few times and motioned that she wasn't ready to leave yet. When she made it back to the table where the ladies were selling the cookies, Melissa wasn't there.

"Austin took her to look around," Melissa's friend Suzanne said. "She said she had something she was looking for. It makes me happy to see her out and about, expressing interest in… anything. She used to be such a vibrant person, always busy doing something."

Even with how much she'd been around Austin, Daisy and Melissa, Ivy didn't know the details of what had happened. She knew it was a car accident that had caused Melissa to lose her second husband and the use of her legs, but that was all.

"She seems to enjoy coming to work with Austin and Daisy."

"I gathered that, though she didn't come right out and say it."

Even though she'd had plenty to eat while at the sale, Ivy still examined the cookie flavors.

"I don't need any of these, but I'm going to buy some anyway."

"Sweetheart, with your figure you could probably eat all these and not gain an ounce," one of the other ladies said.

Ivy laughed. "I assure you that that's not true."

She didn't buy them all, but she did buy two dozen—a variety of chocolate chip, sugar, oatmeal raisin, and cranberry orange. Between her, Austin, Daisy and Melissa, they probably wouldn't last long.

"Are you done shopping?"

Ivy looked over at the sound of Austin's voice and noticed he was alone. "Did you misplace your mom?"

He smiled. "No. She's with Daisy. Mom said she had a couple other places she wanted to go, so off they went."

He motioned toward downtown, and when Ivy looked she could see Daisy pushing her mom down the sidewalk.

"That's a good sign, right?"

He nodded. "I'm almost afraid to hope though. She's had ups and downs before, but it does feel different now."

Ivy hoped for the sake of everyone in his family that he was right.

With her list of purchases in hand so she didn't forget anything, she and Austin began to collect her new furnishings and load them into the bed of his truck. They proved to be a good team, and soon were headed back to her place. When she got out of the truck, she stared at her building. Sometimes it still didn't seem real that it was hers.

"You know, it just hit me we have to haul all this stuff upstairs," she said. "Good thing I bought those cookies. I'm going to need a reward after we're done."

They carried in the lighter items first, then the metal bed frame. When they finally came to the chest of drawers, Ivy groaned.

"You bought it," Austin said, his voice light with laughter.

"Oh, hush."

This caused him to smile fully. Her heart felt as if it had feet that it had just tripped over.

No, she could not let her feelings go down that road. It was too soon. She didn't know him well enough. He was evidently divorced, and there was at least the possibility that the dissolution of his marriage was his fault. He felt like an emotional land mine—one very tall, attractive land mine.

It was likely her feelings were simply a rebound reaction to what she'd gone through with James, some primal but unwanted need to feel as if she was enough—enough that a man didn't have to have two other women on the side, possibly more.

"It's not going to move itself," Austin said, intruding on her thoughts.

"Well, that's just annoying."

They took the five drawers out to make it lighter and easier to hold, leaving them in the bed of the truck. Then they each took an end, Austin the heavier top, and headed across the street. They got it inside and to the foot of the stairs before Ivy said she needed a break. Even without the drawers, the chest was heavier than it looked. It was obviously solid oak with not an inch of plywood to be found.

"Ready?" Austin asked after they'd caught their breath for a few seconds.

She nodded and they picked up their respective ends before heading up the stairs, which creaked slightly under the combined weight of two adults and a heavy piece of furniture that probably dated to the Taft administration.

Ivy's arms strained under the weight as she moved slowly backward, making sure to place her feet with care. Even Austin, who was no doubt used to dealing with cattle, horses and all manner of demanding physical labor on his ranch, grunted as they slowly made their way upward.

"Watch your step," Austin said.

Ivy nodded and made a sound that she'd heard him, but all her attention suddenly fixated on her nose and the powerful need to scratch the itch that had taken up residence there. Distracted, she felt her grip slip a little. On instinct she moved to adjust her hold on the chest, but she released it a bit too much. The next moment seemed to happen in slow motion and in a blur, both at the same time. She grabbed for the falling end of the chest. In the process, her foot turned sideways, slipping off the edge of the step. The weight of the falling chest landed on her fingers. Pain shot up her arm, followed by the feeling of needing to throw up. That had always been her body's response to intense pain—when she'd crashed her bike at age nine and broken her arm, the time in seventh grade when she'd been hit in the head by a spiked volleyball during PE, and when she'd slipped on a patch of ice while hurrying to class her freshman year at UK, which resulted in unintentional splits but luckily no broken bones.

She wasn't that lucky this time.

Austin cried out something, maybe her name or perhaps some other exclamation, but her pain receptors were too busy being overwhelmed for her to make out the actual words.

Miraculously when he set down his end of the chest of drawers, the whole thing didn't go careering back down the stairs. In a blink he was next to her, his eyes wide and his expression full of concern. Ivy was amazed she could even see his face through her tears.

"Can you stand?" he asked.

She tried, but the pain in her ankle joined that of the pulsing in her fingers.

"I need to take you to the hospital," Austin said, then eased her left arm around his strong shoulders and put his right arm around her waist.

Even with him practically carrying her entire weight down the stairs, easing past the still immobile piece of furniture, the pain radiating through her made her stomach heave.

"Bath...room," she said, her voice shaky.

He didn't ask why, simply steered her toward the downstairs bathroom that was thankfully close. Instead of leaving her though, he stayed by her side as she dry heaved a few times then as she splashed water on her face. She made the mistake of putting down her injured foot as she exited the bathroom, and a fresh wave of pain made her cry out.

Austin's arm tightened around her waist. "I'm sorry."

"Not...your fault."

"Ivy, I'm going to carry you to the truck."

"I can make it." She said the words, but even she didn't believe them. It felt as if they made her break out in a sweat instead.

Austin didn't even argue with her. With undeniable strength and ease, he swept her up into his arms and strode toward the open front door, a man with a purpose. Ivy relented and let her head rest against his shoulder, concentrating in a vain effort to contain her pain.

"What happened?" someone asked as he descended the front steps.

It took Ivy a moment to recognize the voice as Melissa's. She and Daisy were evidently back from their excursion.

"She crushed her hand and hurt her ankle," Austin answered, not slowing down. "I'm taking her to the hospital." Once he got her seated and buckled in, he hurried to his side of the truck. "I'll call when I know more."

Ivy knew it was only a short drive to the small local hospital because everything in town was a short drive. As she did her best not to throw up in Austin's truck, she experienced a moment of clarity that she was lucky Jade Valley even had a hospital. Lots of towns of its size didn't, necessitating a long drive to the nearest one.

Austin drove right up to the ER and hurriedly got a wheelchair. If she wasn't hurting so much, she would laugh at how he seemed to be trying to set a new land speed record for getting her into the hospital. Luck was with them as the ER wasn't busy and she was quickly assessed by a nurse. Austin managed to get a cool, wet cloth from somewhere and pressed it against her forehead as she lay on the hospital bed.

Another person appeared at her bedside, a woman who Ivy estimated to be in her late thirties or early forties. She asked about insurance, and Ivy had to explain that she was new to Wyoming and hadn't yet changed her insurance. And that her purse with all that information was not with her.

"I'll go get it and bring it back," Austin said, but didn't make any move to leave.

Maybe it being a small town helped again because the woman, who probably knew Austin, nodded and exited the examination area. Another random thought floated through Ivy's brain, that if this had happened in Louisville, at least one person would likely be looking askance at Austin, as if he might be the cause of the injury.

"I'm sorry," he said, as if on cue.

"It isn't your fault," she said again, more in command of her voice this time. "I had a klutz moment and am paying for it."

A doctor arrived then and performed an examination of both her hand and her ankle, then ordered X-rays of both. Though Ivy knew they were necessary to determine the extent of her injuries, she couldn't help thinking about how much the medical bills would cost because she hadn't yet met her deductible for the year.

The trip to radiology went fairly quickly, even if the movement required brought some fresh spikes of pain. Even though she hadn't been gone from the ER long, Austin had managed to retrieve her purse and get back before she returned to the exam area. One look at his face and she knew in her gut that he felt guilty for what had happened.

"You better not be blaming yourself," she said.

"I should have gotten someone else to help me."

"Don't. Do not act as if this was anything other than an accident. You want to know what caused this? My nose was itching and I got distracted."

Ivy found that despite his help, she was slightly irritated. Was this overprotectiveness and the taking on of guilt that wasn't his to bear at least part of why he got divorced?

Before she could examine that line of thought further, the doctor returned with her X-ray results.

"The good news is that your ankle is not broken, just sprained. You'll need to keep off of it for about a week. The bad news, however, is that your middle finger is broken. It won't require surgery, so that's a silver lining."

The not-so-silver lining was how much it hurt as the doctor set the finger and immobilized it with a splint. She barely kept her not-nice thoughts trapped inside her head. By the time she was dosed with some pain medication and sent on her way, she was ready to crawl into bed and sleep for about three days. The only problem was that her new bed didn't have a mattress and the chest of drawers was still stuck in her stairwell, if it hadn't given way to gravity and crashed into the floor at the bottom of the stairs.

When they arrived back in front of her building, Melissa and Daisy were sitting outside. Before Austin could help her out of the truck, Daisy hurried to push Melissa across the street.

"You're coming home with us," Melissa said.

If it was her own mother offering to take care of her, Ivy would relent without argument. But Melissa wasn't her mother, and Ivy did not want to be a burden the other woman didn't need.

"I'll be fine on my own."

"How are you going to do that?" Melissa asked, a stubborn streak showing that Ivy had never witnessed. "Austin said you have crutches."

"Very slowly," Ivy said, managing to smile.

"Don't be silly." Melissa motioned for Ivy to stay in the truck and for Austin to help her into one of the back seats.

"Trust my thirty-one years of experience, there is no use arguing with her."

"I always knew you were a smart boy," Melissa said as Austin lifted her into the truck.

Considering Ivy couldn't exactly make a run for it and was quite honestly too tired to put up much of an argument anyway, she found herself relenting. After Daisy quickly gathered a few personal items for Ivy, they all headed out of town in a direction she had not yet driven. She relaxed her head on the headrest and watched the landscape roll by, the pastures filled with cattle next to the road moving faster than the towering peaks in the distance. The combination of fatigue, pain medication and the hum of the truck's tires worked to make her drowsy. Her blinks grew slower and slower until her eyes remained closed and consciousness slipped away.

WHEN THEY ARRIVED at the ranch, the sun had slipped behind the mountains. As Austin turned off the truck's engine, Ivy didn't stir. Either the day had worn her out or the medicine she'd been given had knocked her out. By the time he got his mom into the house, Ivy still hadn't stirred. He hated to wake her, but he wasn't going to let her spend the night sleeping in his truck either.

He eased the passenger-side door open. Ivy moved a little, wincing in her sleep. Despite the abnormally strong command she'd given him to not feel guilty about her injuries, he couldn't help it. What-ifs kept going through his head. What if they'd left the chest of drawers on the first floor until Isaac came back to put the finishing touches on the downstairs bathroom? What if he'd been with her when she was considering buying the heavy oak piece and convinced her to choose something lighter?

Austin sighed. His middle name might as well be What-if considering how many times he'd asked himself that question over the past couple of years. He really didn't need to take on worrying about someone else when he had plenty to worry about already. But his mother had insisted on bringing Ivy here. And now he couldn't ignore that he'd found himself increasingly concerned about this unexpected person in his life.

Not wanting to startle Ivy, he tapped her shoulder. "Hey, we're here."

Her eyes opened a fraction, and she looked at him as if she'd never seen him before and was trying to ascertain his identity.

"I'm going to pick you up now."

Ivy opened her eyes a bit more and nodded. She looked as if she wanted to say something, but moved her mouth in a way that told him that it was dry as cotton.

Austin slid one arm below her knees and

wrapped the other around Ivy's back, lifting her easily and pushing the truck door closed with his hip. Now that she'd been treated by a doctor and given medication and orders to take it easy, his earlier panic was replaced by a disconcerting awareness of how her small but feminine body felt next to his. It wasn't right to think of her in that way when she was so vulnerable, but he couldn't seem to stop the insistence of those thoughts. He needed to see her settled and then get out of the house as quickly as he could.

Daisy held open the front door for him and said she'd retrieve Ivy's crutches. He still didn't know how she'd manage using them when she had a broken finger, but they'd deal with that later. Hopefully after he'd banished the thoughts that made him feel way too warm.

"Take her to Daisy's room," his mom said.

Austin didn't bother asking if Daisy had offered or his mom had made the decision, because his sister wouldn't mind either way. It was obvious that she was fond of Ivy and would gladly give up her room while Ivy recuperated.

After laying her on Daisy's bed and covering her with a quilt, he didn't linger.

When he stepped back into the living room, Daisy was coming through the front door with the crutches, the bag from the small hospital pharmacy and Ivy's personal belongings.

"Put them in there where she can reach them," he said, pointing to Daisy's room, "but don't wake her up."

He shifted his gaze and noticed his mother watching him with that observant mom expression he hadn't seen since before her accident. As much as he was happy to see more of her old self surfacing, now was not the time he wanted her to be able to read him like the front page of a newspaper.

"I'll be back later." He didn't explain where he was going or why, because he didn't enumerate the ranch tasks he was off to undertake each day unless it was something out of the ordinary. To do so now would draw more attention to the fact that he was, in fact, putting distance between him and Ivy as fast as he could.

CHAPTER NINE

WHY WERE HER eyelids so heavy? That was the first thought to amble through Ivy's brain when she woke up. The next question to bubble up from her gray matter was, what was that smell? As more of her brain emerged from sleep, she realized that whatever that aroma was it smelled delicious and that she was hungry.

She blinked at the dimness around her. Instead of the view of the inside of her tent, or even the ceiling of her building, she was in a small bedroom. She couldn't make out a lot of what she was seeing, but none of it looked familiar. Then there was the fact she was lying in an actual bed, something she hadn't done since her last night on the road before arriving in Jade Valley.

When she started to roll onto her side, her hand caught on a fold in the quilt covering her and pain shot up her arm, all the way to her eyeball, of all places. That's when everything came rushing back with blinding speed—the chest of drawers falling on her hand, the broken finger now secured with a splint and thick bandaging, the sprained ankle that had led Melissa to insisting she come home with them.

Ivy took a minute to let the worst of the pain recede then slowly sat up. She noticed the daisy pattern stitched onto the quilt she'd been lying under and surmised that she was in Daisy's room. Her gaze landed on her purse and the crutches. She dreaded trying to use them, but she couldn't have Austin carrying her everywhere.

She gasped as she suddenly remembered how she had leaned against his shoulder as he'd carried her into the house. Her face flushed at the memory. No, her whole body did. How was she going to go out there and face Austin?

Ivy pressed her uninjured hand against her face, finding the skin extra warm. She was overthinking the situation. As usual, Austin was just being kind and considerate, the protector that she'd observed him being almost from the moment she'd met him. That protection had simply extended to her in her time of need because her family wasn't nearby to lend her aid.

Her stomach rumbled, making her wonder how long she'd been asleep. She'd eaten enough at the rummage sale that she shouldn't be hungry until tomorrow, and yet here she sat wishing she didn't have a bum ankle so she could race toward whatever was cooking on the other side of the closed bedroom door.

Well, you can't stay hidden in this room forever. Go out there and get it over with. Don't act like Austin carrying you was any big deal.

She closed her eyes, took a few deep breaths, mentally did a couple of *omm*s worthy of a yoga session, then reached for the crutches. After a shaky start and a few bad words she uttered only in her head, she slowly made her way the short distance to the door and opened it. Right then, the door across from her opened, revealing Austin coming out of the bathroom.

"Oh, hey," she said.

She saw him start to reach toward her before catching himself and bringing his hands back down to his sides.

"Do you need help?"

"I can manage." She winced at the memory of how sharp she'd been with him in a bad moment at the hospital. "About earlier today, I'm sorry I was a bit too harsh."

"No worries. It was the pain talking."

That was true, but also not. But she wasn't going to get into all that now.

"Mom made beef stew." He said this in a way that made her deduce it had been quite some time since that had last happened.

"Another good sign?"

He nodded.

"Hmm, I wonder what I would have gotten if I'd actually tumbled down the stairs."

"A broken neck, most likely."

"You're probably right. I'll have beef stew and be happy about it."

Austin let her make her own way up the short hallway toward the combined living area and kitchen. Melissa and Daisy, who must have heard her clunking around, were setting the table and dishing up bowls of the wonderful-smelling stew.

"I hope you're hungry," Melissa said when she looked over her shoulder at Ivy.

"If I wasn't before, the smell of that stew would change that."

She pressed her lips together to keep from groaning as fresh pain rocketed through her finger and up her arm. Austin pulled out a chair for her then took her crutches as she sat.

"Thanks."

"Do you need more of your pain medication?"

She nodded as she slid more fully into her seat at the table. That's when she noticed that while her middle finger was the only one broken, the others were deeply bruised.

"Well, that's colorful," she said as she held up her hand to examine it.

"You're lucky you didn't break all of those fingers," Melissa said as she wheeled to the table, a plate of fresh corn bread on her lap.

"Thank you for inviting me to your home. I'm sorry to be a bother."

"You are absolutely no bother. Quite the opposite." Melissa didn't elaborate, but it was nice to see her in what Ivy instinctually knew was her element—fixing a delicious meal and taking care of others instead of having them take care of her.

The moment Ivy took the first bite of the stew, she knew it was the best she'd ever had. If she'd heard a choir of angels break out into song, she would have only been slightly surprised.

"This is delicious."

"I'm glad you like it." Melissa paused, ever so slightly. "I haven't made it in a long time."

Ivy saw Daisy and Austin glance at each other.

"Well, I think if you made this every day and put up a stand by the road, you'd be a millionaire within a week."

Melissa's sudden laughter, while not loud or lengthy, made Ivy smile. When she glanced at Austin, there was such naked gratitude in his eyes that Ivy felt the sting of tears. To hold them back, she blinked as she returned her attention to her food. She grabbed a piece of corn bread and crumbled it up in her stew.

"What are you doing?" Austin asked.

"What?"

He pointed at her bowl.

"Um, eating."

"No, the corn bread."

She looked at him as if to ask why he was asking a question to which the answer was obvious. "You've never done this?"

"No."

"You should try it then. I do this with white beans, pinto beans, stew."

Daisy was the first to give it a try, giving the combination a thumbs-up after taking the first bite.

"When I can, I'll have to make you all some burgoo." She explained that it was also a stew, native to Kentucky, made up of a variety of meats as well as lima beans, corn, okra, tomatoes, cabbage and potatoes. "Oh, I just had a great idea. When I open the store, I should have a bunch of Kentucky dishes available. Maybe some bluegrass musicians too."

Thinking ahead to how great finally opening her doors for business would be helped Ivy to not focus so much on her current state. At some point, the bad stuff had to stop happening.

"Did you notice the quilt on my bed?" Daisy asked a bit later, after they'd talked about what Daisy had learned about Antarctica for her summer geography club project and how the veterinarian was due to come by the ranch tomorrow to give the cattle a series of summer vaccinations.

"I did. Very pretty."

"Mom made it for me when I was little."

"Oh? You've never mentioned that you quilt."

"I haven't in a long time, even before the accident. I was just too busy."

It was the first time Ivy had heard Melissa mention her accident directly and the first time when there wasn't any hesitation in her speech when talking about the past. Ivy didn't want to give herself too much credit, but maybe her being here had given a little boost to the healing process that was likely already happening, albeit slowly. She certainly would have rather not sustained a broken appendage and a pair of crutches for it to happen, but life worked in sometimes painful ways.

After they finished eating, Ivy noticed that Austin helped Daisy clear away the dishes. It was nice to see that he wasn't one of those guys who didn't pitch in around the house just because he was a guy. In this smaller area, he seemed taller. And with less space around him, she found herself simply watching the way his body moved.

She suddenly remembered how she would catch herself watching James at the office and jerked her gaze away from Austin. Hopefully, Melissa hadn't noticed.

The combination of the filling meal and her medication began to make her drowsy again, but she needed to stay up until everyone else went to bed. She had no intention of ejecting Daisy from her room. She remembered being a teenage girl and how important her own space was to her.

"You should get some more sleep," Melissa said.

"I will later."

"I saw you eye the couch. I hope you're not thinking you'll sleep there."

"I'm sleeping on the couch," Daisy said. "I'm going to read for a while anyway."

"I don't want to take your room," Ivy said.

"You're not. I gave it to you. Big difference." Daisy's smile reminded Ivy of the flowers after which the girl had been named.

Feeling more tired by the moment, Ivy moved to get up. And suddenly Austin was there next to her, not touching or insisting she needed help but close in case she did.

"Does it hurt to use the crutches?" he asked.

"Not as much as I feared it would." She wouldn't claim it wasn't painful, though, because it was. But even if it hurt more than it did, she wouldn't admit it. Because having him carry her while she was fully conscious, and in front of his family, was out of the question.

As she thumped her way slowly back toward

Daisy's room, she tried to forget the fact that he'd carried her twice had happened at all. She hoped he did the same.

What truly annoyed her was that after she managed to get herself into bed and the throbbing pain subsided enough for her to relax, instead of quickly falling asleep, her thoughts fixed on what it had felt like to be carried in Austin's strong arms. Despite the fact she'd been in considerable pain the first time and almost completely out of it the second, certain memories were undeniable. Chief among them were his warmth and strength, how he had acted as if she weighed almost nothing, the way she'd felt protected. As if he was some jeans-wearing, suntanned, modern-day cowboy knight in shining armor.

She supposed he even had a horse somewhere on this ranch. Ivy giggled a little as sleep crept a bit closer and she pictured Austin riding across his ranch wearing a suit of armor and chain mail.

Ivy closed her eyes and gave in to sleep with that image still trotting through her mind and a smile on her lips.

AUSTIN REINED IN his horse, taking a moment to drink a swig of coffee from his thermos. The dawning of a new day was beginning to peek over the mountains that marked the eastern side of the valley, but he'd already been up more than an hour. He had a long day ahead of him, one that was probably going to include a lot more coffee considering how little he'd slept the night before. He hadn't been able to rid himself of the unsettled feeling caused by having Ivy sleeping under the same roof. No one other than his mom and Daisy had shared his space since Grace left.

Even though there was nothing romantic between him and Ivy, it still felt like too much to have her sleeping in a room only a few steps from his own. The way he had caught himself watching her while at work was already surprising and unsettling, but at least there he could leave at the end of the day. At home, he would see her each time he stepped into his own house. And yet he understood why his mother had insisted she stay here. He even agreed with her because Ivy shouldn't try to climb those stairs while on crutches, especially when no one was around in case she fell.

The long day of corralling the cattle, getting them vaccinated, and then returning them to the pasture was arriving right when he needed the distraction.

But as he herded cattle from where they were grazing into the corral near the barn, his thoughts kept straying to Ivy—the way she'd smiled at the rummage sale when she'd found salt and pepper shakers shaped like spools of thread, how she easily struck up conversations with anyone she met, the panic he'd felt when he saw the intense pain in her expression when the chest had slammed into her fingers.

It was a reminder of how quickly someone could be injured or worse. And that he didn't need more people in his life to worry about.

As he maneuvered the last few cattle into the corral, he spotted Dr. Parsons parking in front of the barn. Austin waved a greeting as he hopped off his horse and closed the gate behind the last steer.

"Perfect timing," Austin said as he approached the veterinarian, who had been taking care of the area's animals, big and small, since before Austin could remember.

"I hear you have some company," Dr. Parsons said.

"You'd think I'd stop being surprised how fast news travels around here."

Dr. Parsons laughed as he gathered everything he'd need to make sure Austin's herd was protected from a range of diseases. Austin got the herd circling in the corral and then a few on the outer edge of the group directed into the chute before closing a gate behind them. As he walked up to the head gate where Dr. Parsons was ready with the vaccines, he noticed Daisy walking toward them rubbing her eyes.

Austin experienced some sympathy for her. Not only did she not get to sleep in on her summer vacation, but she didn't even get to sleep in her own bed. But ranch kids didn't really get vacations. He wondered if, in addition to missing her dad, she also missed days spent on the river and spending time meeting people from all over who came to go rafting. Or maybe being around river rafting would be too difficult now, a sad reminder of what she and their mom had lost.

But Daisy wasn't one to complain. If she felt resentful or sad or angry, she kept it inside. He knew what that was like.

"You ready?" Dr. Parsons asked.

Austin nodded and got the first steer into position and closed the head gate, preventing the animal from escaping as the injections entered its hip. The process didn't take long, and when it was over Austin opened the gate to allow the steer to return to the pasture. The three of them worked in a familiar rhythm—Austin guiding the cattle into the chute and closing the gate behind them before moving to the head gate, Daisy urging the cattle in the chute to move forward, and Dr. Parsons administering the vaccines and entering the information in his records. Rinse and repeat, one steer after another.

About halfway through, one of the steers got nervous and put up an extra fuss, trying to back down the chute, which agitated the rest of the cattle behind him.

"Hey, now," Austin said, trying to calm the animal. He nodded at Daisy, who urged the ones in the back forward. As she did so, Austin opened the head gate and a pathway to freedom. But as the steer made a run for it, Austin used his years of practice to close the gate at the right moment.

Dr. Parsons made quick work of the vaccinations, and Austin quickly released the upset beast.

"If you spoke Cow, I don't think you'd like what that one is saying to you," the vet said.

"You're likely right about that."

The sun climbed in the sky, beating down on them and increasing the sweat running down Austin's neck. When they had about ten head of cattle to go, something caused him to glance toward the house. To his surprise, Ivy was standing at the edge of the yard watching what they were doing. Though it was likely just city girl curiosity, her eyes on him caused his skin to heat more than the sun did.

"I see what I've heard is right. She's a pretty girl," Dr. Parsons said.

Austin agreed but pretended as if he was focusing on his work and hadn't heard what the man had said. But it echoed in his brain. *Pretty girl, pretty girl, pretty girl.*

Of course, Austin didn't think of her as a girl. While she was young enough to be the vet's daughter, she and Austin were likely close in age. They'd never discussed the specifics, had no reason to.

But he didn't need for her to answer any questions about herself for him to know that she was indeed pretty. Even more beautiful than her long, wavy hair and petite figure was her wide smile. She'd be able to charm the sun into rising at midnight if she put her mind to it. If her store wasn't successful, it wouldn't be for her lack of trying.

He realized he didn't want to consider that possibility. If she failed, as he had thought she might when he first met her, the likelihood of her returning to Kentucky and him never seeing her again was high.

By the time Dr. Parsons finished with the last steer and Austin released it back into the pasture, he felt as if he hadn't eaten for days. He'd nabbed a couple of the cookies that Ivy had bought the day before along with his coffee early that morning, and it was now midafternoon. Still, Austin thought he might take time to chat with the vet after their business was done. After all, Dr. Parsons was known as quite the talker. As luck would have it, however, he didn't have time to stick around and gab today.

"I've got a lead on a young vet who might want to give me a hand so I can retire one of these days," he said as he loaded his supplies back into his truck. "Cross your fingers."

As Austin waved goodbye to the vet, he noticed that Ivy was slowly making her way back across the yard to the house. Daisy had already disappeared inside. He resisted the urge to run to Ivy before she toppled over and injured herself further. Instead, he walked at a normal pace but was still able to quickly overtake her.

"You're not one to just sit back and take it easy, are you?" he asked as he came up beside her.

"Takes one to know one, as they say."

"Well, I have a ranch to run. It's sort of a never-done sort of job."

She stopped walking and looked back toward where he'd been working.

"I've driven past plenty of farms with cattle before, beef and dairy, but I've never actually visited one. I know this is a ranch, but still. Are all the vaccinations done?"

"Yeah. The last thing I need is sickness in the herd."

"Do you enjoy it?"

"Vaccinating cattle?"

"Ranching overall."

"I do. I mean, I've done it for as long as I can remember. I'm third generation on this land. It's difficult sometimes, stressful, but I wouldn't want to lose it."

"Is there a danger of that?"

"There's always the danger of that."

The approach of another vehicle cut their conversation short. Austin was surprised to see Isaac coming up the driveway. Hopefully nothing was wrong at Ivy's place.

"I finished your downstairs bathroom and you can't even come see it," Isaac said as he stepped out of his truck, pointing at Ivy and her obvious injuries.

"I'll just have to heal quickly so that I can come praise your work properly."

"I'm going to hold you to that."

"What brings you out here?" Austin asked.

"Your mom called and wanted me to bring her a couple of things."

"I could have gotten whatever she needed."

"You can be in two places at once, can you?" Isaac pointed toward the corral and chute, the evidence of how Austin had spent his morning. "I was done for the day anyway. And your mom bribed me with pineapple cake. I was a little surprised, but I wasn't about to argue."

"You're not the only one. She made beef stew and corn bread last night too."

Isaac smiled. "I think having a patient to take care of has given her purpose."

For a moment, Austin resented the fact that his mother hadn't managed to find it in herself to emerge from her quiet and semi-seclusion for him or, more importantly, Daisy. But that wasn't fair to Ivy. She didn't deliberately get hurt. And it shouldn't matter what had helped his mother. What mattered was that she seemed to be turning a corner. Maybe it had taken something new, an outside force, instead of the things and people and situations she lived with every day.

He just hoped his mom's progress stuck after the newness of Ivy wore off, after she went back to her place in town, after his work there was done.

CHAPTER TEN

IVY HATED FEELING like an invalid. Sure, she was mobile and she knew it could be worse, but she had so much to do back at her place. Even while a guest of Austin and his family, she wished she could do more to help. But they insisted that she rest and recuperate, and her body seemed to agree. She couldn't remember the last time she'd taken so many naps. It occurred to her when she woke up in the middle of the afternoon the next day that maybe her fatigue wasn't all attributable to her injuries. Perhaps what James had done was really hitting home. Add to that her sudden decision to completely change her life followed by the upheaval of quitting her job, divesting herself of everything she couldn't fit in her car and driving cross-country to live in a place she'd never been—well, it was a lot of emotional up and down and sideways.

As her thoughts seemed determined to do, they drifted to Austin. Even though she knew she shouldn't even be thinking about another man yet, she couldn't prevent herself from doing so. A man shouldn't look attractive when dirty and sweaty after helping to vaccinate a herd of cattle, and yet he had the day before. It was a different kind of work than what he'd been doing for her in renovating her building, and yet he seemed to be skilled at both.

She heard the commode flush across the hall and wondered if it was him, Daisy or Melissa. Chances were it wasn't him because it was the middle of the workday. She was the only one drifting off to sleep every few hours. Lifting herself to a sitting position on the side of the bed, she was determined to do something productive today, something more than the online window-shopping she'd done the day before.

One thing she definitely needed to undertake was a shower, but that was going to require a couple of plastic bags to protect her bandages and a lot of care to make sure she didn't fall in the shower and injure herself further. The amount of mortification that resulted from something like that would be the end of her.

Her phone, sitting on Daisy's little white nightstand, rang.

"Hey, Lily," she said.

"What's wrong?" her younger sister asked.

"What do you mean?"

"You sound way too chipper."

"I'm always a delight."

Lily snort-laughed. "Spill it."

Ivy told her what happened. Suddenly, Lily's phone was commandeered by their mother.

"You broke what?"

"I'm okay, Mom. Seriously."

"But you're all alone, with no one to take care of you. See, you should have never left."

"Mom, stop. You're getting in a tizzy for no reason. It's not like I'm in traction or something. And I'm not alone. I'm staying at a friend's house until I can walk without the crutches."

"What friend?"

Ivy told her it was Melissa.

"Wait, that's the mom of the guy doing the work on your building, right?"

"Yes." She didn't elaborate because she wasn't a teenage girl who needed to be kept away from spending the night under the same roof as members of the opposite sex. Ivy also was afraid her strange feelings toward Austin might actually be detectable in her voice if she said too much. She didn't need her mother dissecting what Ivy herself didn't fully understand.

"Do you need me to come?"

"No, Mom. I love you, but I'd like your first visit to be after I have everything ready and the store open."

"Okay." Her mom didn't sound happy about agreeing, but she did it anyway.

After a trip to the bathroom, Ivy made her way into the living area only to find it empty. Behind her, a door opened down the hallway. She looked back to see Melissa emerging from her room. Had she been napping too?

"Are you hungry?" Melissa asked.

"I'll just have a couple of cookies if there are any left."

"Would you like some milk with them?"

"Sounds good but I'll get it."

Melissa actually gave her a look that said to not be ridiculous. "I think I'll have better luck pouring it and getting it safely to the table, don't you?"

Ivy looked down at her splinted finger and crutches and said, "You're probably right about that."

At least the container of cookies was already sitting in the middle of the table. Ivy sat and opened the lid.

"It appears as if these have been popular."

"I'm pretty sure that's what Austin had for breakfast yesterday. He was up and gone before daylight."

"Ranch work seems to fill a lot of hours."

"It does. Of course, it's easier when there are multiple people to share the load. But now Austin has to shoulder most of it by himself."

"He said he enjoys it though." Ivy didn't want to risk Melissa falling back into her well of sadness, not after the significant steps to pull herself out.

"He does. Still, it's nice to see him get out and do different things, like working on your building."

"It's been great having all three of you there. It makes me miss my own family a little less."

Melissa smiled as she placed the two glasses of milk on a tray that rested on the arms of her wheelchair then brought them to the table. Ivy got the feeling that Melissa could do more on her own than Austin thought she could. Ivy tried to put herself in his place though. Would she smother her mom with constant help if she'd been through what Melissa had?

As if it was the most natural thing in the world, they began talking about plans for the quilt shop that would be more than a quilt shop. Ivy told her about her ideas for carrying various types of yarn and hosting a knitting club. Melissa suggested a group quilt, housed in the shop but worked on by whoever had time to stop by and work on it, to be raffled off prior to Christmas.

"It could be an annual event," Melissa said. "Like the rummage sale, the proceeds could go to a different cause each year."

"I like that."

Time flew as they added one idea after another to Ivy's growing list of possibilities she kept on her phone—candle-making workshops, making a baby outfit for everyone in the county who had a new baby, monthly music on the lawn that would draw people off Main Street to Ivy's store.

"I've missed this," Melissa said after they'd been brainstorming for a couple of hours. "I used to come up with ideas of how to bring people to the river rafting business I ran with Daisy's dad." She hesitated for a moment, lost in her sad memories. "I was good at it."

"Do you mind me asking what happened?"

Melissa clasped her hands atop the table. "We were hauling the rafts back from the end of a group's float trip when we rounded a curve and a huge RV was half in our lane. My husband instinctually jerked to the right and we went rolling down a steep embankment. I was knocked out at some point before we hit the bottom and I didn't wake up until two days later." She stopped, took a deep breath, collecting herself. "When I did, I just wanted to go back to sleep. I couldn't believe fate had been so cruel to not only take a second husband from me, leaving both of my children fatherless, but I'd been robbed of my ability to fully take care of myself. In those early days, I thought it would have been better if I hadn't woken up. But then Daisy would curl up next to me in the hospital bed, her tears soaking my gown, and I knew I had to keep living."

"Not giving up is often the bravest thing we can do. It takes time to heal from a big blow like that, and no one else can dictate how you do it or how long it takes."

Ivy shared her own mother's struggle to raise three girls alone, how she remembered once overhearing her mother crying in her room late at night when she thought Ivy and her sisters were asleep.

"Loss finds all of us at some point, some more than others," Melissa said.

Ivy looked at her phone lying on the table without picking it up, thought about all the notes that she'd typed into it and how many of those ideas had been Melissa's.

"I have an idea I'd like to run by you," Ivy said.

"Okay."

"How would you like to work in the store once it opens?"

"Oh, you'll want someone more capable than me."

Ivy tapped her phone. "I think you just proved that you're plenty capable. There's no one else I've met who I think would be better suited. Access isn't a problem since there are ramps in the front and back. You said yourself that a lot of the ranch work isn't possible for you anymore, but this would be. I'll be there most of the time, but when I'm not I want to leave the store with someone I trust. You are that person."

Silence settled between them, and Ivy thought she could see the shine of unshed tears in Melissa's eyes.

"Let me think about it."

It wasn't a "no" and Ivy took that as a good sign.

Daisy came in from working in the garden and headed toward the shower. She gave them a quick wave but didn't stop whatever she was listening to on her phone. Ivy would guess it was the travel podcast she liked, one in which two best friends traveled the world off the beaten path. Instead of the typical tourist attractions, they took back roads, visited small towns and villages, and explored the lesser-known historical sites. When she had some time, Ivy aimed to give it a listen herself.

When Ivy glanced back at Melissa, there was a new type of sadness written on her face—the kind that said she knew her baby girl would leave the nest at some point for faraway adventures.

"She'll always come back." Ivy hadn't really meant to give voice to her thoughts, but it was the truth and maybe Melissa needed to hear it.

"I know. Just like I've always known that she'd be the one to leave Jade Valley while Austin would always be comfortable staying here. They're so different, those two."

"But they're also a lot alike. They're both kind, helpful, a bit on the reserved side until you get to know them."

Melissa nodded. "It's good that they're as close as they are, considering the age difference. I thought it might not be that way. When I got pregnant with Daisy, I think it made Austin uncomfortable. But I can still see how he instantly loved her the moment we put her in his arms the first time. His eyes were huge."

Melissa laughed a little at the memory. Some unnamed yearning stirred inside Ivy. Maybe it was for what might have been, all the things she'd lost in that moment when what James had done became clear.

"If Austin ever becomes a father, I think he'll be a good one," Melissa said, a new sadness in her voice.

Ivy admitted to herself that she wanted to know what had happened with Austin's marriage. Whose fault was the divorce? Despite all his positive qualities, was he not a good husband? Had he done something to drive his wife away?

It was entirely possible, of course, that he was not the one at fault and that her trust in men had simply suffered a seismic shaking.

As if he'd sensed that they were venturing close to discussing his most personal information, Austin came into the house through the back door. When she caught sight of him, Ivy had to press her lips tightly together to keep from laughing. Because Austin was covered nearly head to toe in mud.

"Well, I haven't seen that look in a while," Melissa said, as if this wasn't the first time she'd seen her son looking as if he'd wallowed with hogs.

"What happened?" Ivy asked. "I doubt you set up a mud-wrestling ring as a side hustle."

"Let's just say one of the four-legged residents of this ranch was feeling a bit irritated today and took advantage of where I was standing."

A snort of laughter made it past Ivy's best efforts to keep it in check. In the next moment, Melissa joined her. Daisy, who'd just emerged from the bathroom after her shower, joined the chorus of laughter.

"If someone had caught my head in a metal contraption and given me two shots in the rear, I might hold a grudge for a while and push them into the nearest mudhole the first chance I got too," Ivy said, then laughed some more.

"I don't like any of you very much right now."

Austin's words as he headed toward his room only caused them to laugh harder.

DESPITE WHAT HE'D just said, Austin felt exactly the opposite as he stood behind the closed door of his bedroom. He didn't often cry, but he felt the sting of tears at the sound of his mother's laughter. Real, deep-down laughter. And he knew in his soul that it was because of Ivy. Even if he had walked into the house looking exactly as he did now, without her presence he doubted his mother would react in the same way. She might have laughed, but it would have been…what was that word he'd heard Daisy use recently? Ephemeral.

Again he experienced that confusing intertwining of feelings—gratefulness that his mother seemed to finally be emerging from the dark, but admittedly a bit resentful that it had taken an outsider to bring that change about.

He shook his head. This was no time to be selfish or petty. The only thing he needed to feel was thankful.

He definitely didn't need to think about how attractive Ivy was with her hair pulled back into a ponytail and her whole body shaking with laughter.

Grabbing clean clothes, he headed to the shower. When he was finally free of all the mud and dressed again, he walked into the living area to find the kitchen as active as a hive of agitated bees. Daisy was pulling bags of chips out of the cabinet. Ivy, balancing a bit shakily on her crutches, was mixing something in a bowl. His mom saw him and extended her arm. In her hand was a package of hot dogs.

"Fire up the grill."

He took the package. "Did I miss something?"

"We decided it's a junk food and movie marathon night," Daisy said, sounding as if she thought this was the best idea ever.

He headed out back and got the grill going. Usually when he grilled, it was burgers or steaks. He didn't even remember buying hot dogs. Daisy must have gotten them at some point.

They also weren't one of those families that ate in front of the TV, so when they all parked themselves there with their hot dogs and chips with box brownies baking in the oven, it felt like a special occasion.

Daisy commandeered the recliner, she and his mom sharing a foldable TV tray between them. That left him and Ivy to share the couch.

"Daisy, let Ivy have the recliner so she can put her foot up."

"No, I'm fine here," Ivy said.

So much for putting some distance between them. He split the difference between sitting as far from her on the couch as he could and sitting too close. Either option had the potential to cause questions he didn't want forming in his mom's or sister's head.

They ended up playing rock, paper, scissors to decide who got to pick the first movie. He won and picked a newer sci-fi film.

"That surprises me," Ivy said before she stuffed a potato chip in her mouth.

"What? Did you think I'd only watch Westerns?"

"No. I'm not sure what I thought you might like."

He was beginning to think he liked her a little too much, but he wasn't about to say that. It felt a bit too much like walking along the edge of a steep cliff while blindfolded to even admit it to himself.

They stuffed themselves with hot dogs, chips and brownies, and even popped bags of popcorn halfway through Daisy's choice, unsurprisingly a film about a woman traveling through Europe while trying to figure out what she wanted to do with her life.

"Must be nice to be wealthy enough to do that," he said.

"She actually wrote articles about her travels along the way and sold them," Ivy said. "She also would take on daily jobs here and there to make enough to keep traveling."

He'd never had the travel bug like his sister, but even he thought that sounded interesting.

By the time the second movie was over, his

mom said she didn't have another one in her and went to bed. Daisy had fallen asleep in the recliner.

Even though he suddenly felt awkward and as if he wanted to follow his mom down the hall, Austin stayed seated. He picked up the remote and extended it to Ivy.

"Another?"

She shook her head. "I think I'm done, though I'm not sleepy. My sleep schedule is all off-kilter."

"Do you want to go sit outside?" What was he doing? If sitting here next to her with the lights on and his sister in the same room was awkward, what would it be like out under the stars, just the two of them?

"Sure. I could use some fresh air."

He escorted her out the front door, stayed beside her in case she slipped as they made their way slowly toward a bench beneath a large oak tree. When they reached the bench, Ivy sat and stretched the leg with the sprained ankle out in front of her.

"How are you feeling? Still in pain?"

"It's there but manageable. Better than the first day though."

"That's good."

He looked up at the sky, and as his eyes adjusted he picked out a couple of constellations.

"You can sit," Ivy said. "I promise I don't bite."

Though it would be wiser to remain standing, he settled himself next to her. He immediately wished he hadn't because there was way less space between them now than there had been on the couch. Thankfully, he didn't have to navigate pointless conversation. Ivy seemed content to sit quietly and look up at the night sky.

Austin took inspiration from that and did the same. He realized that despite living somewhere with excellent stargazing opportunities, he didn't actually do it often. He was either focused on the task in front of him or in bed so he could get up early the next morning. It was nice to simply sit and be, to enjoy the nighttime beauty he took for granted.

"I liked living in cities," Ivy said. "But every time I've been away from them at night, someplace where I can see the sky like this, I'm always in awe."

"Yeah. I admit I don't take advantage of this view enough."

"I'd tell you not to work so much that life passes you by, but I'd be saying that from a place of privilege. I know you work as much as you do out of necessity. But hopefully you won't forget to do this from time to time."

He looked over at Ivy, and his heart thumped a bit harder when he saw her smiling at him. If he hadn't been through what he had, would he lean forward and kiss her? But abandonment tended to damage your ability to trust.

"You seem to be deep in thought."

He averted his gaze, once again staring up at the sky. "Just trying to remember when I sat out beneath the stars with anyone."

It had to have been with Grace, before the accident, before she had left him to face one of the hardest periods of his life alone.

Ivy grew quiet again, and he got the feeling that this time she was the one thinking about the past. She let out a sigh that was loaded with meaning. He wasn't sure what kind of meaning, but it felt heavy.

"I remember exactly the last time I watched the stars like this. It was when my ex proposed to me."

Austin's gaze went immediately back to Ivy's profile. He certainly hadn't expected that.

"You were married?"

She shook her head. Had her ex broken off the engagement? He didn't pry even though his mind was crackling with questions.

"I know everyone wonders about why someone like me would quit her job and move cross-country to a place she's never been. They probably speculate all kinds of reasons, all of them some version of me running away from something or someone, and they'd be right."

Oh no, had the ex been abusive? His muscles tensed at the very thought that someone had hurt her like that.

"I ran away from the embarrassment of being a fool. I couldn't face going back to work and having to see the man who betrayed me every day."

She told him about how she'd worked with her ex, about how during their engagement party two women had shown up with proof that he had been cheating on her with both of them. No wonder she had wanted to start over somewhere no one knew her, though she shouldn't have had to.

"He's the fool, not you."

A hint of a smile tugged at the edge of her lips. "I appreciate you saying that."

"They aren't empty words. I mean them. A man who would cheat on you isn't worth thinking about."

She looked over at him, held his gaze for several seconds before lowering hers.

"While I agree with you, it's easier said than done. I loved him, was going to marry him. You can't just turn off feelings, even if they betray you."

He knew that all too well.

"I will say that the move has helped, as I'd hoped it would. Being in a new place, around new people, putting everything into a new path has sped up getting over it way more than those days I laid around in my apartment eating self-pity ice cream."

He wasn't sure if that reaction was better or worse than how he'd worked himself to exhaustion after Grace left. He'd told himself at the time that he hadn't had a choice. Someone had to take care of his mom and Daisy, the ranch, the animals. Someone had to pay the bills and hold together what was left of his family.

"I'm going to say something once, and you can either take me up on my offer or forget you ever heard me make it," Ivy said. "I've gathered that you see yourself as your family's protector, their rock. I doubt you ever unburden yourself to them, to anyone. Maybe you're one of those guys who isn't into sharing feelings and keeps everything inside, but if you ever need someone to talk to, I'll listen."

It took him several seconds, but he finally managed a thank-you. But he didn't share his story. He didn't see any good coming from reliving how his wife had gone on a trip to Denver and never come back.

A coyote howled in the distance, and he used that as a flimsy excuse to say they should go back inside. As she had promised, Ivy didn't say anything else about him spilling the beans about his own unhappy past. But the simple fact that she'd offered, right after confessing how she was still healing from a betrayal of her own, meant a lot to him.

Maybe too much.

WHY HAD SHE told Austin about James? That was the first coherent thought Ivy had the next morning. As she lay in Daisy's bed with the early morning light illuminating the collection of maps, posters and teenage mementos, she wondered why it had felt so easy to confess what had prompted her change in life trajectory.

One thing seemed certain though. She had found herself feeling closer to him, more able to open up, than he was with her. Of course, it wasn't a requirement that he tell her about his past in response, but she could now admit that she'd hoped he might. She was curious, yes, but it was more than that. What she'd said to him about how he seemed to keep everything bottled up, so as not to be a further burden to those already carrying a lot of burdens, was true. She had offered to be a willing ear not only as a way to repay him for all of his help but because she really did consider him a friend now. Sometimes she flirted with the idea that if she allowed it, maybe he could be more. But the fact that he'd divulged nothing the night before told her that he didn't feel the same. She reminded herself that he didn't have to. Just because one person felt a certain way didn't mean someone else was required to return those feelings. It was better to know early, before words that ended up being lies were exchanged.

Needing to get back to her new home and to work as soon as she could, she tested putting weight on her ankle. She winced against the pain and sank back onto the side of the bed in frustration. The pain was less than when she'd first twisted the ankle, but it definitely wasn't waitress-worthy. She would have to be satisfied with doing more planning for the eventual opening of her store.

As she left the bedroom several minutes later, wearing an indie band T-shirt and a pair of loose lounge pants, Ivy made her way first to the bathroom and then the living area, which once again she found empty. She glanced back down the hall and saw that Melissa's bedroom door was closed. Not wanting to disturb her, Ivy eased out the front door to sit on the porch. She noticed Austin's truck wasn't in the driveway. Either he was somewhere else on the ranch or had gone into town.

She sighed, wishing she was more mobile so she could explore a bit. Before being brought here, she'd never set foot on a ranch before. Though she could tell it wasn't a huge operation, since Austin largely ran it by himself, it was larger than most farms she was used to seeing back in Kentucky. But the last thing she needed to do was fall and hurt herself further. She couldn't afford that, and it would be a terrible way to pay back Melissa, Austin and Daisy for temporarily housing and feeding her.

Being limited in what she could do made her think about how much harder it must be for Melissa, who was so used to being active and able to go wherever she wanted. Ivy couldn't imagine what it had been like to wake up grateful to have survived such a horrible accident only to discover she'd lost another husband and would never walk again. Some people had to endure more than their share of bad luck. Considering everything Melissa had been through, it made Ivy's recent heartbreak seem small by comparison.

She heard the approach of Melissa's wheelchair before the door opened.

"Ivy?"

"Yeah, I'm here." She pushed up out of the chair where she was sitting and took two steps with the crutches. "Do you need something?"

"Follow me."

Ivy did so, back to Melissa's bedroom. Melissa tapped something under a sheet on her bed.

"I hope you like this, but if it's not what you're looking for, you don't have to use it."

Curious, Ivy crutched her way to the side of the bed as Melissa pulled away the sheet.

"Oh, wow." Ivy let her gaze roam over what Melissa had done with the wood she'd had Austin paint and the old buttons. She'd created a wall hanging depicting a vintage treadle sewing machine using the black and gold buttons, a pin cushion with red ones, and seemingly every color imaginable for spools of thread and a patchwork quilt draped over a ladder-back chair. "This is gorgeous."

"Well, that seems like an overstatement."

"No, it's not. I love everything about this. And it is absolutely going to be hanging in the store where everyone can see it."

Ivy's heart filled with happiness when she glanced at Melissa and saw the pride there.

"I thought about your offer," Melissa said. "If you truly think I could be of use, I'd like to take you up on it."

"This day just keeps getting better and better."

Austin, it seemed, was not as thrilled by his mother's news as Ivy was. Not that he told Melissa this. But after dinner when Daisy went to call one of her friends and his mom was busy in the bathroom, Ivy asked him what was bothering him. He'd been quiet and tense all throughout the meal.

"I wish you had asked me about offering Mom a job before doing it."

"Excuse me? Last I checked she's a grown woman able to make her own decisions."

This was his overprotectiveness speaking, she knew that, but it hit her as a bit patronizing as well.

"Yes, she is, but I don't want her getting hurt again."

"Do you honestly think I'd do anything to put her in danger?"

"You wouldn't mean to, but what if the store doesn't work out? She will have something else taken away from her."

Ivy stared at him. Although a part of her could understand him wanting to protect his mother, it also hurt that he thought all Ivy's efforts would be for naught. The truth was a lot of new businesses didn't make it, but she was determined to not be one of those failures.

"I wouldn't have offered her a job if I didn't think my business would be successful or if I didn't think she could handle it."

Before she said something she would regret, she got up and started for the front door.

"Ivy," Austin said as he followed then blocked the door.

"You had better think twice before you say something like I might get hurt if I go outside.

Remember, I'm a woman armed with two metal crutches."

"I'm sorry. I didn't mean—"

Ivy held up her injured hand. "Don't. You did mean it. But I'm going to prove your doubts—about me and about your mom—are wrong."

CHAPTER ELEVEN

IT TOOK EVERY bit of willpower Austin had not to follow Ivy. He hated the idea of her falling out there in the dark and breaking something else because he'd let his concerns tumble out of his mouth. Ivy was right, of course. His mother was indeed a grown woman, and he should be thankful she was showing enough interest in life again to accept a future job. He *was* thankful. But at some point over the past few days, his positive view of how Ivy's friendship was bringing both his mom and Daisy out of their different kinds of shells had turned to worry. And he didn't think that worry was unfounded. If Ivy's business failed, if she gave up on the wild-hair move to Wyoming and went back to Kentucky, Daisy and his mom would lose yet something else meaningful.

He waited five minutes then stepped outside. Expecting to see her sitting on the bench they had shared when she revealed what her ex-fiancé had done to her, his anxiety spiked when he saw the bench was empty, as was the porch. Holding down the need to call out to her, he stepped off the porch and scanned the fencing along the driveway. No sign of her. Telling himself not to panic, he made his way toward the barn. He noticed the door was ajar and relaxed a little.

Should he go inside or return to the house, trusting Ivy to be okay and to get herself back inside?

"I know you're out there."

He guessed that answered his question. Stepping forward, he slipped into the barn and found Ivy sitting on an overturned bucket. Pooch had his head on her lap, enjoying a good scratch between the ears.

Austin walked past her and leaned his arms on the edge of the stall where Merlin stood. He had so much he wanted to say and yet couldn't find the words.

"I'm sorry if I overstepped," Ivy said, not looking at him. "I shouldn't tell someone else how to handle their family situation, especially when they didn't ask."

He turned to face her. "Part of me knows you're right, but there's also a big part that's afraid. If Mom loses one more thing, she might not be able to recover next time. Daisy and I might lose her too."

Ivy looked as if she wanted to respond but kept her thoughts to herself.

"What is it you want to say?"

She looked up at him then. "Are you sure you want to hear it?"

He nodded once.

"I think you need to trust your mother to find her own pace of healing, to find her own path to whatever comes next."

Maybe Ivy was right. Very likely she was because he thought perhaps she could see the picture more clearly than he could because he was part of the picture.

"I'll try."

Again, he got the feeling that she was holding something she wanted to say in check. Instead, she simply said, "Okay," and shifted her focus back to Pooch.

"Looks like you've made another new friend."

"I've always liked dogs. What's his name?"

"Pooch."

Ivy looked up at him as if he was pulling her leg. "Seriously?"

"Yep."

"That's only one step away from just calling him Dog."

"When he was a pup, he got more than his fair share of the milk so his belly was all pooched out. Daisy thought the word was funny, and since it had a double meaning it stuck."

"Well, no matter your name, you're a good boy, aren't you?"

Austin smiled at how Ivy baby-talked to Pooch and rubbed her nose against his. She had such an easy way with people and animals. If he was being truthful, he envied it a little. If he was being really truthful, he envied Pooch a little.

That admission should startle him, but it didn't. Not really. The change in how he looked at her and felt about her had been gradual, and he realized that he'd been aware of the change on some level despite trying to ignore it. But even if he admitted it to himself, he didn't know if he'd ever admit it to her. Perhaps his ill-advised words earlier had been as much about how he'd feel if she left as it was about his concerns about his mom and Daisy. If he admitted he was beginning to have feelings for her and then she left, it would be that much worse.

Plus, wasn't it too soon to even be considering another relationship? His divorce had only been final for a year. Despite the passage of those twelve months, the wound left by Grace's abandonment still felt raw sometimes. It made him sad and angry by turns.

"Is there a day next week when you would be able to go to Cheyenne with me?" Ivy asked. "I told the coin dealer I had to reschedule, though I didn't tell him why."

"I can go any day."

And hope that spending that many hours alone with Ivy didn't tempt him to give in to his new feelings.

THE MORNING AFTER their talk in the barn, Ivy awoke to find Austin gone from the ranch.

"He said he was going to do some work in your building while you weren't there," Daisy said when Ivy had come into the kitchen.

It had been the first of three days during which she hadn't seen him at all. He left the house early and came back late. She spent the time doing more planning with Melissa, delving into the history of the Stinson Building as well as Jade Valley as a whole with Daisy, and gradually working to put more weight on her ankle for longer periods of time. As the ER doctor had predicted, at the one-week mark she could walk without the aid of the crutches, though she was still careful not to overtax it or make any sudden movements.

Feeling as if she had worn out her welcome, at least with Austin based on how he was staying away from the house during all the waking hours, she got up even earlier than him on the day she'd decided to go home. She eased her way out the front door so she didn't wake up Daisy, who was snoozing away on the couch. Ivy noticed that the girl slept how she did, in the fetal position. An unexpected pang settled in Ivy's middle. She'd miss sharing meals with Daisy and Melissa, laughing with them, planning the store with them.

She'd still see them, of course, but it wouldn't be like this little pseudofamily she'd enjoyed the past week.

She reminded herself that part of the reason she'd moved to Jade Valley on a whim was to prove to herself that she was just fine on her own. And maybe once she returned to her new home and had a few days away from sharing a living space with Austin, the very bad idea of being increasingly attracted to him would fade. Hopefully, his work on her building would be done soon and she'd see him even less, causing the feelings to disappear entirely.

In the meantime, there was something magical about being awake and outside as a new day awoke from its slumber. She heard the first tittering of birds, felt a slight breeze drift across her skin and inhaled the cool freshness of the beautiful mountain valley. Leaning against the wooden fencing that started at the barn and stretched parallel to the length of the driveway, she watched as the peaks of the mountain range to the east became silhouetted by the rising sun. Taking out her phone, she snapped several pictures as the horizon shifted from indigo to yellow then orange.

Right as the top edge of the sun was becoming

visible, the front door of the house opened. Austin was actually getting a later start today. Ivy watched as he headed toward his truck and as his step faltered when he spotted her. For a moment, he seemed to not know whether to continue on his way or cross to where she was standing. Was he concerned he would invade her moment of solitude? Or did he think she was still upset about how he'd reacted to her offering Melissa a job? She'd thought they'd come to an understanding about that, but maybe it still bothered him.

Had he stayed away from her these past few days so they wouldn't argue about it? Or maybe he was using his own alone time to figure out how to balance wanting to protect his family with allowing them to do things where they might get hurt.

"You're up early," he said when he got close.

"Had to get up early to catch my ride to town."

"You're leaving?" He scanned the area around her, evidently only then realizing that her crutches were lying against her bag and not under her arms.

"Yes. I've imposed on your family long enough, though I really appreciate you-all letting me stay here while my ankle healed."

"Are you sure you're ready?"

She lifted her leg and rotated the ankle as a

demonstration. There was still some tenderness, but she didn't tell him that.

"Did you tell Mom and Daisy?"

"No, but I can call them later. And I'll see them soon."

"We'll stay for breakfast."

He wasn't asking, but she also didn't mind. She liked the idea of saying goodbye and expressing her thanks in person, but Austin had been leaving so early and she'd made her decision to go home after they were both asleep the previous night.

"Okay, but I'm cooking."

"I'll help."

"Can you cook?"

"I've lived alone before."

Ivy laughed a little. "That doesn't mean you know how to cook. And a cup of ramen, popcorn and frozen dinners don't count."

"I'll have you know I only had one of those things."

"Popcorn?" It was a logical guess since they'd had some a few nights ago while watching movies.

He nodded. "I don't like spicy food and frozen dinners don't even taste like food."

"I'll agree about frozen dinners, but I love a good hot bowl of spicy noodles. It's great for clearing out your sinuses."

Austin snorted. "I don't consider a food's ability to clear my sinuses a selling point."

He moved to lean back against the fence beside her, watching the sunrise.

"Bet you didn't see anything like this in Louisville."

"You're right about that, though the city has its positives too—lots of museums, concerts and festivals on the river, loads of great restaurants and cool neighborhoods. I've never been one to believe that the small town versus city debate is as cut-and-dried as some people do. I can like the vibrancy and choice available in cities as well as the slower pace and neighbors-helping-neighbors aspect of small towns simultaneously. By the same token, I can dislike the traffic and air pollution in cities while also not being a fan of the lack of choices and the negative side of having everyone know your business in small towns. Life is complicated and so is where you live."

"That's a very enlightened outlook on the world."

"Thank you. I try." The smile she gave Austin came easily. When he smiled back, Ivy felt a tension she hadn't been aware of release in her chest.

When they stepped back inside, Daisy was no longer in the fetal position on the couch. She had kicked off her quilt and was now lying on her stomach, one leg and one arm hanging off the edge. Ivy smothered a laugh while Austin just shook his head.

"How she's comfortable like that, I have no idea," he whispered as the two of them headed to the kitchen.

The girl also managed to sleep through all the unintended noise Ivy and Austin made in their efforts to prepare breakfast.

"I bet she was up late reading," Austin said. "She's been that way even before she could read. Mom used to catch her up past her bedtime flipping through books over and over, as if she knew there was more to them than her little mind could comprehend."

"It's good to have a curious mind. I wish more people did, to be honest."

"You're probably right."

"I usually am."

Austin laughed a little under his breath and tossed a bit of scrambled egg at her. Adept at dodging flying food courtesy of the food fights she'd had with her sisters over the years, she batted the egg away and it hit Austin right between the eyes.

"Oh, it's on." He broke off a bit of biscuit and took aim.

Ivy, in turn, picked up a spatula and assumed the pose of a baseball player at bat. That caused Austin to pause, and then he burst out laughing. Realizing how ridiculous they must look, she started laughing too. She laughed so much that she had to hold her stomach and wipe away tears. Austin was in a similar state. It was as if he hadn't laughed in so long that it was all bursting forth at once. For her, it felt good to see him laughing and to be able to really do so herself. Laughing was so much better than crying.

As she finally started to calm down, she noticed that they had an audience. Melissa appeared to be amused, and Daisy...well, Daisy, with her hair looking like a female version of Edward Scissorhands's, seemed to think they'd taken leave of their senses.

Maybe they had. And maybe that's exactly what they both needed.

"YOU READY?" Austin asked three days later as he and Ivy sat in his truck a couple of blocks from the coin shop.

She smoothed her hands down the front of her dark brown slacks. Today was the first time he'd ever seen her in her professional attire, and he could easily imagine her working as an advertising executive. She'd said she hoped that dressing this way and assuming a professional demeanor in the negotiations would prevent the potential buyer from underestimating her and thinking he could get away with a lowball offer.

"Ready as I'm going to be. I stayed up until a

ridiculous hour last night reading everything I could about these coins."

She had decided to only bring the two most valuable coins. The rest she could sell gradually. And she'd been concerned that bringing in a lot of lesser-valued coins would lessen the impact of the two top-dollar ones or possibly make her seem more desperate for money. She knew the value of what she had, and she said she was prepared to walk away if she felt she wasn't being offered what they were worth. He didn't know if he could walk away from thousands of dollars for two coins, even if offered half of what all the sources were saying they were valued at.

He accompanied her into the shop, which appeared to deal in more than coins. At a glance, he saw an array of pocketknives, cigarette lighters, arrowheads and postage stamps.

"Hello," Ivy said to the older man standing behind one of the display cases as she strode forward with a business professional's confidence. "I'm Ivy Lake and I have an appointment to meet with a potential buyer."

"Well, hello. We've been expecting you." The man motioned her toward a room with the door standing open, part of a round table visible.

Austin saw a slight stiffening of Ivy's spine, but he doubted the other man noticed. But she'd detected something off.

"Great," she said. "I've always liked people who arrive early for appointments."

So that was it. They were trying to knock her off her stride from the moment she entered by claiming she was the one who was late. He smiled to himself at how she wasn't having it. These guys didn't know what they were up against.

Introductions were made once they entered the meeting room, and Austin noticed how Mr. Tifton, the potential buyer, took note of his presence next to Ivy. He'd been right to come with her, and not just so she didn't have to make the long trip alone.

"Where did you get these?" Tifton asked.

"I inherited them."

Not in the traditional sense, but he didn't need to know that and Ivy didn't elaborate.

Tifton took out a magnifying glass to examine the coins, consulted something on his phone. As he did so, Ivy pulled up something on her own phone. When Austin realized she was online shopping for new bedding, he had to bite his bottom lip. Was she playing mind games with Tifton, making him think she was communicating with other potential buyers?

After several minutes, Tifton made an offer for both coins—one that was substantially lower than what all her research had told Ivy they were worth.

"Is that your final offer?"

Tifton nodded, looking confident.

Ivy picked up the coins and slipped them back into her purse. "Thank you for your time."

She pushed back her chair and stood, and Austin followed suit as if he'd been expecting her reaction all along.

To the shop owner, she said, "I appreciate you setting up this meeting."

"Wait," Tifton said. "You're not even going to negotiate?"

Ivy offered up a smile, but it wasn't one of the ones that she wore when she was happy. This one was cool and professional without being frosty.

"I'm not a haggler, especially when I know the worth of something. Have a good day, gentlemen."

Austin held the front door open for Ivy as she walked through with a confident stride. Once the door shut behind them, she said, "Don't look back."

"Are you sure about this?"

"It's a gamble and I'm mentally crossing my fingers, but I think I read him correctly. He wants the coins."

They walked up the sidewalk, back toward his truck. When they reached the crosswalk at the end of the first block, Austin was questioning whether Ivy had read Tifton correctly. Right before they started to cross the street, however, he heard hurried footsteps behind them.

"Here we go," Ivy said so only Austin could hear her.

"Miss Lake." It was the owner of the shop.

Ivy looked back. "Yes?"

"Mr. Tifton would like to make another offer."

"I'm listening." Ivy was making it clear by not taking a step back toward the shop that she was waiting to see if the offer was worth the effort.

The owner looked around, likely to make sure no one was within earshot, then revealed the amount of the new offer, a total of fifteen thousand dollars. Ivy, to her credit, did not squeal or jump or otherwise express the joy he had no doubt she was feeling inside.

"That sounds acceptable."

When they returned to the shop, the transaction happened fairly quickly. Once Ivy was certain the money had been transferred to her bank account, she thanked both men again and headed for the exit. For a second time, Austin followed her. He was amazed at how she kept her cool as they retraced their steps down the street. As they reached the crosswalk, however, instead of continuing ahead, Ivy suddenly grabbed his wrist and pulled him to the left.

The moment they were out of sight of the coin shop, her unaffected facade fell away. She emitted a restrained squeal and performed a little dance that had him laughing. Her smile was the widest he'd ever seen it. In the next moment, she pulled him into a hug that surprised him so much that he almost lost his footing. But she was so happy it was infectious, and he found his arms wrapping around her.

As if she suddenly realized what she was doing, Ivy let go and stepped back.

"Sorry. I just thought I was going to burst if I didn't let out my excitement. I can't believe that just happened."

He knew she was talking about the coin sale, but it was also true of the hug. His body felt abnormally warm, abnormally tingly. He wouldn't have minded if the hug lasted longer, but it was a good thing it hadn't.

"We have to go out to celebrate, someplace nice."

"Nothing too nice because I don't have fancy clothes."

"I'm sure we can find something."

After they checked into the hotel Ivy had booked for the night, they both went to their respective rooms to relax before dinner. He took the opportunity to call his mom.

"Is everything okay there?" he asked when she answered.

"We're fine. Isaac is here. He brought dinner from Alma's."

"That was nice of him." Austin hadn't asked Isaac to check on his mom and Daisy, so did that mean his mom had called him to come over? There couldn't possibly be something percolating between them, could there? That would be... odd. Maybe it was just two longtime friends, both of whom had lost their partners, looking out for each other.

"How did the meeting go?"

"Really well. We're going out to eat to celebrate in a few minutes."

"Have a good time, and don't worry about us. Focus on enjoying yourself while you're there."

He felt as if there was some extra layer of meaning in his mother's words, but he wasn't sure what they were. Did she simply want him to have an evening where he wasn't responsible for anyone? When he might be able to set aside his concerns? Could he do that?

When he left his room a few minutes later, he was determined to try. The feeling of that hug from Ivy still lingered, but he had to remind himself that this night was simply two friends enjoying a night away from their ever-present work. But the moment Ivy stepped out of her room two doors down, the whole only-friends thing flew right out of his head. She had changed into a cute pink skirt and white top. His heart started beating as fast as it had the time he'd almost been trampled by a bull.

The powerful urge to leap back into his room and lock the door, putting a barrier between them, nearly overwhelmed him. How could he feel this way after what Grace had done to him? How could he even consider being with another woman so soon after his divorce, one he hadn't seen coming?

Yet the pull toward Ivy was becoming stronger each day. And today, it had grown stronger by the hour.

"I don't know about you, but I'm ready to do some damage to a plate full of food," she said.

"I could eat."

Ivy smiled, and it made his heart flutter.

They ended up at a place that was nice but not too nice, but the menu looked awesome.

"I don't want you being cost-conscious tonight," Ivy said as they perused the menu. "And no arguments against me buying dinner."

The thought of letting her pay for him didn't sit particularly well, but he was also aware that feeling that way wasn't exactly a modern mindset either.

"Then maybe I'll buy the most expensive thing on the menu," he teased.

"Go right ahead. Except perhaps not the top-shelf drinks," she said, pointing at the liquor behind the bar.

"You don't have to worry about that. I'm not really a drinker."

Leaning into the whole Wyoming cattle rancher thing, he ordered a thick, juicy steak, while Ivy ordered lobster.

"Want to share?" she asked when their huge entrées arrived. "You're not allergic to shellfish, are you? I should have asked before I ordered."

"No, but I've never had lobster."

"Well, you're in for a treat."

"So are you," he said. "Because just the smell of this steak is making my mouth water."

They each cut off a section of their main dish and placed it on the other's plate.

"Oh my, this is good lobster," she said as soon as she took a bite. "Not as good as Maine lobster, but really good."

He had to agree, though the steak was still better in his opinion.

"I have to ask," he said. "How did you know what those guys were doing earlier when they made it sound like you were late for the appointment?"

"I've seen that tactic before, several times. Sometimes it's about the time of appointments, but others it's trying to make you believe you already agreed to some term you know you didn't or pretending that they aren't as interested as they really are. My former boss walked away from buying an old flour mill once when the owner said he couldn't possibly let it go for a lower price. My boss knew he was full of it because that place had at least a decade's worth of vegetation growing all over it. You could barely see the building beneath all the kudzu vines."

"You were impressive today."

"Thanks. Good to know my skills are still useful despite my change in career."

"Speaking of, when do you think you'll be able to open?"

"I'm hoping end of August, right before the weather starts to cool off and people want cozy quilts and yarn to knit."

"And in time to work out any kinks before the fall festival."

"Exactly."

Ivy grew more animated and excited as they continued to talk about her extensive list of plans for the store, ones his mom had helped to create.

"Did you see the wall hanging she created for the store?" Ivy asked.

"Wall hanging?"

"Remember the wood she had you cut and paint? And that box of buttons?"

He nodded.

Ivy looked up something on her phone then

handed it to him. He couldn't believe what he was seeing.

"Mom made this?"

"Yes. Isn't it awesome?"

It really was. How had he not known that his mom had this type of creativity in her?

"I know you have concerns about your mom working, but I honestly think it will be great for her. And for me too, because I'll need help, your mom is a local and knows a lot of people, and she has experience in running a business and dealing with retail customers. Plus I really like her. And Daisy." Ivy looked at him and grinned. "I guess you're not half bad either."

"Wow, high praise."

Ivy laughed before taking a bite of her garlic mashed potatoes.

Their conversation flowed from her business to his. Austin was surprised by all the questions Ivy had about ranching. She seemed genuinely interested, and he liked the newness of the experience in having someone be that interested. He was used to being around people who were already familiar with the ins and outs of the cattle business.

"You really do like it, don't you?"

"I do," he said.

"You've never thought about doing something different?"

"Not really. I like doing the renovation work, but it's always secondary and a means of making sure the ranch isn't at risk. I will do whatever I have to in order to ensure Mom and Daisy don't lose anything else, including their home."

The waiter appeared and asked if they'd like to order dessert.

Ivy placed her hand on her stomach. "While I love dessert, I'm afraid I have no room."

"None for me either."

"I think I need to walk this meal off," Ivy said after she'd paid the bill.

"Sounds good to me."

As they walked along the street, they checked out what was in the various shop windows—Western artwork, Western wear, Western jewelry, books about the West.

"No mistaking where we are," Ivy said, looking amused.

"I'm sure there are places in Kentucky where everything has to do with horses."

"True. Horses, bourbon and basketball."

Though she was now a resident of Wyoming, albeit a new one, Ivy acted like a tourist, snapping photos and buying little Wyoming-themed gifts to send back home to her mom and sisters. When they reached one of the tall cowboy boot public art pieces, Ivy had him take a series of photos of her with it while she struck funny poses—hugging it, pretending to ride a horse like the Pony Express rider painted on the boot, pointing at her pursed lips while kicking up one foot like an old-style pinup model.

He couldn't help laughing at her antics.

"Come on, let's take a picture together." She grabbed his hand and pulled him next to her in front of the boot. "Oh, come on, smile." She elbowed him gently in the ribs, and in response he unthinkingly grabbed her around the waist and pulled her close to his side as he smiled.

After a moment of having a startled expression, Ivy smiled too. He held out her phone with his other hand and took a few pictures of them. They were acting like a couple, and an even larger part of him than earlier liked the sound of that.

As he started to hand the phone back to her, they fumbled the exchange and nearly dropped it on the concrete. Somehow, in the process, he ended up with her hand that was holding the phone clasped between both of his hands. And then their gazes met…and held. Ivy seemed as at a loss for words as he felt.

"Am I imagining…something between us?" He felt as nervous as if he was skydiving for the first time.

Ivy continued to stare up at him, as if her brain

was slowly processing an appropriate answer to his question.

"I don't think so, though I also keep questioning if I'm imagining it."

He understood why she likely felt that way. Not so long ago she'd thought she'd be marrying someone else.

"I know that feeling."

Over the top of her head, he noticed a family approaching the boot, probably wanting to take their own vacation photos. As he shifted his hand to entwine his fingers with hers and guide her away from the boot, it felt natural and nerve-racking at the same time. Was he making a mistake? What exactly did he want to happen?

"Is this okay?" he asked, lifting their joined hands without looking over at her.

"I…think so. Though, to be honest, I feel a bit weird. Like it's too soon or I'm not really feeling what I think I am."

She slowed then stopped next to a bronze statue.

"Are you okay?" He turned to face her but didn't let go of her hand, so small compared to his.

"If I…feel something, does that mean that I didn't really love James? Do feelings change that quickly? I mean, I wasn't just dating him. I was engaged."

"I think as a general rule, feelings are complicated. I've been asking myself some of the same questions, trying to convince myself that I wasn't really growing to like you more and more because I've only been divorced for a year."

"But I was in a relationship much more recently, a serious one."

"Serious for you. Maybe the fact that he betrayed you eroded those old feelings at a faster rate than normal."

"That sounds sensible, but it still feels a bit confusing."

Not wanting to push if she wasn't ready, he started to slip his hand out of hers. But Ivy suddenly tightened her grip.

"Don't." She looked up at him. "I like the feel of you holding my hand. Maybe if you keep doing it, things will become clearer and less confusing."

And so they walked around some more with their hands linked, switching their serious concerns for lighter conversation. Across the plaza, a band struck up a song and they gravitated toward the music. When other couples began to dance, Austin took a leap and pulled Ivy into the flow of dancers.

"I'm not used to dancing to country music," she said.

"Just let me lead."

She did, and the sound of her laughter as she

occasionally tripped over her own feet filled his heart with a brightness that he wasn't sure he'd ever felt before. He'd been happy with Grace for most of their marriage. He remembered happy times when he was a kid, before his father died. There was lots of laughter when Daisy was a baby with impossibly tiny fingers and toes, a toddler who held his hand as she started her first adventures in the world, a little girl who managed to convince him to splash in her kiddie pool with her.

But this, what he was feeling in this moment, was different. He wasn't sure he even had the vocabulary to describe it. Maybe like warmth spreading outward from the deepest part of him, overtaking spaces that had been cold since Grace left him, even before that. The rate at which the intensity was increasing made him wonder if it was visible to those around them.

They danced to a couple of songs before he saw the slightest wince on Ivy's otherwise joyful face.

"We've overdone it with your ankle." It wasn't a question because he already knew the answer. "I'm sorry."

"Don't you dare apologize. I'm having a great time."

"So am I, but we should call it a night. Long day tomorrow." They had a couple places Ivy wanted to go to buy some items she couldn't get in Jade Valley before they made the long drive back.

Ivy sighed as if she hated cutting the evening short. "You're right."

Austin looked back across the plaza and realized how far they'd wandered from his truck.

"Would you like a piggyback ride?"

Ivy laughed. "I am not doing that. We're not in a K-drama."

"A what?"

"Korean TV dramas. Someone is always giving someone a piggyback ride."

They made the walk back to the truck slowly. Austin told himself it was out of consideration for her ankle, but that was only partially true. He was holding her hand again and didn't want to let it go, even though he knew he'd have to.

Ivy didn't seem to be in any hurry either, and he wondered how much of that he could attribute to her ankle and how much to the same hesitance for the evening to end.

By the time they reached his truck, the sky was fully dark, the sun coming up somewhere on the other side of the world. Daisy would likely be able to rattle off those locations.

Austin opened the passenger-side door but still didn't immediately release Ivy's hand. He felt as if he had become a different person from the one who had left Jade Valley early that morning. But that made him wonder if this new version of himself, with all the electric feelings crackling along his nerves, would disappear as soon as they returned to Jade Valley. Would all his memories of what had happened over the past two years rear up like a grizzly with his long, sharp claws ready to rake deep gashes into him? Was this time in Cheyenne just a momentary departure from his constant fixation of taking care of his family, working from dawn till late to make sure they were all safe and wanted for none of life's essentials?

Was his giving in to his feelings for Ivy, even a little, setting himself—as well as his mom and Daisy—up for more heartbreak? He couldn't fully make that question disappear. And yet the pull toward Ivy kept building, so much so that he leaned forward slowly. Part of him wanted her to stop him, to put her hand against his chest to halt his advance, to say it was too soon for both of them. But when she did none of those things, he felt as if he was jumping off a cliff toward an impossibly blue ocean below.

Despite that one voice telling him he was making a mistake, his lips finally touched Ivy's lightly. She didn't pull away but there was a moment of hesitance, perhaps in which her own mind was telling her something similar, before she kissed him back.

The kiss didn't last long, but it left him feeling as if his feet weren't quite touching the ground. He gave her hand a light squeeze before releasing her and walking around to the driver's side. He didn't hold her hand while driving to the hotel either. It was partly because he wanted to keep both hands safely on the steering wheel. Cheyenne wasn't a big city, but it was way bigger than he was used to navigating on a regular day. He also wanted to give them both time to process the kiss they'd just shared, how they had held hands a lot of the evening. He needed time to figure out if he really wanted to go down this road, and he suspected Ivy was examining similar questions. Her earlier one about how she could feel something for him so soon after having been engaged was proof of that.

Honestly, he should ponder the answer to that particular question as well. What if what she was feeling now was just her latching on to someone who made her feel good after her ex had made her feel so bad? What if Austin was only a potential rebound relationship?

When they reached the hotel, they walked through the lobby side by side but still without touching. On their floor, they reached her room first.

"Good night," he said, hesitating only a moment before taking a step toward his room.

Ivy caught his hand, halting him.

"I had a really good time tonight," she said. "And no matter how much I think about it, this feels real."

Tension released all throughout this body. His smile showed outwardly the growing happiness he felt inside.

"For me too."

Ivy smiled in an oddly shy way that made him fall for her a little more. Austin lifted Ivy's hand to his lips and kissed the back of it.

"Get some good sleep. I'll see you at breakfast."

Ivy nodded and slipped into her room. Austin stood staring at her door until he heard the click of her dead bolt locking into place. When he turned toward his own room, he had to resist the urge to whoop and skip down the corridor like a kid who'd just won a year's supply of candy.

CHAPTER TWELVE

DESPITE BEING TIRED from a day that started really early, Ivy could not calm her mind enough to sleep. Instead, she sat in the dark of her room and stared out the window at the lights of Cheyenne. It wasn't as big and busy as Louisville, but she liked the vibe of the small city. It felt like a different world from Louisville or Lexington the same way she felt like a different person here. She wondered whether her mind would be grasping so much for answers if more time had passed since her breakup with James. Would she still question if her feelings for Austin were real or reactionary?

She tried to remember precisely the progression of her feelings as she'd first been attracted to James, as they had begun to talk, their first date, as they'd grown closer, and eventually his proposal. Were those early stages the same as what she was feeling toward Austin now? Why couldn't she remember the finer details?

As she watched the lessening number of cars pass by on the streets, fewer numbers of pedestrians on the sidewalks, the gradual shutting off of lights in various businesses, she thought about all the moments spent with Austin. From the early days when she'd explained to him what kind of work she wanted done and she could see how he wasn't quite sure she was serious but also wanted the work, to how they'd laughed over dinner tonight and then walked hand in hand and danced together.

And then there was the kiss. She wouldn't describe it as hesitant, but there had been a restraint to it. Compared to how James had kissed her the first time, full of a passion that had sent her head spinning, Austin's kiss had felt tender and like he was gauging if it was something they both wanted to happen. When she'd seen what he intended to do, she honestly hadn't been sure. But when his lips had touched hers, it had felt so nice, as if it was beginning to erase all those heavy feelings of betrayal that had trailed her across the country and kept sitting in a corner of her heart waiting to pounce when she was most vulnerable.

But it had been over quickly, too quickly. And yet, at the same time, she appreciated the briefness. Much more and she might have been overwhelmed, unable to dissect her feelings in the aftermath. As it was, it felt as if her mind was deep in the throes of a boxing match. In this corner, common sense. In the opposite corner, trusting her feelings.

Was she placing too much emphasis on the amount of time that had passed since her breakup with James? Was there some unwritten rule about how long you had to wait before starting a new relationship? About how long was necessary between relationships to know the second one was real and not just a desperate search for someone to make you feel loved again?

After almost all the outside activity had come to a halt, Ivy finally crossed to the comfortable bed and crawled under the covers. As she began to feel herself drift, she came to a conclusion. Despite the seeming swiftness of her attraction to Austin, it hadn't been immediate. That seemed to indicate that he wasn't a rebound guy but rather someone she truly liked, more so every day. She would let her feelings lead her where they wanted and see what happened.

ALL THE LATE-NIGHT ponderings and worries seemed to evaporate with the rising of the sun the next morning. Ivy carried her bag downstairs to meet Austin, who was already up and drinking coffee like the super early riser he was. Austin drove them a short distance to a restaurant known for their generous breakfasts.

"I need fuel if I'm going to be forced to go shopping," Austin said.

Ivy shook her head. "You'd think I was going to force you to march across a desert."

"Is that an option?"

They continued to joke over what was, indeed, a large breakfast about which was better—pancakes or waffles—with each enumerating the reasons why the other was wrong. Ivy believed firmly that the answer was pancakes, and nothing would sway that belief. Texture, taste and shape were all superior to waffles, in her opinion.

Despite his comments about hating shopping, Austin was a good sport about traipsing through furniture stores and a couple of antique shops. By the time the truck was loaded with an antique treadle-style sewing machine, some vintage light fixtures, and a fluffy chair and ottoman for her living space, there was only one stop left on her list.

"Do we have enough room for a mattress set?" she asked, hands on hips, as she looked at the back of the truck.

"Yeah, we'll make them fit."

She supposed they'd have to because she couldn't just pop back over to Cheyenne easily. The other option would be either a closer store, which would likely be more expensive, or going the mail-order mattress route. She didn't like the latter idea because she couldn't test it first and, most importantly, she wanted an actual bed to sleep on tonight. She had exhausted her willingness to sleep on the floor in a sleeping bag. If her two old coins had only brought enough to buy a mattress set, that was one hundred percent what she would have bought.

After they had been in the mattress store for a while, her trying out one mattress after another, she sat up on the side of one and said, "I feel like Goldilocks trying out the beds in the three bears' house."

"We get that a lot," a salesman said as he approached them, passing a younger female employee. Then the guy pointed at the mattress where she sat as he looked at Austin. "You should try it out too."

Right as Austin opened his mouth to respond, a baby squalled across the showroom, accompanied by a flurry of exclamations from his parents. The salesman muttered something unflattering as he rushed toward the family. Even though she was still startled by the man's comment, Ivy quickly gathered that the toddler had spilled a sippy cup full of milk on a new mattress.

When her eyes met Austin's, heat raced up her neck into her cheeks.

"I feel like we just saw karma in action, don't you?" Austin said.

Ivy snort-laughed, belatedly hiding her mouth behind her hand. That he'd just dispersed the awkwardness between them in the wake of the encounter with the salesman made her like Austin even more.

"Can I help you with anything?" This question came from the young woman the salesman had jetted past.

"I have a question," Ivy said, still sitting on the edge of the quite comfortable mattress. "If I buy this right now, do you get the commission or does he?" She nodded toward the salesman, who seemed to be in a bit of a heated discussion with the parents of the milk-spilling toddler, who was still making his displeasure known.

"If I process the sale, I get the commission."

"Let's do that."

The young woman, whose name tag read Becca, smiled. "Gladly."

Ivy and Austin followed Becca to the cash register, where she ran Ivy's credit card.

"Thank you for your business," Becca said as she handed back the card and the receipt. "This is only my second day here, and this is my first sale."

Across the room, the salesman handed off the ruined mattress situation to another man Ivy assumed was the store manager and hurried toward them.

"Thank you, Becca," Ivy said when the other guy was within a few feet. "It was nice to meet you, and I think you have a good future in sales. You have a pleasant way with customers."

There was a twinkle in Becca's eyes as she thanked Ivy for her kind words. She knew exactly what Ivy was doing.

"You're bad," Austin said, obviously amused, as they left the building to move the truck around to the side loading dock.

"Who, me?" Ivy asked as she walked backward in front of him, holding her palms to her cheeks and batting her eyelashes in faux innocence.

"Austin?"

At the sound of his name, spoken by a woman with short blond hair, Austin froze. Every speck of humor disappeared from his expression in one blink of Ivy's eyes. He turned his head toward the woman slowly, as if afraid the Grim Reaper might be standing there ready to drag him away to the afterlife. Ivy noticed that he didn't speak.

The woman glanced at Ivy, as if trying to figure out who she was and how she fit into Austin's life, before returning her gaze to him.

"It's good to see you again." Her smile looked

shaky, as if she wasn't sure whether she should smile at all.

Instead of responding, Austin turned away from her and said to Ivy, "Let's go."

The blonde reached out and grabbed Austin's arm. "Wait. Can we talk?"

Austin looked at her fingers gripping his biceps in a way that sent a chill down Ivy's spine and made the woman remove her hand.

"I don't have anything to say to you. That time has passed." He strode past Ivy toward his truck. She gave the woman one more quick look before she hurried after him.

The tight set of Austin's jaw told Ivy that now was not the time to ask questions. Instead, she stayed quiet as he drove around to the side of the building, as he helped the workers load her mattress set and secure it for the long drive back to Jade Valley. She worried that all the fun they'd had on their trip had just been obliterated by the appearance of that woman. If she had to guess the blonde's identity, she'd put money on her being his ex-wife.

The way the woman acted, and how Austin had reacted in turn, made Ivy wonder if she'd been wrong about him. He'd seemed so cold, so distant, so angry at the woman's request to have a conversation.

Possible reasons the two of them had reached

that point spun in Ivy's head as Austin drove away from the mattress store and headed toward I-80. She noticed how tightly Austin held the steering wheel and that he looked straight ahead. It felt very much as if he was doing everything in his power to keep his anger reined in.

Half an hour passed before he finally spoke. "I think we should remain friends."

Confused by his statement, she nevertheless replied, "I do too."

"Just friends."

"Oh." That "oh" was one part shock and one part a sudden pain in her chest. The tears pooling in her eyes surprised her too, and she turned to look out the window as she blinked them away.

"I had a nice time the last two days, but I shouldn't have let it go further."

Ivy pressed her lips together as her eyes stung and *not again, not again, not again* echoed in her head.

"That night you told me about what James had done to you, I didn't reciprocate."

"You didn't have to," she said, doing her best to not let her voice betray how hurt she felt. "I didn't share my story expecting you to do the same."

"Still." He went quiet for several long moments. "You've probably guessed that was my ex-wife, Grace."

"I thought it might be." Ivy cleared the lump in her throat and shifted her gaze to the road ahead, her mind already scolding her for allowing herself to be vulnerable again.

"After Mom's accident, I made plans to bring Mom and Daisy to live with us," he said. "Grace didn't have anything against my family, but she was against the plan. She said we could help out, but that they had their own home. They could sell the rafting business and use the money to hire help. When I told her that there would be no money left after Mom paid off the business mortgage and that Mom wouldn't be able to work to pay the house mortgage, Grace dug in her heels."

Despite her own aching heart, Ivy felt her dislike of his ex-wife growing with each word he spoke.

"She said that she'd spent the latter part of her teens and half her twenties helping to raise her younger siblings when her mother passed, and that she hadn't signed up for more long-term caregiving when she married me. A part of me understood. She had to give up a lot at a young age, but she told me I was going to have to choose—her or my mother and sister."

"That's not a fair choice. It's a cruel one."

"Yeah." He sounded tired, the kind of tired that came from dredging up old memories of things you didn't want to think about anymore.

Ivy tried to set aside her own feelings to understand his.

"So…she filed for divorce?"

"Eventually. She went on a trip to visit a friend in Denver, and she never came back. When she was past due to come home, I called to make sure she was okay. I thought maybe she'd been in an accident. Despite how we'd been fighting, the idea of her being hurt in a car wreck so soon after Mom scared me half to death. When she told me she was still in Denver and that, while she was sorry, I was on my own, I lost my temper and said some not nice things."

"That's understandable." After all, she had done the same to James, even if he hadn't been where he could hear those words.

"Some time later, I'm not even sure how long it was because everything was a blur during those weeks, I was served divorce papers. I was so angry I signed them five minutes after I got them."

His hesitance to start another relationship made even more sense now. So did his understanding of her when she shared what James had done. They'd both been betrayed, both unsure if being in another relationship was worth the potential heartache.

Still, that didn't erase the sting of him saying he didn't want to go any further with her. Maybe he just needed some time to process seeing his ex again. Maybe his calling it quits with Ivy romantically was just a knee-jerk reaction and tomorrow he'd change his mind again.

But that wasn't fair to her. She wasn't the one who'd betrayed him.

"Why do you think she wanted to talk to you today?"

"No idea. Don't care." His words were clipped, and Ivy took it as evidence that he didn't want to talk about Grace anymore. Fine. She didn't exactly have warm, fuzzy feelings about the woman or this entire situation either.

They slipped into silence, and Ivy stared out the passenger-side window at the short green and brown grass of the High Plains. Any other vegetation was sparse on the flat to gently rolling landscape, so different from the western part of the state. Montana might be known as the Big Sky State, but the vastness of the blue sky dotted with puffy white clouds outside her window would give it a run for its money.

Ivy let Austin be alone with his thoughts while she sat with hers, but the longer the quiet stretched, the more antsy and irritated she became. She began to stew because even though she totally understood the hesitance to start a new relationship after being betrayed, she'd opened herself to one with him—and he knew what she'd gone through, how difficult it had to be for her to do so. But she was undecided as to whether she should tell him that. After hearing what Grace had done, would Ivy be showing a different kind of self-centeredness by telling him how she felt? Would it just help verify to him that he was making the right decision in ending things barely after they'd started? Should she take this out to protect herself from further hurt?

As the quiet stretched, the hum of the truck's tires on the road, combined with her limited sleep the night before, made her eyelids drift closed. She forced her eyes open, thinking she should stay awake to make sure Austin did as well.

"You can take a nap," he said, as if he'd heard her thoughts. "I'm wide awake."

She looked over at him. Though she doubted his thoughts about his ex had been left behind them as the miles passed, he didn't seem as tense as when they'd left the mattress store. His grip on the steering wheel was more relaxed, and his jaw wasn't clenched. Maybe the farther they traveled away from Cheyenne, the better he felt.

And that thought made her mad because what if ending things with her was part of what had helped him relax?

She didn't ask him if he was sure it was okay for her to sleep, because he didn't even take his gaze off the highway to glance at her. The invisible barrier between them was growing thicker with each mile he drove.

Instead, she leaned as much as she could to her right, turning her head so that she faced the passenger window. But despite her fatigue, Austin's dismissal made her feel more awake. She watched as the flatter land gave way to more hills as they climbed in elevation. She couldn't help wondering what his ex-wife had wanted to talk to him about. Did she now believe she'd made a mistake and wanted to get back together? From Austin's response to Grace, Ivy didn't see that happening.

But it wasn't totally certain, was it? Despite his obvious anger about what Grace had done, what if they did work things out? They'd loved each other enough to get married before, and stranger things had happened. A larger lump formed in Ivy's throat. Maybe those tentative first steps in her own romantic relationship with Austin had simply been a product of being far away from home, just the two of them. Even without Grace's appearance, would it have disappeared as soon as they returned to Jade Valley? Would being back in his normal environs make Austin think he'd made a mistake, and things would have turned out the same way—with him ending any further development of their romance?

Yes, she was getting good and mad at Austin.

But a part of her still understood on some level why he was acting as he was, and that made her even madder at Grace. She'd like to give the woman a substantial piece of her mind. Despite how she'd unfairly had to shoulder a lot of family responsibility early, it was still an incredibly hurtful decision to abandon Austin when he needed her most. As if having lost his stepfather and nearly losing his mother wasn't enough of a blow, he'd had to find out that his wanting to take care of his mother and sister was the bridge too far for his wife. His caretaker heart was the thing that made Grace bail on their wedding vows.

"I wouldn't do the same thing to you," she said.

"I can't take that chance."

The finality of that statement, how quickly he'd made it and the resulting painful stab in her heart made Ivy glad she wasn't facing him.

It took a long time, but fatigue finally won out over anger and hurt, forcing her to fall asleep. It surprised her when she woke up to discover they'd not only passed through Laramie but were already approaching Rock Springs. They'd be back in Jade Valley in less than two hours.

She glanced over at Austin and he looked pretty much the same as when she'd fallen asleep. Then the anger and hurt came back full force. In the next moment, she made a decision. She wouldn't fight for a relationship the other person didn't want. Back to professional distance.

"Would you like me to drive and give you a break?" she asked.

"No, I'm good."

Once again, he didn't look at her. And his succinct response told her that he wasn't in any more of a mood to talk than when she'd slipped off to sleep. She, however, didn't think she could stand the silence for the rest of the trip. They didn't have to talk about their pasts, but she needed to talk about something.

"How much longer do you think it will take to finish the renovation work?"

"Probably only a week."

"That soon?" She experienced a pang of loss and he wasn't even gone yet. But the way he was acting now, it would be best to get the job finished and both of them back to their separate lives. She wondered if he'd even convince Melissa that working for her wouldn't be worth the time and gas it cost for him to take her to and from work.

"Yeah, if not sooner."

Did he sound like a man who couldn't wait to be rid of having to be around her?

So much for talking to help alleviate the uncomfortable air between them. She pulled out her phone and saw she had a text from Lily.

Who is the hot cowboy?

Ugh. Ivy realized she'd accidentally sent one of the pictures of her and Austin next to that big boot art piece along with some of her solo selfies and scenery shots from around Cheyenne.

That's Austin, the guy who is doing the renovations on the building.

Why do you look like a couple on a date?

We don't. We were goofing off because we had time to kill between yesterday's errands and today's.

Why did he go with you?

He has a truck. I don't. Did you notice any of the other photos I sent you?

Yeah, yeah, all very nice.

Ivy rolled her eyes.

"What's wrong?" The sound of Austin's voice surprised her, coming after such a long period of him not speaking.

"Nothing." He wasn't the only one who could offer short, emotionless responses.

Plus, after what had happened earlier, there was no way she was going to reveal that Lily was teasing her about him. And she wasn't going to tell Lily that she'd kissed the "hot cowboy" either, because it looked as if that was a onetime thing.

Ivy chatted with Lily for a while longer, asking about her and Holly, about their mom, all of their jobs. Yes, she was letting the conversation distract her from the man sitting across from her. Ivy started counting down the minutes until she could escape the suffocating feeling of being trapped in a confined space with a man who'd done a one-eighty where she was concerned.

Good to know now before she was any more invested.

Except that she felt the sting in her heart every time she allowed herself to think about how much she'd enjoyed her time with him yesterday and that morning before Grace had appeared and ruined everything.

When Lily said she had to go, Ivy wanted to reach through the phone and prevent it. Instead, she simply said she'd talk to her sister again soon. She also promised to send pictures of the renovations because they were all dying of curiosity. Now that it looked a lot better than when she'd taken possession of the building, her family would hopefully not freak out as much.

About an hour from Jade Valley, Austin pulled over at a convenience store to fill his truck up with gas. She hurried inside to use the restroom and to get away from Austin for a few minutes. After taking her time to buy a couple of drinks and some snacks, she went back outside to see Austin looking at his phone. When he noticed her approach, he slipped it back into his pocket and resumed his spot in the driver's seat.

"You didn't need to get me anything," he said. "We're not far from home."

"It's okay. I had the munchies."

Anything to occupy their remaining time together. And to make it seem as if he hadn't hurt her as much as he had. Admitting that she'd allowed herself to feel too much too fast was embarrassing and made her feel too raw and pitiful.

When they finally pulled up in front of her building, Rich was there waiting. Had that been who Austin was texting earlier and not his ex-wife? Of course, Ivy had spent so much time in the store that he could have texted both. Back in Cheyenne, he'd been abundantly clear that he had nothing to say to Grace. But what if during all those quiet hours since then he'd changed his mind? Had his anger given way to curiosity about what Grace wanted to say to him? Was it possible they could move past her betrayal and try again?

Ivy hated the idea of that after what Grace had done, hated the idea of anyone returning to someone who'd betrayed them. That feeling stemmed partly from her experience with James, but not all of it. She still remembered how mad she'd been when one of her college friends kept getting back with her boyfriend, even after he'd cheated on her multiple times. She may have yelled something about leopards not changing their spots and stormed off, and their friendship had never been the same until it gradually faded away altogether.

Was that what was happening between her and Austin now, the beginning of fading away despite the fact he'd claimed he wanted to remain friends? Right now, she wasn't sure she even wanted that.

While the two men made quick work of carrying the mattress set upstairs and the old sewing machine to the bottom level, she busied herself taking in the smaller items. It was all done within a few minutes. Rich gave her a curious look before departing for another appointment. That left her with Austin, awkwardness still lying between them like a thick morning fog but at least not trapped in the truck together with miles to go.

"Thanks for all your help," she said, trying to act as if nothing had changed between them since they'd set off from Jade Valley yesterday.

"No problem. I'll be back in the morning to work out back."

She nodded, glad that he would be working

to clean up the small courtyard area behind the building and mostly out of her sight.

Without saying anything else, he got in his truck and drove away. Her heart sank way more than it should have, proving that she hadn't learned her lesson. She'd come to Wyoming with the mission of forging an independent life for herself, and she'd instead allowed herself to start to fall way too easily for another man.

If he wanted to go back to a purely boss/contractor relationship, well, that was fine with her.

At least that's what she told herself.

AUSTIN WALKED STRAIGHT to the barn when he got home, bypassing the house because he needed time to get his sour mood hidden away before he encountered his mother and sister. Both of them were too observant for him to get away with some flimsy excuse like he was tired.

He was as upset with himself as he was with Grace. He hated that he'd allowed her to get in his head so much that he'd been twisted in tight knots all the way back to Jade Valley. Worse, he'd shut out Ivy, ended things with her. Having Grace show up out of the blue had felt like a sign from the universe that he was making a mistake starting a new relationship.

Even if it hadn't felt like a mistake as it was

happening. While he'd held Ivy's hand, danced and laughed with her, he'd felt better than he had since before his mom's accident. If it was only him he had to worry about, maybe he'd be okay by morning and he could go apologize, tell Ivy that he hadn't meant it and hope they could pick up where they left off. But his own feelings were not his only concern. And after the way he'd told Ivy he only wanted to be friends, how he'd let her know that he couldn't take a chance on more, he figured she was done with him anyway. He certainly would be.

He knew sometimes people had whirlwind vacation romances, but one limited to twenty-four hours seemed ridiculous. If he'd hurt Ivy, especially after what she'd been through in her last relationship, kicking himself repeatedly sounded like a just punishment.

He'd been in the barn about an hour when the sound of approaching footsteps told him that his mom had likely sent Daisy out to see why he wasn't coming into the house.

"Hey, kiddo," he said as Daisy entered the barn.

"Mom said to come in and eat."

"I'm not hungry. I had a lot to eat today."

"What's wrong?"

"Nothing."

"You're lying." She didn't say it harshly, but rather using a matter-of-fact tone.

Instead of denying it, he said, "You should have seen the size of the breakfast I had. It was enough for a basketball team."

"Fine, don't tell me. But I've got five dollars on Mom not letting you off with that flimsy excuse. Wouldn't you rather talk to me instead?"

Austin stopped sharpening the lawn mower blade but kept staring at it.

"I ran into Grace in Cheyenne this morning."

"Seriously?"

He nodded.

"What did she say? Not that I care."

"That's pretty much what I told her, that I wasn't interested, and walked away. Didn't look back."

"Good."

This was the most fire he'd seen out of his little sister in a long time. It took a lot to make her mad, so when it was apparent that she had been angered it was best to stay far away until she cooled down. Daisy might be on the quiet side most of the time, but she was like him—protective of her family.

"Don't tell Mom. I don't want to upset her," he said.

Daisy agreed to keep his secret.

"How did it go at the coin shop?"

"Really well. Watching how Ivy handled the

situation, it's easy to assume she was very good at her previous job."

And that if anyone could make a quilt shop in the Stinson Building into a success, it was her.

"I'm glad Mom is going to be working in her store. I think it'll be good for both of them."

"Both?"

"Yeah. Mom will be out and around people, and she'll feel useful. And Ivy won't be alone all the time. She tries not to show it, but I think she gets lonely. She probably misses her family."

All because James had been the biggest of fools, cheating on a beautiful, funny, talented woman. The man really was an idiot.

But Austin probably was as well, because he'd gone from kissing Ivy to almost completely ignoring her on the long drive back home, telling her that being with her wasn't worth taking a chance. If he could rewind time, even by only a day, he wouldn't have given in to his growing feelings. Everything was now much more complicated. What was she thinking at that moment? Did she think that he'd taken advantage of her vulnerability after she'd told him how she'd been betrayed by James?

"Hello?"

He pulled himself out of his thoughts when Daisy waved her hand in front of him.

"You have on your thinking-too-much face,"

she said. "She doesn't deserve you hurting your brain over her."

"I'm not." At least not the *her* Daisy was referring to.

His sister didn't look convinced.

"I promise."

He knew she still didn't believe him as she turned to head back inside, but she didn't press him further. Once she was gone, he finished sharpening the lawn mower blade, put it back on the mower, then sank onto a wooden bench. His thoughts drifted to the night before, to how nice it had felt to give in to the feelings he'd tried to deny and kiss Ivy. He pressed his hand to his chest, still able to feel how it had seemed as if his heart had expanded and floated within him like a heart-shaped balloon. And then Grace had appeared and popped it with a huge pin.

Deflated. That's exactly how he felt now, and he didn't know what to do about it. Should he find a way to reinflate that balloon or toss it away altogether?

CHAPTER THIRTEEN

WHEN FIONA CALLED Ivy to see if she could cover her early morning shifts at Trudy's because she was sick with some respiratory virus that had her coughing like a seal's bark, Ivy accepted. Her ankle might protest some, but she figured she could wrap it to give it extra support. She'd have to be careful with her healing finger, but the extra hours at work would serve a dual purpose—earning more money that she could invest in her store and staying away from Austin.

She did her best to understand how seeing his ex-wife would rattle him, but she still couldn't help feeling hurt. When she did see him, she could almost believe their romantic twenty-four hours hadn't even happened. He avoided eye contact, was all business. Maybe she should be thankful for that because it would make moving on again easier. But the truth was, her heart felt badly bruised.

When her extended shift was over for the day, she ran a few errands before finally heading home. As she turned the corner at Main and Yarrow, her heart did a weird combination of sinking and speeding up when she saw Austin's truck was still there. Of course it was. He wasn't one to cut a workday short. Plus he seemed in a hurry to put the renovation project behind him. Today, he'd been working on light fixtures inside plus moving the old wood-and-glass display cases that she had sanded and stained to the spots she'd indicated.

If her brief romance with Austin was over, she could at least be excited about how soon she could start the process of stocking her store.

When she stepped into the building, the first thing she noticed was that Austin was not inside. The next was that not only were the antique display cases and the new light fixtures in the appropriate spots, but the button wall hanging Melissa had made was now hung on the wall.

"That looks awesome," she said as she approached Melissa, who was busy on Ivy's laptop computer.

"I'm glad you like it."

"I love it, so much so that I think you should make some more pieces like it and we'll sell them in the store."

"Funny you should mention that. I just bought a cheap collection of old buttons online, and they'll be here by the end of the week. I already have several ideas if Austin can stop being grumpy long enough to cut some boards for me."

Ivy fixed her gaze on the wall hanging so that Melissa didn't see how the sound of her son's name affected Ivy.

Once again telling herself to only focus on the positives, she thought about how much having a purpose and a creative outlet had breathed new life into Melissa. Even if Ivy and Austin weren't going to be a couple, she was happy with the friendships she'd made with his family. Sure, it would take a while to get past things not working out with him, but hopefully they could return to being easy friends again at some point.

"Are you okay?" Melissa asked. "You look like you have a lot on your mind."

"I do. It's not every day that a girl starts a brand-new business." Ivy infused her answer with excitement, which wasn't entirely fake. The closer she got to actually ordering products and setting up the store, the more it seemed as if it was really going to happen.

As she climbed the stairs to her home, however, she couldn't maintain the smile she'd offered Melissa. Though she knew she shouldn't, she looked out the back window. Austin and Daisy were behind the building, cleaning the old stones that made a sort of patio area. Most of them had been covered with years of dirt and vegetation, but enough were visible to know they existed. She'd found a couple of outdoor chairs during her culling of the building's contents. Some cleaning and a new coat of paint would make them perfect for the patio area. Who would sit with her, she didn't know. Maybe it would just be her and Sprinkles.

Though she knew she should move away from the window, stop watching Austin, she couldn't quite make herself do so. As she watched him use a shovel to remove some of the accumulated years of disuse, she noticed how his T-shirt stretched across his back, how his strength made the work look easy. She remembered how she liked seeing him smile and hearing him laugh. She'd gotten a glimpse of the man he could be if he didn't have so much weighing on his shoulders. Mixed with her anger at him for not believing in her enough to give them a chance was the realization of how much she was going to miss seeing him every day. She'd swear she could hear the ticking of the minutes until he was gone getting louder and louder.

AUSTIN SHOULD HAVE known something was up by how quiet his mom was on their way home after work, but he'd been so caught up in his own thoughts that he hadn't really noticed. It had started to dawn on him that something serious was on her mind as he watched the way she cut her chicken breast during dinner. Warning lights started blinking red and Daisy headed to her room after loading the dishwasher, leaving him alone with his mom.

"I'll go feed Pooch," he said as he started to get up from the table.

"Sit." It wasn't a request. The way she said that single word took him back to when he was a kid and had made a decision that got him into trouble. Now, as then, he complied.

"Is something wrong?"

"That's what I want to ask you," she said. "Why have you and Ivy been avoiding each other ever since you got back from Cheyenne?"

"We're not. We see each other every day."

"My legs may not work any longer, but my eyes are perfectly fine. And I know what I've been seeing. Something happened between you two while you were gone, didn't it?"

He sighed. "It's nothing for you to worry about."

"So you're the only person in this family who gets to worry about anyone?"

Now his mom sounded irritated, bordering on angry.

"I didn't say that."

"You didn't have to. It's been abundantly clear for some time now." She took a slow, deep breath, seeming to gather herself so she didn't outright explode. "I appreciate everything you've done for me and Daisy, everything you continue to do, but you're holding on too tight and your focus is too narrow."

He must have looked confused because his mom's expression softened a bit.

"You and Ivy like each other. I'm fairly certain the cattle could see that if she spent time in the pasture with you. Even if you don't tell me what happened on your trip, I know something did. When you left, the two of you talked and joked easily with each other. Now you can barely meet each other's eyes when you're not avoiding each other entirely. And I can't tell if Ivy is sad or mad. Maybe it's both."

So he hadn't been imagining it. But he had been trying to ignore it, telling himself over and over that ending things before they went any further would protect them both.

Austin considered how to handle the conversation so that after it was over he didn't have to address the topic of Ivy and him again.

"We thought maybe there could be something, but there isn't."

"You mean that you won't let there be anything." She made this accusation so quickly that it showed she had it at the ready, that she'd been dissecting his actions well before tonight.

"Don't you think I'm old enough to make my own decisions?"

"Yes, but I also have the right as your mother to tell you when you're being stupid."

He jerked a little at that jab.

"I don't have to have a crystal ball or be able to read minds to know what is going on," she said. "You are refusing to allow yourself to find happiness again because of what Grace did. That's giving her too much power over your life."

Amazing how similar his mom and Daisy sounded sometimes.

"Mom, I have my reasons."

"If one of those reasons has anything to do with me, I'm going to be really angry."

"Why? Because I don't want you and Daisy hurt again? Because I don't want to be hurt again?"

"So you're going to just be alone the rest of your life?"

"I'm not. I have you and Daisy."

"Do not use us as an excuse. You know someday Daisy will go off to college and then to see the world. And I won't live forever."

"Don't say that." The idea of losing either of them ripped him apart inside.

"It's a fact. I'm twenty-two years older than you. And even if I live to be a hundred, it is not the same as having a life partner and you know it."

"Well, I don't have a very good track record with that, do I?"

"Austin, I remember distinctly when you were a little boy and you fell off your pony. You didn't even cry. You got up, dusted off your little jeans and climbed back on. You've done that about everything your entire life—except trying to find love again."

"It hasn't been that long, and I have plenty else on my plate."

"And I'm sorry for that."

"It's not your fault."

"Part of it is. I know I've not been much help since the accident."

"You've been grieving."

"And I will continue to do so, but I'm also still here and I have to keep on living. You and Daisy deserve a mother who is fully here, not one who might at any moment sink into depression. I loved Sam and I miss him with my whole heart. Same as with your father. But I am tired of living in a fog. I'm going back to work, and I'm going to contribute to the family finances so everything isn't on you."

He started to interrupt her, to say he was fine, but she held up her hand to stop him.

"I'm excited about the opportunity to work in Ivy's store. If what you're worried about is the store not making it and Ivy leaving Jade Valley, you can put those worries to rest. That girl has a great head for business. She's ambitious and determined but isn't overstretching."

"But even good businesses fail. People you think would never leave do. And then you're left to pick up the pieces. I don't want to go through that again. I can't put you and Daisy through that again either, because I know how close you both have gotten to Ivy."

"So you think that by not allowing yourself to like her, to date her, we magically wouldn't be sad if Ivy decided to go back to Kentucky? Do you realize how foolish that sounds? You've gotten so good at self-sacrifice that you've forgotten who you used to be."

Those words felt like a bomb going off, one he hadn't known was approaching. Had he really gone too far in his protectiveness of his mother and sister? Of himself? Had he used protecting them as a convenient excuse to not open himself up to being hurt again?

He realized he'd used seeing Grace again as another convenient excuse.

If he really thought about it, Ivy didn't seem like a person who would deliberately hurt someone else—especially considering how she had suffered because of her previous relationship. But he'd already pushed her away. The fact that she had been avoiding him to the fullest extent possible, coupled with his mom's observation about Ivy's mood, told him that he'd likely already blown his chance.

He looked across the table and saw his mom watching him, likely interpreting every small change in his expression the way she had his entire life.

"What if I've already messed up my chance?"

"What if you haven't?"

Not able to wait until tomorrow to find out the answer, he grabbed his keys, gave his mom a kiss on the forehead and ran to his truck.

Please don't let me be too late.

IVY KNEW SHE had to get past thinking about Austin every time she looked at her refurbished floors, her freshly painted ceiling and the new pane in the window that had been broken when she first arrived in Jade Valley. This was her home and would soon be her business, so she would be spending a lot of time in the building. Maybe once it was filled with patterned fabrics, colorful yarn and various sewing notions the memories of Austin standing in a certain spot and moving in a certain attractive way would fade.

Until then, memories of him seemed to be everywhere. She would get past her hard-and-fast fall for him—because, no matter that she'd so recently been engaged to someone else she loved, she had fallen for Austin. Maybe this was her cosmic punishment for opening her heart too easily.

Feeling antsy, she decided to try out the new firepit she had constructed out of some old left-over bricks that had been hidden under weeds and grass next to the back of the building and some fast-drying cement. Tonight felt like a night for s'mores. After a quick trip to the grocery and locating an appropriate stick, she lit a fire and watched as it grew to a useful size.

The first bite of gooey marshmallow and choc-olate squeezed between graham crackers burned her tongue a little, but she didn't care too much. It was delicious and just what she needed. It didn't escape her notice that the s'mores were serving the same self-pity purpose the copious amounts of ice cream had after her disastrous engagement party. But sometimes you just needed an infu-sion of sugar to make you feel a little bit better.

Tomorrow she would be better. She would shift the part of her thoughts stuck on Austin over to join the ones focused on the work that lay ahead of her. Each day after deciding to move, it had gotten a bit easier to not think about James and his betrayal. Throwing herself into work had helped her heal faster than if she'd stayed in Louisville, having to see him every day. She could do it again, even if Jade Valley's size and the fact Melissa would be working for her meant Ivy would inevitably see Austin from time to time.

But tonight she would allow herself to remember all the fun and lovely moments she'd spent with Austin, particularly during their trip to Cheyenne. The laughter, the hand-holding, the shared excitement over how much she'd gotten for the coins. And the kiss. Her heart ached at the knowledge that they would never share another.

Trying to not sink too far into sadness, she focused on the fire. She followed the sparks as they floated up toward the twilit sky. It was a beautiful, peaceful evening despite her new heartache.

As she was finishing off her second s'more and about to assemble a third, her phone rang. Not in the mood to chat with her sisters or mother because they would immediately be able to tell something was wrong, she almost ignored it. But she glanced over in time to see the call was from Austin. Her heart leaped in surprise and hope, but immediately on the heels of that was worry. Had something happened to Melissa? Or even Daisy?

"Hello?"

"Where are you?" Austin sounded breathless, which made her worry even more.

"At home."

"I just knocked on your front door. I guess you didn't hear it."

"I'm out back."

Why was he here?

She'd just set the makings of the next s'more on the paper plate sitting on the little metal table between the two old metal chairs when Austin rounded the corner of the building in front of her. Somehow he looked even taller than normal. He stopped suddenly, as if he'd forgotten why he was there or perhaps because he was telling himself that he shouldn't be.

"Did something happen?"

Still, he didn't say anything. Worried, she took a step toward him. "Austin?"

"Did I ruin everything?"

"What?" She glanced toward the building, wondering if he was talking about something he'd worked on earlier.

This time, he moved toward her. His steps were slow, hesitant.

"Us," he said. "I was wrong when I pushed you away. I know I don't deserve it, but I want to ask for another chance."

Ivy's heart started beating faster. Was he really asking her that?

"You made it clear you weren't interested in anything beyond what happened in Cheyenne.

I got the distinct impression you even regretted that."

"I know. I'm sorry. I…" He looked up at the darkening sky for a couple of beats before fixing his gaze on her again. "Running into Grace less than twenty-four hours after we admitted we had some feelings for each other felt like an ominous sign." He shook his head. "This sounds out there, but it felt like the universe was reminding me of what happened the last time I trusted someone, cared about someone. I was bombarded with all these thoughts that I had to protect Mom, Daisy and myself from having to go through that again."

"I told you I wouldn't do that to you. I know what it's like to be betrayed, hurt by the person you care deeply about."

"I know. I also know I'm an idiot and may have ruined everything. I can't blame you if that's the case, but I hope you give me another chance."

Only minutes ago she'd been sitting by the fire sad that things hadn't worked out, but now that Austin was here and saying he was actually still interested she grew wary. She'd had enough of the ups and downs of romance, the never knowing what drop was right around the next corner.

"I don't think you'd ever deliberately hurt any of us," he said. "I knew that deep down, but I let the fear take over. I can't stand the thought of Mom or Daisy losing anything or anyone else."

"Life is filled with losses. We can't avoid all of them, no matter how hard we try. And some of us suffer more than our share. It's not fair, but that's life. You know what else life is filled with, though? Good moments. Great moments. Wonderful people."

"You're right. I know you are."

"But you've been in protective crisis mode for so long that it's hard to stop. And it causes you to hurt others rather than be hurt."

He looked at her for several heartbeats, as if wondering how she had figured it out, before nodding.

"But I want to stop. And start with you for real."

She stared at him for a few seconds, trying to decide how she wanted to respond. "Are you sure?"

"Yes. But if it's too soon for you, I'll wait. It hasn't been long since your breakup."

"Trust me, I've asked myself countless times if what I feel for you makes any sense, how much it hurt when you called things off, whether it means that I didn't love James. But then I wondered who set the time limits—how long we have to wait after we lose someone to think about being with someone else, how long is too short and why. And you know what I think? We have to go with our instincts, and it's no one else's business but the people directly involved."

After a moment's hesitation, Austin took a slow step forward.

"You have such a healthy way of looking at things. I'm not sure I'm smart enough to date you."

The word "date" made Ivy feel giddy, more so than even when James had first asked her out.

"Don't underestimate yourself. A person has to have a good head on their shoulders to juggle all the balls you have been."

The light in the sky was growing dimmer, but the orange glow of the fire illuminated Austin's smile.

"I'm really sorry I hurt you," he said. "I'll do my best to never do that again."

"See that you don't."

"Does that mean we can give us a second try?"

"Yes." She refused to think about how the last time she'd said yes to a man, it had been a proposal for a marriage that never happened. That was the past. James was the past. The present was about her reclaiming her happiness in all its forms, and one of those definitely included Austin.

CHAPTER FOURTEEN

AUSTIN PAUSED IN assembling a set of display easels he'd built for the history exhibits Ivy had ordered based on Daisy's research about the Stinson Building. He glanced out the window that faced Main Street.

"It's only been about thirty seconds since the last time you looked," his mom said.

Though it was good to hear amusement in her voice, he still blushed a little at her teasing. He hadn't felt that way since he'd first started seeing Grace, which seemed ages ago.

Daisy snickered beside him, and he acted as if he was going to grab her. She squealed and ran to hide behind their mom.

"Don't use me as a shield."

Daisy acted affronted. "You started it."

"Technically, your brother started it by looking out the window so often, as if that will make Ivy appear faster."

"I should have left the two of you at home."

Daisy and his mom looked at each other for a

moment then laughed in unison. Austin would be irritated if seeing them happy didn't make his heart feel full. Still, he quickly finished his task and headed outside. A few days ago he'd wanted to hurry to complete all the tasks this job had required, but now that he was basically finished he dreaded reaching the end of the day.

He scanned the front yard of the building. It could really use some landscaping, but Ivy said she'd tackle that later. Now that the building was livable and usable for her store, her focus had shifted to ordering stock and finalizing how she wanted to display it. That was definitely more in his mother's wheelhouse than his. Soon he'd be back to full-time ranch work, only able to see Ivy when they made plans to spend time together or when picking up his mother after work. They hadn't gone on an official date yet, but it had only been two days since their decision to make a go of it, followed by sitting next to the fire and eating s'mores until all the marshmallows were gone.

He looked up the street, and there she was. His smile was instantaneous when she waved from a block away. He resisted the smitten teenager urge to run to her, but only barely.

"Are you waiting for me?" she asked when she got close.

"Maybe."

Her smile would light up the deepest cave.

"So, you want to go on a date?" she asked.

"Sure. What do you have in mind?"

"How about a hand-in-hand walk through… Fizzy's?"

That was not at all what he'd been expecting. "Fizzy's?"

"Well, you did talk the place up and I haven't been yet. What's better for a first date than a treasure hunt?"

Dinner, a movie, a nice walk along the river.

But when he thought about it, it made a sort of sense. So much of their time together had revolved around the way she was rebuilding her life here in Jade Valley. It had been nice watching not only the building come back to life, but also his family. And when he thought about it, Ivy fit that description too. While she'd been nice and friendly right from the start, there was a new brightness in her eyes now, the proverbial bounce in her step that hadn't been there when they'd first met. If she wanted to go picking at Fizzy's, a-picking they would go.

He hadn't counted on his first date with Ivy including his mom and sister tagging along, but Ivy said the more the merrier. And an hour after arriving at Fizzy's, he had to agree. While Daisy went off in search of books and things that appealed to her sense of adventure, his mom and

Fizzy sat on Fizzy's front porch drinking cold sodas in glass bottles and laughing at something or another.

"They sound like they're having a good time. Aren't you glad they came with us?" Ivy gently poked him in the ribs to tease him.

"Yes, though at some point we're going to go on a proper, 'just us' date."

"I like the sound of that." Ivy slipped her fingers through his as they moved from one of Fizzy's buildings full of stuff to the next.

"What about these?" Austin pointed toward several large cubby shelves.

Ivy's eyes lit up like it was the best Christmas morning ever. "Those are perfect for yarn skeins. I wonder how much they are."

When she started to step forward, he gently tugged her back.

"You won't find prices on anything here. You make an offer and Fizzy either takes it or he doesn't. If he likes you, he'll be willing to haggle."

"I can do it, as you saw at the rummage sale, but I don't especially like to haggle." She stared at the shelves. "But I have an offer in mind. Let's keep looking though."

Austin was surprised by how much he enjoyed shopping with Ivy. He'd never enjoyed shopping with Grace, but to be fair this was an entirely different type. This was shopping to make a dream come true.

As he watched Ivy looking through an old cigar box full of thimbles, he couldn't help smiling.

She glanced up at him and stopped riffling. "What?"

"You look so happy right now."

She smiled as she let the box lid close.

"That's because I am." She walked toward him, gripped the front of his shirt and pulled him down to where she could plant a quick kiss on his cheek.

It was over so quickly that for a moment Austin was left a bit wobbly on his feet.

"What was that for?"

"I just felt like it." And with a mischievous smile she turned back to her personal treasure hunt.

When they finally returned to Fizzy's front porch, the older man and his mother were laughing so hard that they were wiping away tears. Austin stopped in his tracks and stared. Though she'd begun to laugh more easily lately, he literally could not remember the last time he saw his mother laughing with her entire body and soul. Next to him, Ivy squeezed his hand. When he looked down at her, he felt such a wave of gratitude that it almost felled him right there in the middle of Fizzy's years of accumulation.

After a few moments of simply appreciating how much his mother's outlook on life had changed since Ivy's arrival in Jade Valley, he and Ivy continued toward the porch.

"What is so funny?" he asked.

His mom waved off his question. "You don't need to know."

"Well, now I'm really curious."

"A tale from the past that is going to stay there."

Austin decided his unsatisfied curiosity was a price he was willing to pay for his mom's happiness.

After Fizzy got his laughter and resulting coughing under control, Ivy made her offer for the cubby shelves.

"I've had so much fun this afternoon that I'm going to let you have them for half that."

"Wow, thank you."

"Mom, do you have something on Fizzy?"

That question caused his mom and Fizzy to look at each other and start howling with laughter again.

"That must be some story," Ivy said to him as the two older adults laughed themselves silly.

By the time they loaded up Ivy's purchases and Daisy had paid for a book of world maps from the early 1900s, Austin helped his mom back into the truck and they all headed back into town. As they got closer, it started to rain. Austin

291

wanted to hurry so that Ivy's items didn't get wet, but he wasn't about to endanger her or his family. When they arrived in front of Ivy's building, his mom said that she'd sit in the truck so the rest of them could hurry to get the truck unloaded.

When everything was safely inside and thankfully only a bit damp, Daisy went back to the truck. Left alone with Ivy, he tugged her gently out of sight of his mom and sister.

"I had fun today," he said.

"I'm glad."

"That said, I get to choose what we do on our next date."

She looked up at him and grinned. "Deal."

Feeling his heart fill with happiness, he pulled her close and kissed her. It was more than a quick peck this time, but he didn't let himself get carried away either. They'd agreed to take things slowly to make sure they did things right and that they both really were ready to move on.

He didn't feel any doubt anymore. He was falling in love with Ivy, and it took a lot of restraint not to tell her that. But she'd been in a relationship more recently than him, and it wasn't fair to her to go back on his word that they'd take things one day at a time. She had a lot on her plate right now, and he didn't want to add any stress to her life.

"I know today was my official last day of work,

but you can still call me any time you need help. I'm your..." He trailed off, not sure how Ivy would define their relationship.

"Boyfriend?"

"Are you okay with that term?"

"Absolutely."

The way she said that with her whole being made Austin feel as if he was floating all the way home.

"ARE WE ALMOST THERE?"

Across the truck from Ivy, Austin laughed at her question. Though her eyes were closed, she could picture him so clearly. Over the past couple of weeks, they'd spent as much time together as work allowed. He'd picked up another job rebuilding a porch and adding a wheelchair ramp for an elderly couple after word got around about the work he'd done on her building, including the addition of the ramps.

"You sound like Daisy when she was a kid asking, 'Are we there yet?'"

"All kids ask that at some point or another. I remember me and my sisters asking Mom that every time we went anywhere outside of Lexington."

"In answer to your question, yes, we're almost there. But don't you dare peek."

"This better be good."

After he finally parked the truck, assisted her out of it, then led her forward for a couple of minutes, she was allowed to open her eyes.

The view that greeted her wasn't merely good. It was magical.

"Oh, it's gorgeous here." She walked a few steps to the top of a hill overlooking an expanse of the valley through which the river meandered. The sun glinted off the water, the sky was an impossible blue and the surrounding mountains seemed straight out of a fantasy realm.

"I'm glad you like it."

"How could anyone not like it?" She turned to look at him and noticed the picnic basket in his hand. "Oh, and food too? I think you might be a keeper."

Ivy hoped Austin didn't read too much into that last statement, even though she believed it with her whole heart. She hadn't told her family about him yet because she knew they'd think she was moving on to another relationship too fast. Lily had teased her about the "hot cowboy," but if she knew that Ivy was now seriously falling for him, she would sound the family alarm. It wouldn't surprise Ivy if both sisters and their mother showed up on her doorstep to try to talk some sense into her.

She relaxed when Austin didn't seem to mind her allusion to a long-term relationship. In fact, his smile gave her hope that he was feeling the same way. She needed that boost after the dream she'd had the night before, one in which Grace had shown up in Jade Valley with an apology that swayed Austin. That scene had drifted away to be replaced with one of Austin and Grace getting married a second time on the front steps of Ivy's building. But somehow she didn't own the building anymore. Austin had managed to take it away from her and give it to his new bride.

Ivy had woken up with her heart racing and her jaw clenched so tightly that it hurt.

"Are you okay?"

"Yeah, more than okay." She stepped away from memories of the nightmare and toward Austin. "Did you get a picnic lunch from Trudy?"

With the summer weather so nice now, they had been making lots of picnic meals for tourists to take with them on their outings. Trudy always slipped in a flyer about how to stay safe in bear country with respect to food.

"I'll have you know I made all of this myself."

Ivy grinned. "Is it sandwiches and chips?"

Austin gave her an affronted look. "No, it's *premium* sandwiches and chips."

Ivy laughed. "Oh, I stand corrected."

But he hadn't lied. The thick roast beef sandwiches were delicious, and he had paid attention to what she liked and brought her favorite sour cream and onion chips. His thoughtfulness, the postcard view and sharing it all with the man who meant so much to her made it no less than a perfect day.

"What's in the storage container?" she asked as she pointed inside the basket.

"You'll find out when you finish your sandwich and chips."

"Okay, Mom."

Austin made a *pffft* sound before taking a big bite of his sandwich.

Ivy was happy to just sit in the incredible quiet, a type of quiet that it was hard to believe still existed in the modern world. Other than the sounds of their eating, all she heard was the breeze in the pines and the tittering of some bird in a nearby tree.

"It's so peaceful it makes me not want to leave," she said.

"I know that feeling. I happened upon this spot several months ago when I felt like the stress was going to crush me. Most of the time I dealt with it fine, because there was no other option. But there was something about that day where I couldn't breathe all of a sudden and I just started driving. Somehow I ended up here. I think I sat here for like two hours, but by the time I left I felt lighter and able to handle everything again. Like you said, it felt peaceful. When I was trying to think of someplace special to bring you, I thought of this." He pointed toward the valley spread out before them. "Being with you makes me feel the way this place does, lighter and able to handle anything."

Ivy was so touched that she couldn't find the right words to respond. Instead, she placed her hands on his cheeks and kissed him. When she pulled away, Austin smiled at her.

"Well, that's better than the dessert I brought."

"Hmm, I'll reserve judgment. I do like dessert."

"If you like the dessert better than kissing, I might have to leave you here."

"There are worse places to be left." As soon as the words left her mouth, she realized how he might take them. "I'm sorry."

He shook his head. "It's okay. We don't need to tiptoe around each other anymore, don't you think?"

She considered that for a moment. "I agree."

Still, she didn't immediately ask the question that had been sitting in her mind unanswered since that day in Cheyenne. But they were moving forward, getting closer every day. Best to get it out there in the open.

"Are you curious about what Grace wanted to talk to you about that day?"

"No." His answer was immediate and sounded

decisive. "I suspect she wanted to say she was sorry, even ask how Mom was doing. Maybe part of her would have even meant it, but it doesn't matter to me anymore. Someone who just wants to stick around when times are good isn't someone I want to be with."

Ivy entwined her hand with Austin's. It was amazing when she thought about how they'd both been betrayed, both thought they didn't want to be in a relationship again, and then they'd found each other. Louisville and Jade Valley were almost like two different worlds. If not for her seeing that contest to win the Stinson Building at nearly the last minute, she and Austin would have never met.

"You ever think about what the odds must have been for us to ever even cross paths, let alone get together?"

"More than once," he said.

"It's weird how life works. When I was standing in that hotel and those women showed me proof of what James had done, it felt as if the world fell out from under me. I didn't know how I was going to go back to work and not be angry every time I saw him. I sat in my apartment eating buckets of ice cream and wondering how I could avoid dying of mortification every time I saw someone who was there that day. When

I won the building, it felt like a lifeline and I took it."

"I'm glad you did."

Ivy looked up at Austin and felt happiness suffuse every cell in her body. "I am too. I really am."

Hopefully someday the little voice inside her head would stop telling her to be careful how happy she was or she might tempt fate to snatch it away again.

She leaned her head on his shoulder and they sat like that for a long time, simply enjoying the beauty of Wyoming and the comfort of each other's company. Eventually, however, curiosity had her lifting her head and tapping the picnic basket.

"Where did you get this?"

"My mom bought it when she decided my dad was the one for her. She made him a big lunch and brought it to the ranch. Unfortunately for her, Dad was at the back of the ranch working with my grandfather when she delivered it, and my grandmother wasn't keen on her being so forward."

"Did your dad get it eventually?"

"Grandma grudgingly gave it to him that evening. He didn't know how to respond and didn't want to disappoint his mother, so he ended up not saying anything to my mom for a long time.

She was heartbroken and thought he didn't like her. It took overhearing another boy saying he was going to ask Mom to a school dance to kick Dad into action. They went to that dance and were a couple from that night until he passed."

"My heart breaks when I think about everything your mom has been through, more than any of us."

"Which is why I'm so thankful that she's doing better now. Even if you and I had never started dating, I would be eternally grateful for how you've helped her and Daisy. And me." He laughed a little. "Even the stray cat, who I swear is going to let you pet him one of these days. I think you're just a fixer of broken things."

"That's a nice compliment but gives me too much credit."

"You don't give yourself enough credit. There's something about you, like…an inner light or something. People feel good just being around you."

"That's the nicest thing anyone has ever said about me."

"It's the truth."

Ivy blinked against sudden tears. In that moment, she knew that she loved Austin. But some instinct told her that it was still too soon to say so. The timing, despite being in this stunningly beautiful place he'd chosen to share with her, still wasn't right. But she knew it, and it filled her heart with a joy that was hard to contain.

"So, now for the most important question of the day…"

"What I made for dessert?"

"Bingo."

Austin reached inside the picnic basket and retrieved the plastic storage container.

"Prepare to be amazed," he said as he gripped the edge of the lid. "This is some of my finest work."

"I'm overcome with anticipation."

He slowly pulled back the lid to reveal…

"Are those bourbon balls?" Gone was her teasing, replaced by genuine shock.

"They are."

"You really made these?"

"With the help of online videos."

Ivy picked up one of the round candy balls made of bourbon, chocolate, wafer crumbs, pecans and butter, originally created in Kentucky.

"Austin, this is so good," she said after taking the first bite.

"Thank goodness. I had to throw out two batches before this."

Ivy's immediate laughter almost had her snorting bourbon ball bits out of her nose. It was so good to laugh with her entire soul and have someone with whom to share that laughter.

After they were full, they took a few minutes to snap pictures of the valley and some selfies together. Austin surprised Ivy by planting a kiss on her cheek when he took one of them with the valley in the background. Even before looking at it, she knew it was going to be her favorite. She might even make it her lockscreen since there was no hiding their relationship anyway. She was fairly certain half the town somehow knew about them within twenty-four hours of Austin arriving at her s'mores-filled pity party.

A bit of thunder rolled in the distance right as the wind picked up a bit.

"Seems Mother Nature is putting the kibosh on our perfect outing," Ivy said.

Austin pulled her into his arms and said, "We'll come here again."

"I'll hold you to that."

THE PHONE RINGING woke Austin. He glanced at the clock and his heart started thudding harder. No call that came at nearly one thirty in the morning was a good one. He didn't recognize the number but he answered anyway.

"Austin, this is Angie Lee."

Waves of panic threatened to drown him when he remembered the last time Sheriff Lee had called, to tell him about his mom's accident. But now his mom and sister were safe in their own bedrooms. What could…

Please no.

"Is Ivy okay?"

"She's safe but distraught. Lightning struck her building and it's on fire. She's wet and cold from the rain, but she refuses to even sit in my car."

"I'll be right there."

More thunder rumbled as he quickly got dressed and grabbed his keys.

"What's wrong?" Daisy asked as soon as he stepped out of his bedroom.

He noticed his mom had already gotten up and was wheeling herself out of her room. Quickly he shared with them everything Angie had told him.

"Go," his mom said. "But be careful."

He knew what her fear was, and he promised that he would take care.

"And bring Ivy back here. We'll have things ready for her."

Even though he was in a hurry, he took a moment to kiss both his sister and his mom on the tops of their heads then raced for his truck. As he drove toward town, the sky was almost continually lit with lightning. Chances were high that the fire at Ivy's wouldn't be the only one caused by the weather tonight. By the time he hit Main Street, the rain was gone even if the lightning and wind weren't. His heart was beating fast as he made the turn onto Ivy's street. The fire department was still there, but the fire was either out or at least under control.

His heart sank when even in the darkness he could see that a large part of the roof was damaged or gone. When he spotted Ivy standing on the sidewalk on the opposite side of the street, she looked even smaller than her normal petite stature. He quickly parked, already opening his door as he turned off the ignition.

When Ivy spotted him, her face crumpled and the tears started to flow. He erased the distance between them and pulled her into his arms. He hugged her close, placing his hand against the back of her head.

"Thank God you're safe," he said.

Her only response was to cry harder. Austin let her and had difficulty not crying himself. Over the top of Ivy's head, he made eye contact with Angie. She gave him a sympathetic look then went back to her conversation with the fire chief.

Austin didn't know how long he stood there holding Ivy, but her sobs gradually lessened in intensity then faded into an occasional sniffle.

"It's ruined," she said against his chest.

He knew she meant more than the actual building. Her dream, her new beginning had a literal and figurative jagged hole in them.

"You don't know that. Wait until daylight to assess how bad it is."

She sneezed and that's when he noticed that she was barefoot, though she'd managed to grab her purse and phone. Without asking, he picked her up and carried her to his truck and set her inside. He used a flannel shirt that he kept in the truck to wrap her cold, wet feet. He wanted to scold her for putting herself in danger of getting sick, but he was so thankful that she wasn't hurt or worse that he held his tongue. He would bring her home with him where they would take good care of her while she worked with the insurance company to make things right again.

They sat in the truck with Austin holding Ivy's hand until the fire department left. But when he put his hand on the key to start the truck, Ivy suddenly said, "No, wait."

"We'll come back in the morning." Right now she needed to get dry and warm. If he knew his mother, she would have some hot food waiting when they arrived, no matter that it was the middle of the night.

Ivy pointed out the window toward where Angie was pulling something out of the back of her sheriff's department SUV. When he realized that it was the wall hanging his mom had made, he had to blink rapidly. Ivy had paused in the midst of escaping to rescue the piece his mom had put hours into.

"You should have just left it," he said, his voice cracking a bit at the thought that her taking the time to get the wall hanging could have cost her life. "It's replaceable. You aren't."

"I had to save it."

He didn't argue with her because she was already upset, had already lost so much. Even if the damage wasn't total, it was still a huge setback after they had all worked so hard to enable her to be ready to open before the fall festival rolled around.

He got out of the truck to retrieve the wall hanging. Angie sent a sympathetic look in Ivy's direction.

"Go ahead and take her home," Angie said. "I'll wrap up things here."

Behind her, a couple of deputies were already stretching caution tape around Ivy's building. It wasn't a preventive barrier, but he knew that Angie would make sure that no one went prowling around to see if they could scavenge anything inside.

"We'll come back when it's daylight, but call me if you need anything."

"Don't rush. Make sure she gets some sleep. I'll be surprised if she doesn't end up with at least a cold."

After he settled the wall hanging on the floor behind his seat, Austin drove out of town toward the ranch. Even though he needed to be careful on such a dark, wet night, he held Ivy's hand the entire way because he wanted to remind her that she hadn't lost everything. He was still there. So were Melissa and Daisy, Trudy, all the people Ivy had befriended since her arrival in Jade Valley.

By the time they arrived at the ranch, the storm system had moved out. The moon was even peeking out from behind the dark clouds. Again, he lifted Ivy in his arms and carried her inside.

"Oh my," he heard his mom say when she saw Ivy's bare feet.

He set Ivy down and framed her face with his hands. "Why don't you go take a warm shower? We'll have some dry clothes and hot food for you when you're done."

"I'm sorry," she said.

He smoothed some of her damp hair away from her cheek, tucking it behind her ear.

"There's no reason for you to be sorry."

Daisy gave him a look that said she would take over now. She hurried to her room to gather the things that Ivy would need. When they'd both left the living room, his mom motioned him into the kitchen.

"How bad is it?" she asked softly.

"It was too dark to tell for sure, but it's not

good. At least part of the roof is…" His voice broke, thinking about how Ivy may have been asleep right under that roof when the fire started. What if she had fallen down the stairs in her panic to get out? "It's gone."

His mom took his hand and squeezed it. "She's safe. We'll take care of her. She's family now."

He and Ivy were a long way from that type of relationship. They hadn't even said they loved each other, though he knew without a doubt now that he did love her. But even without the words, she felt like part of their family. For the first time he believed he might be able to make that type of commitment again. He just had to wait to see if she felt the same way.

CHAPTER FIFTEEN

IF THE DAMAGE to her new home had been frightening during a dark, rainy night, seeing it in the light of day was devastating. If Austin hadn't been standing next to her with his arm around her shoulders, Ivy was certain that her legs would have buckled beneath her. As she walked carefully across her living space, the bright blue sky she saw when she looked up through the giant hole in her roof felt incredibly out of place.

Sadness settled in her heart as she examined the damage to the original floors that Austin had revived with hours upon hours of repairing, sanding, sweeping and refinishing. The chest of drawers that had led her to the ER and the mattress she had purchased in Cheyenne were no more than soggy trash now. Shoes, clothing and mementos she had hauled all the way from Kentucky were completely lost as well.

Ivy felt like weeping all over again, but she'd already cried so much the night before—first in Austin's arms outside as the firefighters fought the fire and again when she'd finally curled up in Daisy's bed. All that crying resulted in the pounding headache she'd had all morning. The fact she might have slept only an hour didn't help. Neither did the question that kept banging against the sides of her skull like a mallet.

What now?

Needing something proactive to do, she gathered what few things had survived the combination of fire and water, including the coins she hadn't yet sold. It was sad when all of your worldly possessions were a car and what fit in a two-by-two-by-three-foot plastic tote. She sighed so deeply that it felt as if it fell all the way to the center of the earth.

"It'll be okay," Austin said as he came up behind her and placed his strong, supportive hands on her shoulders.

She appreciated his words of comfort, but she wasn't at all sure things would be okay after this. She'd already sunk everything she had into revitalizing a building that had been in worse shape than she'd anticipated. But at least then the roof had been intact and a rainstorm hadn't found its way inside.

She nearly laughed as she remembered finding the box of matches and candles and marveling that the building hadn't burned down before. The building had sat vacant but whole for years, but right when it was going to realize a new purpose it had sustained what was likely life-ending damage. Her business hadn't even been able to open before it had gone belly-up. Maybe the building was cursed and that's why nothing ever lasted there.

"Let's go," she said. "I don't want to look at this anymore."

As she turned to leave, she caught a glimpse of what had been the lovely bathroom Isaac had built for her. Odd that a bathroom could make her teary again. She swiped at her eyes and headed for the stairs.

"I can carry that for you," Austin said.

"I'm good." It was strangely important for her to hang on to her possessions with her own hands.

"Are you okay to drive?" Austin asked after she put the tote in the back seat of her car.

She nodded, and they got into the driver's seats of their separate vehicles. Ivy would never tell Austin that as they reached Main Street and Austin turned right, she almost turned left and took the same road out of town that she had taken in when she'd arrived in Jade Valley. But she felt as if wherever she landed, the dark cloud of failure would simply follow and start planning its next attack.

When they reached the ranch, she didn't get

out of her car. The energy it would take to do so seemed impossible to muster.

Austin noticed that she wasn't moving so he came toward her car. She rolled down the window as he reached her door. Thankfully, he didn't ask inane questions like "Is something wrong?" or "Are you okay?" The answers were obviously yes and no.

"I'm going to call my family before I go in," she said.

"Okay."

The fact that he knew she needed some time alone made her love Austin all the more. That's when she started to panic. What was she going to do now that she didn't have a home or a place for her business anymore? How was she going to make a living? Working at Trudy's was nice for getting to know people and bringing in a bit of money, but it wasn't what she'd moved across the country to do. Why did her happiness keep getting snatched away?

She tried to work up the nerve to call her mother to tell her what had happened. She rehearsed how she would launch into the topic for the least possible freak-out on the other end of the call, but she knew that no matter what she said and how she said it her mom and sisters were going to…well, freak out. And to be fair, if she found out any of them had escaped a house fire in the middle of the night, she'd be quite freaked out too.

To put it off a little longer, she first called her newly acquired insurance agent. Of course, Shelly Deneen already knew all about the fire. Something like that didn't happen in the middle of Jade Valley without everyone knowing about it. When she was finished with that call, however, it was time to get the dreaded call over with.

"Hi, Mom," she said when her mom answered on the second ring.

"What's wrong?"

Why were her mother and sisters so dang good at detecting when something was wrong based on no more than two words?

"What makes you think something's wrong? I can't call my mother?"

"I can hear it in your voice."

Ivy sighed. So much for easing into the news.

"I'm totally fine, but I can't say the same for my building." She swallowed hard, determined to get through the next few minutes without crying again. Her head already felt as if it was going to crack open.

"Come home," her mom said when Ivy finished telling her about the fire.

"Mom, it's too soon to make that type of decision. I haven't even met with the insurance adjuster yet."

"At least for a visit. We miss you, and having some distance might help you decide what you want to do next."

Maybe her mom was right. After what had happened with James, putting a lot of distance between her and him had really helped. But she couldn't keep moving across the country every time something went wrong. She looked up at the house, and her heart ached. Should she have allowed herself to get so close to Melissa and Daisy? To fall for Austin? Had he been right to worry that she would end up hurting all of them? She certainly hadn't planned to, but she hadn't planned for literal lightning to strike her new home either.

"I'll think about it and let you know."

They talked for a few more minutes, but only about a quarter of her mind was paying attention to the conversation. The rest was being bombarded with questions for which she had no answers.

After they ended the call, Ivy continued sitting in her car for a couple more minutes. She wasn't ready to go inside where she wouldn't be the only one with questions. Needing more time to sort out her thoughts, she got out of the car and started walking along the path she'd seen Austin take to access his back pastures. She hadn't seen any of the ranch land beyond the areas where the house and barn sat.

A couple of minutes later, she crested a hill and saw a small, curving flow of water. She knew here they would likely call it a creek though it wouldn't even merit that title back in Kentucky. Wyoming was way more arid than her home state, so she suspected what lay before her was often just a dry creek bed but now had flow because of the previous night's storm.

Even with Wyoming's vastly different landscape, Ivy had grown to love that difference. It, as well as the people she'd met and the work she'd done, had helped her to jump-start the healing process necessary after her breakup. She didn't want to leave here for many reasons, not just her feelings for Austin. But would she really have a choice? Her winning the building at just the right time had been a fluke, one that wouldn't be repeated. Even though she had insurance, she had a horrible feeling in the pit of her stomach that the payout wasn't going to be enough.

The longer she was out walking, the more she expected Austin to come looking for her. But he continued to give her space. By the time she was ready to retrace her steps, she still didn't know what she was going to do regarding her future but had decided that she did want to visit her family. She'd grown to care about Melissa a lot, but nothing compared to being enveloped in the arms of your own mother.

The distance she'd covered came as a surprise to Ivy as she made her way back to the house. She stopped a couple of times to take photos because she'd thankfully been able to save her phone if not her laptop. If she was going back to Kentucky for a visit, she wanted lots of beautiful shots to show her mom and sisters. Towering mountain peaks, a hawk in flight, colorful wildflowers for which she hadn't learned the names yet, even Austin's herd of cattle.

When she finally reached the house, she found Austin replacing the roof on Pooch's doghouse.

"Did you have a good walk?" Austin asked as he paused in his work.

Ivy gave Pooch a rub on his head, which he seemed to greatly enjoy.

"It was nice. I don't think I'll ever stop being amazed at how pretty it is here."

"You won't. I've lived here my whole life and it still catches me unaware sometimes."

Ivy crouched and gave Pooch a hug. Something about the action almost made her cry again. The tears were constantly right there ready to spill. She noticed Austin glancing her way, and the fact that he was holding back questions of his own was painfully obvious.

"My mom told me to come home for a visit,

and I'm going to take her up on that. I can't do anything with the building until all the insurance stuff is settled anyway. I... I need some time to think about how I want to proceed."

Austin didn't reply beyond a simple "Mmm."

Was he worrying that she wouldn't come back the same way Grace hadn't?

She stood and walked up to him, wrapping her arms around his waist. Now was not the right time to tell him she loved him, but maybe she could show him.

He hugged her back and placed a gentle kiss on her head. "Do what you have to do."

Those words were still echoing in her mind and her heart as she took off from the Denver airport the next day, bound for Lexington. The problem was she still had no idea how to proceed with her life, but she knew she hated the idea of not having Austin in it.

AUSTIN FINISHED BUILDING the porch and ramp for Mr. and Mrs. Harbin in record time. Then he attacked his normal ranch chores and every task he'd put off for lack of time. He had to keep busy so that he didn't give his mind the opportunity to worry that he'd never see Ivy again. It didn't work, but he kept trying. She'd only been gone for four days but it felt like four years.

After clearing and cutting up some limbs that

had fallen in the storm that led to Ivy leaving Jade Valley, he headed toward the house for a cold soda. Even thirsty, he still didn't want to go inside. He'd seen the looks his mom and Daisy had been giving him, ones filled with concern, but they hadn't commented on his long hours and the reason for them. To put off encountering them for a little while longer, he headed for the garden.

"Okay, now I know you're avoiding us," Daisy said as she exited the house via the back door. "You hate weeding the garden."

"Thought I'd give you a break from it."

"Yeah, right."

He looked up at his sister's uncharacteristically disbelieving tone. There was an edge of annoyance in her words too.

Daisy crossed her arms, and the way she looked at him made her seem way older than her actual age.

"You're worried Ivy won't come back, aren't you?"

Austin jerked out a weed with more force than necessary and pitched it aside.

"When did you get so smart?"

"You know I've always been smart. And observant."

"The attitude is new."

"I'm tired of all the adults in my life doing frustrating things."

"What exactly did I do?"

"It's what you haven't done. You're moping around worried that Ivy won't come back to Jade Valley, but you haven't done anything to make sure she does."

"I talk to her every day, ask how she's doing, how she's enjoying seeing her family despite the circumstances."

"Have you told her you love her yet?"

That question startled him.

"How do you know I do?"

Daisy tilted her head a smidge. "Are you serious right now?"

He continued staring at his sister, wondering why she suddenly seemed more mature than him.

Daisy came to crouch in front of him.

"If it was any more obvious how the two of you feel about each other, it would literally smack everyone nearby on the face."

"You think she loves me?"

Daisy rolled her eyes. "Why are men so dumb?"

A moment passed but then Austin laughed. "You sure got sassy. I'm not sure I like it."

"People grow up. At least some of us do."

"Okay, that's enough." He pulled his little sister into a gentle headlock and messed up her hair.

"Hey!"

He released her and let himself fall back to sit on the grass at the edge of the garden.

"I don't want to tell her how I feel on the phone, and I can't go flying across the country."

"Then show her instead."

"How?"

"You'll have to figure that out."

"Well, you're no help."

Daisy smiled then surprised him by planting a quick kiss on his cheek before shooing him away from the garden so she could finish the weeding he'd started.

He stepped into the house to grab a soda from the fridge. His gaze landed on the wall hanging made of buttons and knew that whatever he did to convince Ivy that Jade Valley was still her home, it had to center around making sure her dream could still come true here. Hoping that a drive would knock some usable ideas loose, he got in his truck and headed toward town. He first went to the grocery and bought some cat food. Ivy had been feeding the stray she'd named Sprinkles, and he could at least do that for her.

The cat was nowhere to be seen when he filled the bowl at the back of the little patio area, but that wasn't surprising. While the cat had gradually been coming closer to Ivy, the same could not be said for him.

After he finished, he walked slowly around the outside of the building. Then he did the same inside, assessing how much damage there was and how much it would take to make the building usable again. Was it possible? Could he somehow make it happen?

"Austin?"

He turned and saw Trudy standing at the top of the front steps. Not wanting her to come inside, he hurried back to the entrance.

"Did Ivy get home safely?"

A pang hit him that Trudy referred to Kentucky as Ivy's home rather than Jade Valley. He knew what she meant, but it still stung.

"She did."

"Any idea how long she's going to stay there?"

He looked behind him at the mess Ivy had left behind. He wouldn't blame her if she never wanted to see this place again…at least not in its current state.

"I don't know, but I have an idea and I need someone to tell me whether it's crazy or not."

"That sounds intriguing."

He didn't know if it was really intriguing or even feasible, but he told her anyway.

"You know, that's the best idea I've heard in a long time."

Austin found his smile again. He was going to make this work, no matter what it took.

IVY HANDED THE credit card back to the man who'd just bought two dozen red roses.

"Good luck with your proposal," she said.

"Thanks. If only these roses would make my nerves go away."

"That would be nice, wouldn't it?"

As soon as the man exited the floral shop, the smile dropped off her face. Though it was nice to spend time with her family, even kind of fun to work in the shop again, her life still felt as if it was drifting untethered. As she had expected, the insurance payout wasn't going to give her the funds she needed to get her own store up and running. With each day she spent back in Lexington, she felt that dream moving farther and farther away. Though she talked to Austin every day, either by phone or text, she wondered whether he was moving farther away as well. Sometimes he seemed distracted, as if he was already forgetting her.

Had she fallen for someone else who didn't care as much for her as she did for him? Did she have some fatal flaw that made her pick the wrong men over and over?

She shook her head. Austin wasn't like James. She knew that deep in her heart.

Didn't she?

The fact that she hadn't seen James's betrayal coming kept haunting her, making her doubt what she believed. Suddenly, the smell of fresh flowers and the hopeful expression of the man about to propose to his sweetheart overwhelmed her.

"Mom, are you okay if I leave?"

Her mom looked worried, as she had since she'd picked Ivy up from the airport.

"It's such a nice day I think I want to go for a walk."

"I'll go with you," Holly said as she came out from the back storage room.

Ivy wanted to be alone, but her family seemed to have made a pact before her arrival that they were not about to let that happen. But if she went back to Jade Valley, she wouldn't see her mom and sisters for a long time so she agreed to let Holly tag along.

They ended up at the UK Arboretum and fell into step beside each other on the loop trail. After some throwaway comments about the nice weather and the pretty flowers and plants, Holly got to the point of her tagging along.

"Have you made any decisions yet?"

"No. What I want to do and what I can do may be two different things."

"But you want to go back?"

Ivy stopped and looked at her sister. "I do. I just don't know how, or whether I'm making yet another in a string of mistakes."

"If it wasn't for Austin, would you be as conflicted?"

She'd told her family about Austin on her second day home when they'd grown suspicious of how much she was looking at her phone. To her surprise, they hadn't warned her to be careful about moving too fast. In fact, they'd seemed happier for her than she'd imagined they could be. Lily had commented about how Ivy's face lit up way more when she talked about Austin than it ever had whenever she mentioned James. That had surprised Ivy because she had loved James, even though now she hoped she never crossed paths with him again.

"I'm not sure," she finally said in answer to Holly's question. "He's a big part of the reason, but I also really like the town and the people. I just don't know how to make it work."

Which was why she'd been home for a month already. With each day that went by, she worried more that Austin was moving on without her—either because his feelings weren't as strong or because he was protecting himself from being hurt yet again.

Her phone buzzed with a text. When she saw it was from Austin, she experienced a wave of the conflicted feelings she'd started having the last few days. Was he texting to say he missed her or that he wanted to call it quits yet again, and for real this time? If it was the latter, could she really blame him? She knew what Grace had done to him, and yet Ivy had stayed away longer than she'd intended. But with each day that passed, one thing led to another, one doubt to another. She told herself she wanted to have everything figured out before she returned to Jade Valley so that she wasn't a burden on Austin, Melissa and Daisy. But the truth was she was scared that her new dream and new romance were both over and that if she returned to Jade Valley she'd have to face those truths in person.

Can I video call you now?

Ivy was surprised by Austin's question, and panic ensued. He was a decent guy, so maybe he was calling to break up with her as close to face-to-face as he could manage under the current circumstances. Her hands shook as she responded with a simple affirmative.

When she saw his smiling face on her screen, hope replaced fear. He wouldn't be smiling if he was about to break up with her.

"Where are you?" he asked.

"On a walk at the arboretum with Holly." She turned her phone so that Austin could see her sister, who smiled and waved.

"Nice to sort of meet you," Holly said.

"You too."

"I'll let you two talk now. I need to walk off the strawberry shortcake I had for lunch."

After Holly set off down the path, Ivy found a shady spot to sit.

"I have a surprise for you," Austin said.

"Yeah? What's that?"

Instead of replying, he lifted his phone so that she could see behind him.

"Surprise!" The chorus of voices startled her.

Those voices belonged to a lot of familiar faces—Melissa and Daisy, Trudy, Stephanie and Fiona, her neighbors Evangeline and even Reg, Angie Lee, Eric Novak, Sunny and Dean Wheeler, Maya Pine and Gavin Olsen, Isaac and Rich, Fizzy, Melissa's garden club friends, several of the business owners from around Jade Valley. She wondered what was going on that had brought them all together. And then she realized where they were and her breath caught. It was her building, but it had somehow acquired a new roof while she'd been gone.

"What is happening?"

"I told you, it's a surprise."

He turned the camera and she saw Daisy pull a cloth away from a new wooden sign in the front yard, one that said Quilters' Dream. The sign and building were surrounded by landscaping that hadn't been there before. Scattered among the new shrubs and flowers was a collection of painted stones. She wondered if they were the ones she'd collected while cleaning away the overgrowth.

The bigger question, however, was why would they put up a sign and do landscaping for a business that wasn't likely to ever open?

"Austin, I appreciate all this, but I think—"

"Before you finish that sentence, let me take you on a tour."

"A tour?" Had he cleaned up some of the mess in the hope it would weigh the scales in favor of her returning to Jade Valley?

She watched as he walked toward the front door of her building with everyone he passed smiling and waving. When he stepped into the building and panned the camera around, she couldn't believe what she was seeing. The vintage display cases looked much like they had before the fire. The floors appeared to be replaced. Melissa's wall hanging was back in its spot.

"Daisy did this," Austin said as he focused on the corner Ivy had dedicated to the history of the building and Jade Valley, which now held an impressive collection of historic photos and text to explain them.

Ivy was speechless as Austin climbed the stairs to the second level. Yet another surprise awaited her at the top. The door that had gotten damaged during the fire had been replaced by a beautiful wooden door painted dark blue. In white script, someone had painted "There's no place like home."

Austin opened the door and emerged into a room that no longer had a hole to the sky above it.

As he panned the camera, she had to blink back more tears. Her living space was fully outfitted with items that hadn't been there when she left.

"I don't understand. How did this happen?"

"Community effort. Almost everyone in town donated time, supplies or money to make this reality. By the way, Fizzy was extra generous. I think he has a little crush on you. I had to remind him that you have a boyfriend already." Austin turned the camera back toward him. "You've made an impression on a lot of people since you arrived here. We all want you to come back."

Ivy swiped at the tear that escaped, but at least this time it was born of happiness instead of loss.

All her questions about the future became answers. She was going back home.

Back to Jade Valley.

Back to the man she loved.

AUSTIN TOOK OFF his hat and wiped the sweat off his forehead. The temperature had shot up the past couple of days, but ranching required outdoor work no matter the weather. Thankfully, however, his herd was looking good.

He'd been so busy with organizing, overseeing and contributing to the community's overhaul of Ivy's building that he now had to focus on his ranching duties, especially since he'd been hired to build a shed for a couple who had a vacation home several miles north after Trudy had recommended him. He'd found out that any time she heard of those types of jobs, she had a rotation of people she suggested to do the work and he was on the list. As a thank-you, he'd given her a package of steaks from his freezer and bought two of her pies.

He looked out across the pasture toward the mountains and remembered what Ivy had said about constantly being amazed by how beautiful it was here. He couldn't wait to see her again. Not knowing when she might return was difficult, but her reaction to the video tour led him to believe she was in fact coming back. She'd been so overcome with what he, her friends and new neighbors had done for her that it had been difficult for her to speak. He'd finally told her that they could talk again when she was ready.

An out-of-place sound drew his attention, and he turned quickly in case a predator was nearby. When instead he saw Ivy running toward him, he thought maybe he'd been out in the heat too long and she was a mirage.

But then she nearly crashed into him and pulled

him down into a kiss that made him stumble. He wrapped his arms around her and kissed her back, putting into it all the words he hadn't yet said.

"How are you here?"

"Plane, car, my two feet," she said. "I needed to get here as fast as I could."

Austin smiled. "There was no rush. I'm not going anywhere. Although I'm really glad to see you."

"I needed to tell you something in person."

His heart thumped hard against his rib cage. Was she—

"I love you. No pressure if you're not ready to say—"

He halted her words with another kiss, not holding anything back. "I love you too. So much."

"Really?"

"Really." He picked Ivy up off her feet and swung her in a circle, whooping his unbelievable happiness.

Ivy laughed as if joy filled her entire body.

He knew exactly how she felt.

EPILOGUE

FALL HAD ALWAYS been Ivy's favorite season. Turning leaves, cooler temperatures, harvest festivals, Halloween—she loved it all. So it felt perfect that the grand opening of her quilt shop coincided with the Jade Valley Autumn Extravaganza. If she had thought the rummage sale crowd had been big, it was nothing compared to how full Jade Valley was for the festival. It felt as if all of Wyoming was filling the sidewalks and shops, including her own. In fact, people had been waiting outside when she unlocked the front door that morning, and there had been a steady stream since.

Locals were stocking up on sewing and knitting supplies. Tourists were buying everything from hand-dipped candles to expensive quilts to boxes of the quilt-themed Christmas ornaments Melissa had suggested might be big movers. She'd been right.

Ivy glanced across the room to where Melissa was talking with a group of women from Provo,

Utah. Bits of their conversation floated over to Ivy, and it sounded as if the ladies were part of a quilting club back home. They were loading up on the unique fabric patterns that Ivy and Melissa had spent hours together selecting.

When the Pinecone Pickers, the bluegrass band she'd hired for the day, struck up "Blue Moon of Kentucky" outside, Ivy smiled. The day's "Kentucky Meets Wyoming" theme had been Austin's idea. He, Isaac and some other guys were busy manning the food booth that featured both pulled pork barbecue made with sauce that she had ordered from a famous restaurant in Kentucky, and prime rib sandwiches. Daisy and her geography club were selling chips and drinks, as well as handling the payment transactions for all the food concessions. The garden club ladies were once again selling their impressive array of cookies.

Trudy, who was busy at the restaurant, had nonetheless managed to get her church to donate the use of all their folding chairs for the day. The last time Ivy had a moment to glance outside the open front door, most of them were filled with people eating and tapping their toes to the music.

"Are you ready?" Ivy asked the older lady who stepped up to the cash register.

"I better be or my credit card is going to literally start crying."

Ivy and the woman both laughed.

"Your mother was telling me how you moved out here by yourself to start this store," the woman said, pointing to where Ivy's mom was chatting up another customer. "I like that kind of adventurous spirit."

"Thank you. It's a great place to live. Wonderful people and you can't beat the view."

"You're right about that."

As the woman left, Ivy noticed Lily bringing another large box of yarn out of the storage room Austin had built during the second renovation of the building. With no one currently in line, Ivy moved to help her refill the cubby shelves that had miraculously survived the fire and subsequent dousing.

"Where's Holly?"

"She went to buy some more bags of ice for the drink coolers outside. I also ordered us all some fountain drinks with the good ice."

"Bless you."

It was beyond wonderful to have her family here for her grand opening. Despite her telling them to go enjoy the festival, they had insisted on lending a hand.

"I think your hot cowboy has sold the equivalent of a dozen cows and several pigs outside. It's as if people haven't eaten for days."

Ivy laughed. "Maybe they have been eating light so they can gorge themselves this weekend."

"Sounds like a solid plan."

As the hours passed, Ivy kept expecting the flow of customers to dwindle. The fact that they didn't gave her hope that her venture was really going to be a success. Several customers, both local residents and those who had traveled hours to attend the festival, had assured her that they would be back.

After she finished another transaction, her mom joined her behind the counter and wrapped her arm around Ivy's shoulders in a quick hug.

"I'm so proud of you."

"Thanks, Mom. That means a lot to me."

Her mom pointed toward the exit. When Ivy looked that way, she could see Austin outside laughing with an older gentleman she'd seen a couple of times at Trudy's but whose name she couldn't remember. Now that she was in Jade Valley for good, however, there was plenty of time to get to know people better.

"I also approve of him," her mom said of Austin. "He is perfect for you."

Her mom had never said anything so complimentary about James, although she'd gotten along with him fine.

"You think so?"

"Any man whose eyes light up the way his do

when he looks at you or even when he talks about you when you're not around is a keeper."

"I'm glad you think so because I plan on keeping him."

When things finally slowed down enough in the store to allow Ivy to go outside, the band was playing "Orange Blossom Special." She hummed along as she headed for the barbecue booth.

"What can I get you, ma'am?" Austin asked, his mouth spreading into a wide grin.

It struck her how much easier his smiles came now than when she'd first met him.

"Pulled pork sandwich, please."

He handed over a sandwich. "What else can I get for you?"

"How about a dining companion?"

"Go on," Isaac said. "We can handle this."

Austin grabbed a bag of chips for her as he left his post. She still had her huge soda with the good ice from the convenience store. They sat in two chairs in the back row, and when she sat down she realized how much her feet ached. It would have been more comfortable to wear her broken-in sneakers, but she'd chosen some cute white sandals instead because she'd been determined to wear her new dress. It seemed almost a lifetime ago when she'd chosen the blue fabric with the dandelion design.

"Oh, it feels good to sit down."

"I'd say your grand opening has been a success."

Ivy looked over at him. "It wouldn't have been possible without you."

"And a lot of other people."

"And a lot of other people." She leaned toward him and whispered, "But you're still special."

"So are you." He planted a kiss on her forehead then draped his arm along the back of her chair. "Now eat."

She smiled. Austin may have changed in some ways, but the man was always going to take care of the people he loved. Her mom was right.

He was a keeper.

* * * * *